My Lord Eternity

IMMORTAL ROGUES

ALEXANDRA IVY

ZEBRA BOOKS
KENSINGTON PUBLISHING CORP.
http://www.kensingtonbooks.com

ZEBRA BOOKS are published by

Kensington Publishing Corp.
119 West 40th Street
New York, NY 10018

ISBN-13: 978-1-4201-2861-1
ISBN-10: 1-4201-2861-2

First Printing: October 2003

10 9 8 7 6 5 4 3 2 1

Printed in the United States of America

Praise for *New York Times* bestselling author Alexandra Ivy and her *Guardians of Eternity* series!

DARKNESS UNLEASHED

"*Darkness Unleashed* is oh, so hot and wonderfully dangerous. I can't wait for the next installment!"

Gena Showalter, *New York Times* bestselling author

DARKNESS REVEALED

"A darkly erotic adventure with a vampire hero who can bite me anytime! Readers will adore Cezar's deliciously romantic craving for feisty, idealistic Anna Randal."

Angela Knight, *New York Times* bestselling author

DARKNESS EVERLASTING

"Ivy again provides vast quantities of adventure, danger and sizzling passion, ensuring her place on the list of rising paranormal stars."

Romantic Times

EMBRACE THE DARKNESS

"Delivers plenty of atmosphere and hot-blooded seduction."

Publishers Weekly

WHEN DARKNESS COMES

"Hot author Ivy bursts onto the paranormal scene and her vampire trilogy launch is not to be missed. A big plus in this novel are the excellent characters, which help build a believable world with paranormal elements and a highly passionate romance. Vivid secondary characters help set the stage and anticipation level for further chapters. Ivy is definitely an author with huge potential in the paranormal genre."

Romantic Times (Top Pick!)

Books by Alexandra Ivy

WHEN DARKNESS COMES

EMBRACE THE DARKNESS

DARKNESS EVERLASTING

DARKNESS REVEALED

DARKNESS UNLEASHED

BEYOND THE DARKNESS

DEVOURED BY DARKNESS

BOUND BY DARKNESS

FEAR THE DARKNESS

MY LORD VAMPIRE

MY LORD ETERNITY

MY LORD IMMORTALITY

And don't miss these *Guardians of Eternity* novellas

TAKEN BY DARKNESS in YOURS FOR ETERNITY
DARKNESS ETERNAL in SUPERNATURAL
WHERE DARKNESS LIVES in
THE REAL WEREWIVES OF VAMPIRE COUNTY

Published by Kensington Publishing Corporation

Prologue

"You will keep in mind the importance of your mission? And the fact that all vampires are depending upon you?" the tall, gaunt-faced vampire intoned, his expression one of cold censure.

It was an expression that Lucien Valin was accustomed to enduring. In truth, he tolerated open displeasure with monotonous regularity.

Unlike his brethren, he did not rejoice in devoting his days to hunching over musty books and brooding upon the philosophy of the elders. He did not desire to debate the nature of life. What did it matter to know of life if one was not allowed to truly enjoy it to its fullest?

It was that delight that had led him into trouble more than once. And even had him hauled before the Great Council on one memorable occasion.

Vampires could be humorless creatures when their tedious peace was disturbed, he had been forced to acknowledge. Especially when he had briefly transformed the library into a sultan's harem. The Great Council had taken a very dim view of his prank.

Now Lucien attempted to appear suitably subdued as he gave a low bow. "I understand the importance, Valkier," he murmured.

"The Veil must not be allowed to fall," the elder vampire continued in his dire tones. "'Tis failure enough that Tristan, Amadeus, and Drake managed to enter the world of humans in their determination to steal the Medallion. If they gain command of the ancient artifact, the power they will be able to summon could do untold damage."

Lucien gave a nod, his expression becoming uncharacteristically somber.

He had been deeply shocked when he had been called to the Great Council and told of the treacherous vampires who plotted to put an end to the Veil.

It had been two centuries since vampires had walked among mortals. In her infinite wisdom, the Great Nefri, leader of all vampires, had used the Medallion to create a Veil that had protected vampires from the world of men, and from the curse of bloodlust that had plagued them with the savage desire for human blood. A desire that made them vulnerable to the light of day.

For two centuries they had lived in peace.

A peace threatened by the devious traitors.

"I will not fail."

"You cannot." A surprising hint of frustration tightened the stern features. "Unfortunately our task has been made more difficult by Nefri's choice to divide the Medallion and give it into the hands of mortal females. You must protect the female as well as search for the vampires who hunt her."

Lucien was rather curious at Valkier's note of censure. The Great Nefri had taken care to bind the pieces of the Medallion to the very souls of the mortal maidens. The traitors could not steal or force the women to give over their gift, and not even death could undo the binding. The only means of acquiring the Medallion was if it were freely given. And as an added precaution Nefri had requested three vampires be sent to keep guard of the Medallion, even if it meant death to the traitors.

Far more wise than hoping to hide the powerful artifact or facing the renegades on her own, to his mind.

"It will be my pleasure to protect the maiden," he retorted smoothly.

The cold disdain returned to the gaunt countenance. "That I do not doubt. You possess a lamentable fondness for mortals, especially female mortals."

Lucien shrugged. "They are fascinating creatures."

"They are weak, impulsive, and violent, at best. It

is only because they breed like maggots that they have managed to survive at all."

Lucien was not surprised by the scathing contempt. As Immortals, it was only to be expected that vampires would look down in disdain at the lesser mortals. Few shared his own delight in their burning passions and lust for life. Most of his brethren chose to ignore their existence.

Of course there were a handful, such as the renegades, who believed mortals were no more than chattel to satisfy the hunger of vampires.

Unwilling to enter into a futile argument with the powerful elder, Lucien offered a bow.

"I should be on my way. Gideon and Sebastian will be awaiting me."

"You have the dagger?"

Lucien reluctantly nodded.

The powerful blade had been blessed with a magic that would destroy a vampire. He dearly hoped he would have no use for the weapon. The mere thought of destroying one of his brothers was enough to make him shudder in horror.

"I am prepared," he murmured.

"I sincerely hope that you are, Lucien," Valkier retorted. "If it had been the choice of the Great Council, you would not be leaving the Veil at all. You are boastful, irresponsible, and utterly lacking the ability to comprehend the dire threat that we face. It was I alone who overruled the other

Council members. I, perhaps foolishly, believe your unseemly fascination with the humans will be an asset in your task. I can only hope that you do not fail my trust too miserably."

Lucien could not prevent the urge to offer a mocking bow. "Your confidence is overwhelming as always. I can only attempt to live up to your high expectations."

"Go."

Chapter 1

Although Miss Jocelyn Kingly had never before encountered the devil, she was fairly certain he was currently sitting in her front parlor.

It was not so much his appearance that made her think of the Lord of the Netherworld, she grudgingly conceded.

Indeed, he might have been a beloved angel with his long, tawny curls that framed a lean countenance and brushed his wide shoulders. His eyes were a pure, shimmering gold with long black lashes that would make any woman gnash her teeth in envy. His features were carved with a delicate male beauty.

But there was nothing angelic in the decided glint of wicked humor in those magnificent eyes and sensuous cut of those full lips.

And, of course, the indecent charm of those deep dimples.

She should have sent him on his way the moment

he arrived upon her doorstep. Not even for a moment should she be considering the notion of allowing such a disturbing gentleman into her home.

She would have to be mad.

When she had first been struck with the notion of renting her attics, it had been with the prospect of discovering a quiet, comfortable tenant. Someone who would not disturb the peace of her household.

Unfortunately there were few such tenants who desired to live in a neighborhood that hovered on the edge of the stews. The local pickpockets and prostitutes did not possess the funds to pay the rent, even if she were to consider allowing them into her home. And the few gentlemen who possessed businesses in the area already owned their own property, usually far from St. Giles.

Which left Lucien Valin.

A shiver raced down her spine.

If only she were not in such desperate need of money.

If only it were not a full two months until her quarterly allowance.

If only . . .

Her lips twitched with wry humor. She could devote the next fortnight to listing the "if-onlys" in her life. Now was not the time for such futile longings.

She better than anyone understood that the

mistakes of the past could not be altered. One could only ensure that they were not repeated.

Unconsciously straightening her spine Jocelyn forced herself to meet that piercing golden gaze. It came as no surprise to discover her visitor's lips were twitching as if he were amused by her obvious hesitation.

"So, Miss Kingly, was the newspaper in error?" he prodded in that husky, faintly accented voice. "Do you have rooms to let or not?"

The voice of a devil. Jocelyn sucked in a steadying breath. Devil or not, he was the only potential tenant who offered the cold, hard coin she so desperately needed.

There had to be something said for that. Unfortunately.

"There are rooms," she agreed in cautious tones. "However, I feel it incumbent to warn you that they are located in the garret and are quite cramped. I am uncertain that a gentleman of your large proportions would find them at all comfortable."

His slender, powerful hands moved to steeple beneath his chin, the golden eyes shimmering in the slanting morning sunlight.

"Do not fear, I am tall, but thankfully, quite intelligent. I need hit my head upon the rafters on only a handful of occasions to recall to duck."

"There is also our unfortunate proximity to the

slaughterhouses. The stench can be unbearable on some days."

"I have discovered that there are few places in London that are not plagued with one unpleasant odor or another. Not even Mayfair is unaffected."

Jocelyn maintained her calm demeanor with an effort. She never allowed herself to be ruffled. She had learned through painful experience that to lose control was a certain invitation to disaster.

"Unlike Mayfair, however, this neighborhood can be quite dangerous as well."

His dimples suddenly flashed. "Surely, my dear, you do not suppose Mayfair to be without its dangers? Just imagine . . . marriage-mad mamas, overdressed fops fragrant with the stench of rosewater, and a prince who insists upon keeping his chambers as smothering hot as the netherworld. It is enough to terrify the stoutest of hearts." He lifted one broad shoulder. "I should be able to hold my own against a handful of thieves and street urchins."

There was no reasonable argument to refute his confident words. Although he cloaked himself in a lazy charm, there was no mistaking the fluid power of his male form or the hint of ruthless will that was etched upon the lean features.

Only a fool would underestimate the danger of Mr. Lucien Valin. And Jocelyn was no fool.

"If you say," she reluctantly conceded.

"Is there anything else?"

"There are my rules, of course," she swiftly countered, not at all surprised when his lips curled in open amusement.

"Of course."

"This is not a lodging house. I live very quietly. I will not countenance loud gatherings or drunken carousing."

A tawny brow flicked upward. "I am allowed no callers?"

"Only if they are discreet."

For some reason her cool response only deepened his amusement. "Ah."

That unwelcome shiver once again inched down her spine, and Jocelyn discovered herself battling back the words to order this Mr. Valin from her house.

She did not have the luxury of turning away a perfectly suitable tenant just because of some vague fear.

"And the arrangement will be of a temporary nature," she instead retorted in an effort to reassure her faltering nerve. "No longer than two months."

"That suits me well enough."

It appeared everything suited the devil.

Jocelyn narrowed her gaze. "I also must insist that you respect my privacy. You are welcome to eat in the kitchen with Meg, but the remainder of the house is not to be entered."

There was a brief pause as he studied her carefully

bland countenance. Then he gave a vague nod of his head.

"As you wish. Is that all?"

It was, of course.

She was charging him an outrageous sum of money for cramped rooms and meals he would be forced to eat in the servants' quarters.

She had also made impossible rules that would annoy the most even-tempered of gentlemen.

The mere fact that he had so readily agreed made her even more suspicious.

"Why are you here?" she demanded in abrupt tones.

His hands lowered as he regarded her with a bemused smile.

"I beg your pardon?"

Jocelyn deliberately allowed her gaze to drop to the deep burgundy coat cut by an obvious expert and white waistcoat stitched with silver thread. Her gaze continued over the hard, muscular thrust of his legs to linger upon the glossy Hessians that cost more than many families could earn in a year.

At last she raised her head to discover him regarding her in a curious fashion. "It is obvious that you are a gentleman of means, Mr. Valin. Why would you desire to take inferior rooms in a neighborhood most consider fit only for cutthroats and whores?"

"Does it truly matter what my reason?" he demanded softly.

"I will not harbor a criminal."

He gave a sudden chuckle. "I assure you that I am not hiding from the gallows."

"Then, why?"

"Let us just say that there was a slight misunderstanding with my cousin."

The explanation was a trifle too smooth for her liking.

"You had a slight misunderstanding with your cousin and now you desire to hide in St. Giles? You shall have to do better than that, Mr. Valin."

The devilish glint in the golden eyes became even more pronounced. "Perhaps it was more than a slight misunderstanding. Gideon can unfortunately be tiresomely unreasonable when he chooses, and I believe there was some mention of a nasty duel. It seemed best to avoid him for the next several weeks. Just until his temper is recovered."

"What is the nature of this misunderstanding?"

His features unexpectedly firmed to uncompromising lines. "That is a private matter."

A woman, Jocelyn silently concluded, caught off guard by a traitorous prick of disappointment.

What else could she expect from such a gentleman? He was, after all, born to break the heart of susceptible women.

Then she was severely chastising herself for her unworthy thoughts.

She knew nothing of this gentleman. Certainly not enough to brand him as a womanizing letch. And in truth, even if he were, she was in no position to judge another.

"I respect your privacy, but you must understand that I have no desire to discover an angry gentleman upon my doorstep with his dueling pistol."

The incorrigible humor swiftly returned to the bronze features. "He has no means of discovering I am here. Besides, Gideon would never harm a lady. He far prefers to charm them." His smile became decidedly suggestive. "As do I."

Jocelyn carefully laid her hands upon her tidy desk. This flirtatious banter was precisely what she had feared from Mr. Valin. It was important that she put a swift end to any hopes he might harbor of a casual seduction.

"That is all very well, but do not imagine for a moment, Mr. Valin, that I am remotely interested in any charms you might claim to possess."

Far from wounded by her firm words, the gentleman stroked a slender finger down the length of his jaw.

"Surely you exaggerate, Miss Kingly? Not even remotely interested?"

"No."

He heaved a teasing sigh. "A hard woman."

"A sensible woman who has no time for foolish games," she corrected him firmly. "You would do well to remember my warning."

"Oh, I possess a most excellent memory," he drawled, reaching beneath his jacket to remove a small leather bag that he placed upon the desk. "Indeed, I even remembered this."

She eyed the bag warily. "What is it?"

"The two months' rent in advance, just as you requested."

Jocelyn made no effort to reach for the money. She knew the moment her fingers touched the coins she would be irrevocably committed to allowing this gentleman into her home.

And yet, what else could she do?

There was nothing particularly noble in bare cupboards and empty coal bins. And besides, she had Meg to consider.

Her old nurse was the only one to stand beside her when the scandal had broken. She was the only friend she had left in the world.

How could she possibly allow the older woman to suffer even further hardship?

The answer, of course, was she could not. This money would pay their most pressing creditors and put food on the table. At the moment that was all that mattered.

Grimly thrusting aside the warning voice that

whispered in the back of her mind, Jocelyn gave a nod of her head.

"Thank you."

As if thoroughly aware of her inner struggle, the devil lifted his brows in a faintly mocking manner.

"Do you not wish to count it?"

"That will not be necessary."

"So trusting, my dove?"

"You will not be difficult to track down if I discover you have attempted to cheat me."

"There is that," he agreed with a chuckle. "When may I take possession of the rooms?"

Although not always meticulously devoted to truth if a small bit of subterfuge was more practical, Jocelyn discovered herself unable to form the lie that would allow her a few days' grace from Mr. Valin's presence.

Not that it truly mattered.

She would no doubt merely waste the days brooding upon what was to come. Surely this was like swallowing vile medicine. It was best to be done with quickly.

"The rooms have been cleaned and prepared," she forced herself to admit. "You may have them whenever you desire."

"Good. I will collect my belongings and be here later this afternoon."

This afternoon.

She absolutely refused to shiver again.

"What of your cousin?" she demanded. "Will he not shoot you when you return for your belongings?"

"I have it on excellent authority that he devoted the goodly portion of the evening to his current mistress. It will be several hours before he awakens."

She unconsciously grimaced. "I see."

An odd hint of satisfaction touched the handsome countenance. "You disapprove of such pleasurable pastimes, Miss Kingly?"

Jocelyn was swift to smooth her features to calm indifference. "I do not possess sufficient interest to disapprove, Mr. Valin."

His lips twisted wryly. "No, of course not."

Having strained her nerves quite far enough for one morning, Jocelyn rose to her feet.

"I believe we have covered everything, Mr. Valin."

Efficiently dismissed, the tawny-haired gentleman reluctantly pushed himself from his chair.

"I shall return in a few hours," he was swift to warn.

Jocelyn, however, was prepared on this occasion.

"If you have need of anything, please speak with Meg. She is quite capable and is in full control of the household."

The golden eyes narrowed as she easily maneuvered him firmly into the hands of her servant.

"More capable than you, Miss Kingly?" he demanded in those husky tones.

"Without a doubt." With a crisp nod of her head

she regained her seat and reached for her ledger book. "Good-bye, Mr. Valin."

He remained standing beside the desk, but as she kept her gaze upon the pages of her accounts, he at last gave a low chuckle.

"Until later, my dear."

Jocelyn maintained her charade of distraction until she at last heard the sound of the door closing behind his retreating form. Only then did she lean back in her seat and close her eyes in an odd weariness.

There would be dinner on the table tonight.

But what was the cost?

And was she prepared to pay it?

The kitchen was surprisingly clean and filled with the delicious aroma of fresh-baked bread and drying herbs.

Seated at the scrubbed table, Lucien leaned back with a deep sigh.

His surroundings could hardly compare with Gideon's vast town house or even the elegant hotel he had chosen upon his arrival in London. The house might be tidy with sturdy furnishings, but there was no ignoring the neighborhood was a breath from utter decay and that the air was rancid with the stench of rotting trash and sewer.

Still, he was not overly disappointed that his trail

had led him to this narrow house in the shabby cul-de-sac. His rooms might be cramped and his delicate senses offended by the derelict surroundings, but it all became meaningless the moment he had stepped into the small study.

Even now he could feel the shock of utter bewitchment when he had beheld Miss Kingly.

She had quite simply stolen his breath.

Her face was a perfect oval with large eyes the impossible blue of tropical waters. Her hair, which had been ruthlessly wrenched into a knot at the base of her neck, possessed the rich luster of sable that contrasted sharply with the flawless cream of her skin. She possessed the timeless beauty of a Madonna, with lush curves that could make a man's thoughts stray in dangerous directions.

As a collector of beautiful objects, he had been stirred by her loveliness.

As a vampire with his passions unleashed for the first time in two centuries, other parts of his anatomy had been stirred.

Just for a moment he had briefly considered how swiftly he could woo her into his bed. How magnificent she would be stretched upon snowy white sheets, her hair a river of silk, he had thought with a decided yearning. In the candlelight her skin would glow with the pale luster of fine porcelain. Her lush curves would fit his hands to perfection.

Ah, to possess such a woman would surely bring untold pleasure.

But even as his blood had tingled with anticipation, he had gazed into those well-guarded eyes and sensed the bleak loneliness deep within.

His calculated passion had died with a regretful sigh.

This woman was not in need of a lover.

She was in need of a savior.

The knowledge had been as unwelcome as the stench of the nearby slaughterhouse, and just as inescapable.

He was here to protect this maiden.

He could only hope his rusty sense of chivalry could be persuaded to overcome the lust that even now swirled through his blood.

Pushing back his plate, he cast a roguish smile toward the undoubted general of the household. The servant was a large woman with iron-gray hair and features cast in granite. He could only hope her heart was not similarly unyielding.

"Exquisite, my dear Meg," he complimented her. "As savory as any I have ever tasted. A true masterpiece."

The charm he had once presumed irresistible appeared woefully ineffective. As woefully ineffective upon the servant as it had been upon her mistress.

"'Tis shepherd's pie, hardly a masterpiece."

"Ah, but in the hands of an artist even shepherd's pie can be a masterpiece. And you are, indeed, an artist."

If anything, the woman regarded him with even sharper suspicion. "Miss Jocelyn warned me you possessed the silver tongue of the devil. I now understand why."

Lucien was not remotely surprised.

He had known from the moment he had entered this house that the young maiden had felt uneasy in his presence.

Unfortunately the Medallion she wore about her neck made any attempt to use a Compulsion spell impossible. The ancient artifact was powerful enough to protect her from even the most devious skills a vampire possessed. He would have to win her trust by more difficult and time-consuming means.

Not one of his more notable talents.

"Did she?" he murmured. "A most intriguing and unique young woman."

"And far too wise for the likes of you," the woman retorted.

"Ah, Meg, you wound me."

"Not yet I haven't, but I certainly will if you take it in mind to toy with Miss Jocelyn."

Lucien gave a startled laugh, discovering he quite enjoyed bantering with this gruff old tartar.

For all her crusty manners, it was evident that she was utterly devoted to Jocelyn.

"I beg your pardon?"

The servant planted her hands upon her ample hips. "Miss Kingly is a fine, decent maiden who has endured far more heartache and disappointment than any lady should. I would willingly thump my frying pan upon the head of anyone foolish enough to bring her pain again."

Lucien was instantly intrigued. Heartache and disappointment?

Knowledge was always power, and he very much desired to know as much of Jocelyn as possible.

"How very distressful. She is far too young to have endured the pains of this world. Tell me, what was the source of this heartache?"

"It is her story to tell if she so chooses. Just remember that I shall be keeping a close eye upon you."

He met the warning gaze squarely. He could, of course, force her to speak of Miss Kingly's past, and anything else he might desire, but he resisted temptation. Other than himself, this woman was the only person in London willing to stake all to protect the vulnerable maiden. He might very well need her with her wits clear.

"I have no intention of harming Miss Kingly," he retorted. "I would never harm any young maiden.

But neither will I ignore her. She has an obvious need for my company."

"Need for your company? And what can you mean by that?"

"There is a deep sadness in her eyes."

"Fah. That I already know. As does all of London. As I said, she has endured betrayal in her past."

"And she does not allow the wounds to heal," he said softly, keeping Meg's reluctant gaze trapped with his own. "A fatal mistake. Bitterness is like an infection that will destroy her soul if it is not cleansed."

As obviously aware as Lucien of Jocelyn's brittle wounds, the woman grudgingly lowered her guard.

"Perhaps. How do you propose to cleanse this bitterness?"

"First by revealing that there is still joy to be found in this world."

The pale eyes narrowed. "How much joy?"

His lips twitched at her blunt suspicion that he intended to seduce her young mistress.

A suspicion that was well founded.

"As much as she desires, and no more," he reassured the older woman. "Do you not believe she has earned a share of happiness?"

"Yes. No one is more deserving."

"So if I chose to prod Miss Kingly out of her icy shell of composure, then I need not fear being greeted by a frying pan?"

"That depends," she warned, her gaze straying meaningfully toward the frying pan upon the counter.

"Upon what?"

"On whether this prodding endangers Miss Jocelyn's heart. She is not nearly as invulnerable as she would have others believe. Especially when it comes to a devil with a silver tongue."

It was no doubt a genuine concern, but Lucien swiftly shrugged it aside.

He needed to be close to Jocelyn if he were to protect her.

Any unfortunate complications would have to be dealt with once the traitors were returned to the Veil.

"I wish only to see her laugh," he at last murmured.

Meg heaved a faint sigh. "As do I."

"Then we shall have to work together."

"We shall see." The woman was not about to give any more than absolutely necessary.

"You intend to keep that frying pan quite handy, do you not?"

"Oh, yes."

With a laugh Lucien rose to his feet. "We are going to get along just fine, Meg."

Chapter 2

Amadeus stalked the woman with a cool precision.

Remaining in the shadows of the derelict shops and lodging houses, he kept a steady pace as she searched for the prostitute known on the streets as Molly.

A prostitute whom he had murdered less than an hour earlier.

For nearly a fortnight he had studied this woman's every movement.

He knew precisely when she would leave her home each evening. When she would bring food to the various street children. When she would seek out the pathetic whores and urge them to abandon their tortured lives and travel to the small cottage she had purchased outside of town. He even knew that on this night she would seek out the young, hapless Molly as she did on every Wednesday evening. In vain she would plead with the prostitute to leave the brutal husband who forced her onto the streets to pay for his gin.

Which was precisely why he had disposed of the whore and laid his minions into hiding just around the corner.

Miss Kingly's very predictability would be her undoing.

Giving a sharp whistle, Amadeus watched for the three slovenly servants to stagger around the corner and surround the unaware maiden.

Just as he had commanded, the men quickly grasped Miss Kingly and covered her mouth to prevent her from crying out in alarm. Amadeus waited a moment to ensure that she was properly frightened by the sudden attack before he stepped forward to complete his well-plotted scheme. Only to halt in surprise.

With a detached appreciation he watched her fierce struggle to free herself from her determined attackers.

There were no tears, no fainting, no traces of panic.

Instead, she grittily kicked at the men, using her hands and even her elbows to attempt to win her freedom.

This woman was different.

A sharp, unexpected curiosity flared into existence deep within Amadeus's icy soul.

As a true scholar, he was always intrigued by the

unexpected. Especially when it came to mortals. It was not the heat of their passions, nor their tedious loves and hatreds. It was their simple mortality that lured his interest. Perhaps once he had retrieved the Medallion that she now wore about her neck he would allow Miss Kingly to become a part of his ongoing research.

She would certainly enhance the rather disappointing selection of humans he was currently examining.

Of course, first he must ensure that the Medallion was given to his grasp.

With a calculated motion he continued his path toward the struggling maiden. As he neared the first of his henchmen, he lifted the ebony cane he carried and hit him across the shoulders. The man cringed, although he felt no pain through the spell of Inscrollment that Amadeus had cast upon him.

"Begone, you fiends," he dramatically commanded, sharply smacking the other two servants. "The Watch is on its way, and you shall soon be lodged in Newgate."

At the word "Newgate," all three abruptly halted their assault and turned to stumble down the darkened street.

Perhaps a careful eye would have noted the manner they had so easily capitulated at his threat, or even the fumbling shuffle of their gait as they hurried away, but thankfully the maiden was far more concerned with pulling her shawl about her to conceal the large rip in the bodice of her gown.

"My dear, are you harmed?" he asked in soft tones that befitted the image of a modest, well-intentioned vicar. He had chosen the voice with the same care that he had altered his shape to a slender elderly gentleman who had lost most of his gray hair and possessed the features of a man dedicated to good works. Precisely the sort of gentleman a woman Miss Kingly would turn to in times of trouble.

And she was soon to have ample trouble.

"No." She smoothed the dark hair that had been tumbled from the tidy knot. "I am unhurt."

Amadeus made a mental note of her steady tone and cool composure. Oh, yes, she was worthy of experimentation, indeed.

Already he itched to bundle her back to his hidden lair and begin, but as she turned, the muted light from a nearby gin house shimmered against the golden amulet around her neck.

His breath caught.

Although only a portion of the original Medallion, he had no doubt that it contained a power more potent than any he had ever tasted before. And once made whole again, he and his fellow traitors would command the vampires. They would at last bend to his will.

Unfortunately he had already discovered that

the Medallion was protected by a powerful spell. It had been bonded to the mortal's soul, making her impervious to Inscrollment and any other spell he might be able to conjure. Not even death could part the Medallion from the maiden.

The only hope of gaining control of the ancient artifact was to have it given to him of Miss Kingly's free will.

Which was precisely why he had been forced to conceive this ludicrous scheme. He had to win the trust of Miss Kingly and somehow convince her that she must offer him the amulet.

"Thank the good Lord," he said as he offered her an encouraging smile. "I feared I might have been too late."

Despite his humble manner, she seemed to instinctively sense danger in the air, and she took a step backward even as she attempted to appear suitably grateful for his display of courage.

"You were very brave."

He pressed his hands to his chest in a modest fashion. "Very kind of you, but I merely did what any other gentleman in my position would do."

She glanced toward the shuffling figures disappearing into a nearby alley. "Not every gentleman, I fear."

"No, perhaps not," he regretfully agreed. "The streets can be dangerous for a young maiden on her own. May I escort you home?"

She unexpectedly squared her shoulders. "I thank you, but that will not be necessary."

Amadeus paused. While he found her valor a source of interest, it did not suit his plans to have her quite so independent. With an effort he determinedly curbed his flare of impatience. He was an Immortal. He had learned that patience was a virtue that could not be underestimated.

"Are you certain?" he coaxed. "I may have momentarily frightened those louts, but there is no telling when they might return. Besides which, they are not, unfortunately, the only scoundrels who would be willing to harm a maiden."

She clutched her shawl about her. "I do not live far."

"It does not take far to discover yourself in danger in such a neighborhood."

"I am accustomed to traveling these streets," she retorted, although Amadeus did not miss the manner in which her gaze strayed toward the now-empty darkness.

"Ah, but on this night it is unnecessary. I stand eager to offer my arm and my escort."

He held out his arm, but once again she stepped back from his advancing form. Briefly he wondered if the Medallion somehow gave her the ability to sense the fact he was not mortal. Or perhaps even his evil intentions. It was a complication that did nothing to improve his thinning temper.

"You are very gracious, Mr. . . . ?"

"Vicar Fallow." Amadeus bowed low, careful to ensure his expression remained impassive. Even if the woman did sense something unnatural about him, she would have no notion of what it meant. Or the danger that threatened her. "And you are?"

"Miss Kingly."

"A pleasure to make your acquaintance."

"And you, sir. However, I have a task I must complete on this evening, so if you will excuse me?"

Realizing that she was about to slip from his grasp, Amadeus smoothly blocked her path.

"May I offer my services in performing this task?"

Forced to halt, she barely managed to hide her flare of impatience. "I merely wish to speak with Molly."

"Molly?"

"She can always be found on this street."

Amadeus raised a hand to his heart and offered a soulful shake of his head. "Oh, my dear."

She frowned at his sudden expression of sorrow. "What is it?"

"Does this Molly have red hair and a freckled countenance?"

"Have you seen her?"

"I very much fear I have."

Forgetting her revulsion of him, Miss Kingly suddenly stepped forward. "What is it?"

He pretended to consider the matter for a

moment before speaking. "I am uncertain how to tell you this, but she was discovered in a nearby alley just half an hour ago."

Her hand reached up to clutch the Medallion upon the chain as if seeking strength.

"Discovered? What do you mean, discovered?"

Amadeus briefly recalled the sweet delight as he drained the life from the struggling, terrified whore. It had been a hurried affair, without his usual finesse, but the blood still raced through his body with a potent force.

"She has been murdered," he announced simply.

Predictably the maiden's eyes widened in shocked horror. Humans could become so illogically attached to one another.

"Dear heavens," she breathed.

"A shock, I know," he sympathized.

"Are you certain it was Molly?"

He heaved a deep sigh. "Unfortunately it was I who found the body."

There was a moment of silence as Miss Kingly struggled to come to terms with the disturbing news of her friend, then she abruptly straightened her shoulders with commendable fortitude.

"Where have they taken her?"

Once again she managed to catch Amadeus off guard with her display of courage. His brows rose at her firm words.

"No, you must not attempt to see her," he retorted in solicitous tones.

"Of course I must."

"My dear, it would not be at all prudent."

Her expression hardened to one of determination. "I do not care for prudence. She may have been a prostitute, but I cared for her."

It was the opportunity he had been awaiting. He would display just how kind and compassionate he could be.

"A most honorable sentiment, my dear, and I fully applaud your generous nature. I myself have pledged my life to helping these poor wretches who nightly struggle just to survive. However, my desire in preventing you from joining the poor child stems from the knowledge you would be deeply disturbed by her grievous attack. The murder was quite savage."

She paled at his soft words, her hands trembling as they clutched the shawl. "Oh."

"It is truly best that you return home."

Clearly disturbed by the unexpected end to Molly, the formidable woman gave a reluctant nod of her head.

"Yes, perhaps you are right."

Once again Amadeus held out his arm. "Shall we?"

"No, no, I thank you," she stammered, still uneasy in his presence. "I prefer to be on my own."

Incensed, Amadeus took a step forward, his

fangs instinctively lengthening in anticipation of the kill. He would teach this vexing chit a lesson in daring to defy him. Then, with an effort, he regained his composure.

All things would come to him in their proper time.

Patience.

"As you wish." He performed a stiff bow. "I do hope that you will not hesitate to seek me out if you ever have need of my services. Until then, good night, my dear."

"Good night." With an absent nod the maiden turned and soon disappeared around the corner.

On his own, Amadeus clenched his hands in frustration. The evening had not progressed nearly as well as he had hoped. Miss Kingly had not readily embraced him as her savior, nor had she eagerly turned to him for his assistance. Instead, she remained wary and far too distant.

Still, he would not allow himself to press matters. Unlike Tristan, who was always brutal and impulsive, or Drake, who was far too arrogant, he knew that it was his keen intelligence that would allow him to succeed.

He had planted one further seed this evening. In time it would lure Miss Kingly into his clutches. Of that he did not doubt.

Until then he would simply enjoy the undeniable pleasures of his various experiments.

* * *

Watching Miss Kingly safely walk away from the deadly vampire, Lucien slipped the dagger beneath his jacket.

It had been rather a nasty surprise to nearly stumble over the traitor. When he had impulsively decided to follow Miss Kingly through the dark streets, he had been more concerned with the mundane dangers. Thieves, rapists, murderers. The sight of the Inscrolled slaves, followed closely by Amadeus, had made his blood run cold.

Keeping close enough to rush to the maiden if the vampire desired to harm her, Lucien had remained in the shadows to discover precisely what the renegade would do. For all his frivolous ways, he knew it was imperative that he understand precisely how Amadeus intended to acquire the Medallion.

It had taken only moments to realize that the renegade was intent on wooing the maiden with his supposed sympathies to those poor individuals who littered the streets of St. Giles. And that he was quite willing to kill without remorse to achieve his goal.

The realization hardened his determination.

He would not allow Miss Kingly to be harmed. For once in his existence he possessed a true responsibility. He would not fail.

Waiting until he was certain that the maiden was

on her way home, Lucien silently stepped from the shadows and confronted the vampire with a mocking smile.

"My, my, Amadeus," he drawled. "How terribly clever of you to save Miss Kingly in such a daring manner. But then, you have always been clever."

With a smooth motion Amadeus turned to confront him, a cold glitter in his pale eyes.

"Ah, Lucien, I have been expecting you."

Lucien narrowed his gaze in dislike. He had always found the vampire a pompous, ill-humored man. He was also cruel in nature and took unpleasant delight in causing pain in others.

Unfortunately he was also cunning and dispassionate. Two qualities that would ensure that he would not make a foolish mistake.

Keeping his guard raised, he leaned against the derelict gin house and folded his arms over his chest.

"Poor Molly. I do not suppose she ever realized that she was being butchered just so you would have an excuse to insinuate your way into Miss Kingly's life?"

The thin lips curled into a humorless smile. "In truth she revealed little interest in the reasons for her torture. Like most humans, she was predictably swift to succumb to her terror. They can be so tediously mundane."

"An unfortunate tendency of being mortal, I have discovered."

"Yes." Amadeus gave a mockingly sorrowful sigh. "And as I was pressed for time, I was forced to be wretchedly clumsy. Her throat, I fear, was quite mangled and her head barely remained attached."

Lucien refused to be goaded into revealing his revulsion. He did not doubt Amadeus was deliberately attempting to prod for some response.

"My sympathies. I know how you dislike a messy kill."

Amadeus gave a delicate shiver. "I do. Unlike Tristan and Drake, who have joined me in the battle for the Medallion, I do not allow bloodlust to make me into a savage. It is only a means to a greater power."

"That is no doubt a great comfort to Molly," Lucien drawled.

The false vicar gave an indifferent shrug. "Sacrifices must be made."

"Why?" Lucien demanded.

"I beg your pardon?"

Lucien slowly pushed himself from the wall. "As you said, you are unlike Tristan and Drake. You have never placed yourself forward to be considered as a member of the Great Council, nor sought privilege for your undoubted powers. You are a scholar. Why are you here?"

Amadeus smiled in a condescending manner. "I

am a seeker of knowledge, not a scholar," he corrected Lucien. "I do not read the words of others or endlessly debate philosophy with those of lesser intelligence. I search for the truth in all its various forms. An impossible task when I was imprisoned behind the Veil."

His arrogance would have been astonishing to all but those acquainted with Amadeus. He rarely disguised his sense of superiority over all others.

"You find truth in the killing of mortals?"

An odd glitter abruptly entered the pale eyes. "Actually I believe that there must be a startling clarity that can be found when confronted by impending death. What other moment can offer such a rare opportunity to thrust aside all frivolous distractions so that one is allowed to concentrate on the meaning of life? As an Immortal I am denied such a moment of enlightenment, so I search for it among the humans. For all their weaknesses, they must gain some knowledge in that final breath. Now that my experiments can continue, I possess great faith that I shall uncover the most fascinating revelations. It is all a matter of discovering the proper mortals for my research."

There was a fevered edge in his tone that struck a chill in Lucien, but he determinedly kept his expression impassive. The vampire had obviously lost all sense in his thirst for knowledge.

"You are now free of the Veil. What need have you for the Medallion?"

A sudden sneer twisted Amadeus's features. "I am not so naive as to believe Nefri will tolerate my peculiar studies. Like you, she possesses an inexplicable fondness for mortals. And, of course, the lure of power is undeniable. With the Medallion I shall be beyond the tedious strictures of the Great Council and free to indulge in my thirst for knowledge, no matter where it might lead."

Lucien slowly straightened his shoulders, his own expression grim. "All very commendable, no doubt, but I fear I cannot allow you to claim the Medallion."

Amadeus gave a sharp laugh at his firm warning. "You believe you can halt me?"

"If necessary."

"Then we are destined to be enemies." The vampire gave a mocking bow. "May the best vampire win. Adieu, Lucien."

With supreme nonchalance Amadeus turned on his heel and moved down the darkened street. Lucien briefly fingered the dagger beneath his coat before giving a shrug. He truly hoped that there would be no need to actually put an end to the vampire. No matter what his distaste for Amadeus and his torture of humans, he was a brother to him. It would be a terrible thing to destroy him.

Giving a shake of his head, Lucien shrugged off

his dark thoughts. For the moment his concern was for the Medallion—and Miss Kingly. He could not allow himself to be distracted.

With movements too swift for human eyes, Lucien disappeared into the shadows and made his way back to the small house that was now his home. His fleetness ensured that he arrived upon the doorstep only moments after Miss Kingly, and with silent steps he slipped in behind her. It was only when he lightly touched her upon the shoulder that she gave a startled jerk and turned to regard him with a wide gaze.

"Oh, Mr. Valin," she breathed, not completely able to hide her relief that he was not some villain intent upon harm.

"Good evening, Miss Kingly," he murmured softly, his gaze deliberately moving to the smudge of dirt upon her cheek and down to the torn bodice of her gown. "What has occurred?"

She belatedly attempted to hide her wounds with the well-worn shawl. "'Tis nothing."

His expression firmed at her ridiculous words. "'Tis more than nothing."

Without awaiting her approval, he grasped her elbow and sternly steered her toward the small front salon. She attempted to protest, but it was obvious she was still too unnerved by the murder of her friend to conjure her usual spirit.

"What are you doing?"

"Those wounds must be attended to or they will become infected," he retorted, leading her to a chair and pushing her onto the threadbare cushion. He crossed toward the sidebar near the window. "I presume you have brandy? Ah, here we are."

Grasping the small bottle of brandy, Lucien returned to the dazed maiden. He paused to remove a handkerchief from beneath his coat and poured the brandy onto the clean linen before gently pulling the shawl aside.

"This is not necessary," she protested as her cheeks filled with heat. "Meg is quite capable of assisting me."

He lifted his head to meet her embarrassed gaze. "Why would you disturb Meg when I am here? Now, hold still, this might burn."

He pressed the handkerchief to the scrape on her shoulder, his lips thinning as she flinched in pain. Amadeus would pay for causing her injury, he silently promised himself, determinedly cleaning the bits of dirt from the wound.

"Oh," she choked as he continued his ruthless cleansing.

He gave a rueful grimace. "I fear I have no means of making this painless."

She gritted her teeth. "It does not matter."

"May I inquire how you managed to find yourself in such a condition?" he demanded, hoping to take her mind off his ministrations.

"I encountered some ruffians."

"Ah. Hardly surprising in such a neighborhood. I suppose it would be a waste of time to warn you that a young, lovely maiden should not be wandering the streets at this hour?"

"You suppose correctly," she retorted in tart tones, no doubt having been warned of the dangers on more than one occasion.

"At least you should take along a companion. A lone woman is far more likely to be attacked."

"I will not endanger Meg."

His gaze met her own squarely. "Only yourself?"

She gave a lift of her shoulder, only to wince at the movement.

"It is my decision to make."

He smiled wryly at her stubborn tone. She would not easily be dissuaded from her reckless behavior. Not when she was convinced she was saving those poor souls upon the street. And unable to reveal the truth of her danger, Lucien was stuck in the unenviable position of somehow charming her into accepting his assistance.

A task that he would not wish upon his most dire enemy.

"Undoubtedly, my dear," he soothed as he continued to work upon the deep scratch. "An independent woman such as yourself has no need to request permission to go where she chooses."

She eyed him with open suspicion, as if sensing his devious intent. "Precisely."

"And yet, surely a wise woman would take more care?"

Her features abruptly hardened at the unshakable truth in his accusation. "Are you finished?"

"In a moment." Lucien carefully considered his words, knowing that any misstep could take days, if not weeks, to repair. "Do you go out often at night?"

"Yes."

"You help those in need?"

"When possible." The beautiful eyes darkened. "Unfortunately I cannot help them all."

Knowing that she must be thinking of the recently murdered Molly, Lucien offered a smile of sympathy.

"No one person can."

"No, I suppose not."

Lucien slowly straightened to gaze down at her pale countenance, his heart once again struck with her gentle beauty. A beauty that was reflected in her generous heart.

"I have a proposition for you, Miss Kingly," he said in low tones.

She swiftly stiffened in wary confusion. "I beg your pardon?"

"I am willing to pay you . . . let us say one

pound . . . for each occasion you allow me to accompany you during your visits to the street."

There was a moment of shocked silence before she slowly rose to her feet.

"What?"

"I believe you heard me."

"But . . . why? Why would you be willing to offer such wealth for the inconvenience of accompanying me as I meet with pickpockets and fallen women?"

His lips twisted with wry humor at the sharp disbelief in her tone.

"You are not the only soul who feels compelled to help those in need. And I happen to believe that at the moment you are very much in need."

"Me? Absurd." Her chin tilted to a proud angle at the implication she might harbor a hidden vulnerability. "I am not in need."

Unable to help himself, Lucien reached out to lightly touch the perfect skin of her cheek. His fingers tingled with pleasure as they traced over the satin softness.

"You make your choice as to whom you offer your service, Miss Kingly. Surely I am allowed to make my own choice as well."

She allowed his touch to linger a delicious moment before she was sharply pulling away.

"This is ridiculous."

He arched a golden brow at her unsteady accusation. "Will you toss away the opportunity to acquire such ready coin because you think me ridiculous?"

"I think you mad."

"Perhaps." He gave an indifferent shrug, his eyes twinkling with his irrepressible humor. This maiden was certainly not the first to call him mad. "But does it truly matter? You shall have your money and I shall be allowed to rest easy knowing you are safe."

She opened her mouth to condemn him to the devil for his audacity, but even as her pride rebelled at his implication that she was incapable of caring for herself, common sense began to intrude. She hesitated, gnawing her bottom lip as she was forced to consider his rash offer.

"One pound for every night?" she demanded in thick tones.

"Yes."

"Just to accompany me?"

He paused, deciding to take full advantage of her momentary wavering. He was determined to save her not only from the streets, but from past wounds as well.

"And there is one more condition."

"What is that?"

His smile widened as he stepped close to her stiff form. "That each evening we also indulge in less serious pursuits."

An expression of outrage swept over her countenance. "I should have known."

Chuckling at her predictable reaction, Lucien laid his fingers gently upon her arms. "Hold a moment. I mean only harmless pastimes such as cribbage or backgammon."

The outrage slowly faded, to be replaced with a faint frown. "I have no interest in such frivolous games."

"So you will not accept my bargain?" he teased lightly. "Not even to help those you claim to care so deeply about?"

The challenge was undeniable, and again she hesitated.

One pound might be meaningless to Lucien, but to a woman in Miss Kingly's position it was a veritable fortune. And while she might scorn material gain for herself, she was far too determined to help others to easily turn her back upon any help that might be possible.

Even if it meant making a bargain with the devil.

Or a very devious vampire.

At long last allowing her compassion for others to overcome her pride, she settled her hands upon her hips and flashed him a glare that would no doubt have slain him had he not been an Immortal.

"Very well. If you wish to toss away your money with such reckless disregard, I accept. But, I warn you, I will endure no nonsense. I will expect you to remember you are a gentleman."

"So be it, my dear." Taking her hand, he lifted her fingers to lightly brand them with a kiss. "Our bargain has been sealed."

Chapter 3

After a night spent chastising herself for her stupidity in agreeing to Mr. Valin's ridiculous bargain, Jocelyn awoke with the determination to put the foolishness from her mind.

She had been shaken to learn that Molly had been savagely murdered, and oddly disturbed by her encounter with Mr. Fallow. The unknown vicar may have shown his bravery and compassion by rushing to her aid, but she had found his presence disturbing in a manner she could not explain. Indeed, she had almost wondered if she would not rather have faced the villains alone.

All in all, the evening had been a horrid reminder of the savage world she now inhabited. It was little wonder that she had been caught off guard and easily manipulated into the devilish bargain.

Now she could only attempt to make the best of

the unfortunate situation with as much grace and dignity as possible.

She grimaced wryly as she sat behind the desk in her study. Somehow it seemed extremely difficult to maintain any grace or dignity when in the presence of Mr. Valin. He was too impertinent, too brazen, and too utterly charming. His irreverent spirit was a constant threat to her calm composure.

Resolutely putting aside all thoughts of Mr. Valin and the unfortunate Molly, Jocelyn carefully checked over her most pressing bills. Many she would be able to attend to with the rent money she had received, and the others could wait until her quarterly allowance arrived. There was not much extra, but with great care she knew that she would be able to buy the additional food necessary to help the street urchins who depended upon her.

She was busily making a list of supplies, when Meg abruptly stepped into the room with a decided air of annoyance.

"There's a gent here to see you, Miss Jocelyn," she announced in disapproving tones. "He says he's a Runner."

"A Runner?" Jocelyn rose to her feet in surprise. Although the Watch haphazardly controlled the rough streets, it was rare for a Bow Street Runner to take an interest in the refuge of humanity that huddled in the darker streets of London. "You had better show him in, Meg."

Meg folded her arms across her ample chest with a loud sniff. "Not that it's my place to judge, but I would think that a man like that would have more important matters to attend to than bothering law-abiding maidens and tracking dirt onto my freshly scrubbed floors."

Jocelyn could not halt a small smile at the disgruntled tones. Meg had never fully approved of her desire to live in such a neighborhood and help others. And she liked it even less when she felt Jocelyn was being put upon.

She was far more protective than any mother.

"No doubt he considers his business here of some necessity," Jocelyn murmured.

There was another decisive sniff. "It had best be is all I can say. Otherwise he can clean them floors himself."

Meg reluctantly turned to leave the room, stomping away in a manner that indicated that she was intending to severely chastise the caller for daring to interrupt Jocelyn.

Stepping around the desk, Jocelyn was kept waiting only a moment before the large, surprisingly young man with a smiling countenance and thatch of unruly brown curls entered the room. He appeared more an innkeeper or merchant than a dangerous Runner, and Jocelyn found her initial unease lessening as he offered a dashing bow.

"Forgive me for intruding, Miss Kingly. I am Mr. Ryan."

"Mr. Ryan." She gave a nod of her head. "I understand you are from Bow Street."

He smiled ruefully. "Alas, it is true, but please do not hold that against me. I am merely a simple chap attempting to do my poor best to make a living."

Jocelyn was swift to sense this man used his decidedly boyish charm to his full advantage. If not for the shrewd glint of intelligence in the blue eyes, it would be easy to mistake him for an easily deceived fellow.

She could only wonder how many criminals had been lured into admitting far more than they should.

"Will you have a seat?" she asked as she perched on the edge of a chair near the desk. She waited until he had settled his own large form onto a chair opposite her before continuing. "What can I do for you?"

Thankfully he came directly to the point. "I am investigating the death of Molly Chapwell."

Jocelyn lifted a hand to press it to her heart. The pain was still too fresh to be easily accepted.

"Poor Molly."

He lifted a brow at her words. "You knew she had been murdered?"

"Vicar Fallow informed me last evening." She

grimaced at the memory of the small man who sent chills down her spine. "I was searching for her."

"Ah, yes." He ran a hand along his jaw in a thoughtful manner. "The vicar who discovered her body."

"He said that it was a savage attack."

Mr. Ryan's smile faded. "I won't lie to you, miss. It was as bad as I've ever seen."

Jocelyn shivered, unable to imagine anyone able to hurt the simple, kindhearted maiden, no matter whether she was a prostitute or not.

"Why? Why would someone harm Molly in such a vicious fashion?"

He paused for a moment. "To be honest, I was hoping that you could answer that question."

"Me?" she retorted in surprise.

"You did know her."

"Only from the streets." She heaved an unconscious sigh. "I attempted to convince her to leave her life as a prostitute and travel to the small property I own outside of London. Unfortunately she would not heed my urgings. Now it is too late."

"You did not perhaps know if she was fearful of any person in particular?" he demanded.

Jocelyn briefly considered Molly's drunken husband, who had more than once left her with a black eye. He was obviously violent. And yet she could not believe he would readily dispose of his one source of income. He may have been despicable, but he was not entirely stupid.

"Not that she revealed to me," she at last conceded.

"Would she seek you out if she discovered herself in danger?"

The question caught Jocelyn off guard. Would Molly come to her if she were in need?

"I do not know. Perhaps." She gave a lift of her hands. "Why do you ask?"

"Because this was found clutched in her hand." Mr. Ryan leaned forward to press a crumbled piece of paper into Jocelyn's hand.

Startled, she glanced down to discover her name roughly scrawled across the torn sheet.

"It has my name on it," she breathed in shock, then her brows drew together in confusion. "But . . ."

"What is it?"

She slowly lifted her gaze to meet his steady regard. "Molly could not read or write."

The blue eyes narrowed at her sudden exclamation. "Most astute, Miss Kingly. That was what I presumed as well."

Jocelyn could not halt a deep shudder. It had been disturbing enough to know that an acquaintance had been brutally murdered. To discover she was clutching a paper with her name upon it made the horror even greater. It suddenly seemed very personal.

"Why would she have my name on a scrap of paper?" she whispered.

Mr. Ryan regarded her somberly. "It appears that there are two possibilities. Either she was given the paper for some unknown purpose. Or . . ."

"What?"

"Or the paper was placed in her hand after she was murdered."

She dropped the note onto the floor, her fingers unwittingly rubbing against her skirts, as if to rid herself of the nasty sense of menace that tingled through her.

"Why? For what purpose?"

The large man grimaced. "That I cannot say."

"Dear heavens," she breathed, more disturbed than she wished to admit.

"I tell you this only because I believe you should take care, Miss Kingly. It might well be that your work among those less fortunate has made you a dangerous enemy."

With an effort she gathered her calm about her. She would not be panicked into abandoning those who depended upon her support. After all, she had been terrified when she had first taken this house so close to the stews. And even more terrified when she had first ventured into the streets at night. Whatever came along she would face squarely, not cowering behind her door.

"That is absurd," she said in crisp tones. "I do

nothing more than offer hope to those who have none."

"There are always those who earn a profit from the misery of others," he pointed out with more than a hint of warning. "They would not appreciate your interference."

She could hardly argue the truth of his words. There were always people like Molly's husband. And those horrid men who sold children to brothels. She would not doubt that several cursed her name. Perhaps even desired to rid the streets of her presence.

But there were also countless others who viewed her as their rescuer from starvation or worse.

"Do not ask me to halt my efforts, Mr. Ryan," she said in low tones. "I will not."

He slowly smiled, as if expecting her staunch response. "I only ask you keep in mind that there is danger in what you do. And perhaps when you are upon the streets that you notice anything peculiar."

Jocelyn rose to her feet, offering a small nod. "Very well."

Shoving himself upright, the Runner allowed his inner resolve to chase away his air of jovial goodwill.

"Do not fear," he assured her in relentless tones. "We shall soon have this monster in Newgate."

She did not doubt for a moment that this man would be tireless in his search for the killer. Unlike most, he did not sneer when he spoke of Molly, or dwell upon the fact she was a mere prostitute. Instead, there was a grim determination etched into his countenance.

"I do hope so. He should be punished for what he did to poor Molly."

"He will. Until then, please take care."

"Yes, I will."

"Then I will bid you good day." With a bow the man turned to leave the room.

Jocelyn remained standing as she considered the unexpected visit. She was determined not to overreact to the announcement that Molly was clutching her name in her hand. There could be a dozen explanations. It would be foolish to plague herself with concerns that might very well be imaginary.

All the same, if she were perfectly honest with herself, she could not deny a renegade flare of relief that Mr. Valin had forced his way into her home.

For all his rakish charm, she sensed that he would make a dangerous adversary.

And at least for the near future she would not be alone.

The hack pulled to a halt in the shadows of St. Giles. With care Lucien helped Miss Kingly to alight complete with a large basket she had insisted she bring with her. He had been rather surprised when she had made no protest at his determination to accompany her to the streets on this evening, and he could only wonder what had occurred with the Runner earlier in the day.

Obviously something had unnerved her enough to lower her pride to the point of welcoming his assistance. And while he was relieved not to endure a lengthy argument, he could not help but ponder what danger she faced.

Whatever it was, he would do well to be on his guard, he sternly assured himself, his gaze lingering on the delicate lines of her face. No matter how invincible she might consider herself, he knew that she could never be prepared for what hunted her now.

No mortal, no matter how brave or determined, could be prepared for a vampire.

As if sensing his concern but misunderstanding the cause, she regarded him with a lift of her brows.

"You are determined upon this?" she demanded.

He smiled as he firmly took her hand and placed it upon his arm. "Quite determined, my dove. I will be at your side each night you travel to the streets, and even pay for the privilege."

She gave a faint shrug, but she could not entirely disguise her relief. "'Tis your money."

"Indeed it is. And soon to be yours."

"Yes." She glanced down the darkened street. "We go down that way."

Lucien gave a nod, but before he could take a

step, a familiar tingle raced down his spine. He stilled, searching through the darkness with his mind to locate the source of the malice that was nearly tangible in the air. It took a moment to locate the vampire in a nearby alley, and he reluctantly removed Miss Kingly's hand from his arm.

"A moment, my dear."

She glanced at him in surprise. "What is it?"

"Remain here. Do not stray."

"Mr. Valin, where are you going?" she demanded with a hint of impatience.

"To rid us of a pest." Removing the dagger from beneath his coat, he moved with a fluid stealth down the street and slipped into the alley. He confronted the silver mist with a frown. "Reveal yourself, Amadeus."

With an eerie chuckle the mist swirled, forming into the shape of the nondescript vicar.

"Just keeping a guard on my property, Lucien. Neither of us would desire harm to come to the Medallion."

Lucien narrowed his gaze in distaste. "I intend to keep a close guard upon Miss Kingly. Your concern is unnecessary."

The vampire gave an impatient click of his tongue. "The female is meaningless. All that interests me is the power that she unwittingly holds. As long as she maintains possession of the Medallion, I shall be near."

It was a threat that Lucien did not doubt for a moment. Amadeus possessed a single-minded purpose that would make him relentless in his quest to gain command of the Medallion.

"It shall never come to you," he swore in low tones.

Again Amadeus chuckled, his expression mocking as he regarded Lucien.

"It will be mine within the month. There is nothing you can do to halt me."

Lucien clutched the dagger in his hand. "Do you wish to settle this now?"

"Now? That would hardly be logical," the vampire retorted. "The moment is not yet ripe to put my plans in motion."

Plans? Lucien experienced a flare of unease. He deeply disliked the knowledge that the cunning vampire was patiently plotting in the shadows. He was devious and utterly ruthless. Worst of all, it appeared that he would not be easily swayed into giving up his desperate desire for power.

"I do not desire to destroy you, Amadeus," he said in dark tones, his reluctance unmistakable. "But I will if I must."

"You?" Amadeus stepped forward, his eyes glittering with cold amusement. "Within a few days you will be bored of your role as heroic knight and be seeking more enticing entertainments. You have never been worthy of being a true vampire."

The condemnation struck deeply. There was no denying that many among the vampires had considered him a plague rather than an equal among brothers. Even the Great Council had chastised him for his frivolous nature and lack of responsibility.

And perhaps, deep inside there was a faint doubt that he was equal to the great task laid upon him. A task that might very well have been given to a far more worthy vampire.

He would not, however, reveal any weakness to Amadeus.

"I will not fail," he pledged softly. "I will not."

"Of course you will," Amadeus mocked. "It is as inevitable as my undoubted success. I always win, my poor boy. You would be wise to stay out of my path."

The air around the vampire suddenly shimmered, and in a blink of the eye Amadeus had changed into a large black dog. With one powerful vault he was past Lucien and bounding down the street.

With a curse, Lucien turned to follow, but even as he left the alley, the slender form of Miss Kingly was appearing from the shadows.

"Mr. Valin."

He grimaced with impatience, knowing he could not abandon this maiden to pursue the vampire.

There were more dangers than Amadeus in the dark streets.

Calming his fiery desire to discover precisely what the renegade was plotting, Lucien regarded the pale face with a lift of his brow.

"I thought I told you to stay put."

Her pride was instantly ruffled by his stern words. "I do not take orders from you, Mr. Valin."

His irritation was swift to fade at her stiff defiance, and a smile curved his lips as he held out his arm. "So I see. Shall we go?"

There was a moment's pause before she at last laid her fingers upon his arm, although she made no move to continue down the street.

"What were you doing?"

Lucien grimaced, still able to feel the faint choking sense of malevolence. "Having a word with an old friend."

"A friend." Her eyes abruptly narrowed. "In this neighborhood?"

He abruptly laughed as he realized the direction of her thoughts. "Stop glaring at me in such sour disapproval. My friend was not a poor lady from the local brothel. It was an acquaintance from my homeland."

A faint color touched her cheeks at the realization she had leapt to conclusions, but her gaze remained steady. "Where is your homeland?"

Lucien shrugged. "At the moment it is in the garret of your house."

"That is not what I meant."

"No?"

"No."

Although he was uncertain that he could keep his secrets forever, Lucien was not about to confess to truth until he had proven to this maiden she could trust him.

"I believe we should be about our task. The night is swiftly passing."

She frowned into his impassive countenance. "What are you hiding?"

"All things in their time, my dear. For now I think we should concentrate upon what we set out to do this evening."

Perhaps sensing he was not about to satisfy her curiosity at the moment, she gave him a last probing glare before reluctantly nodding her head.

"As you say. It is this way."

Allowing her to lead the way down the street, Lucien kept a watchful eye upon the various drunks and ruffians that tumbled from the local gin houses. More than one allowed their gazes to linger with hunger upon the beautiful maiden at his side, but one glance into his set countenance was enough to convince them to move along to less dangerous game.

He was so intent upon his vigilant guard that he

nearly stumbled over Miss Kingly when she came to an abrupt halt before a tumble down building.

"An empty warehouse?" he demanded in puzzlement.

"It is not empty." She headed toward a narrow door. "Come, but be on your guard."

He smiled ruefully at her warning. "I am always on my guard, my dove."

Coming to the door, Miss Kingly knocked sharply upon the splintering wood. From within, a muffled voice could be heard.

"Who passes?"

"It is Miss Kingly."

There was a moment of silence. "Do you know the password?"

"Thomas," Miss Kingly retorted in stern tones.

"Sorry, that ain't be it."

"Thomas, open this door at once."

With ready speed the door was pulled open to reveal an urchin with a round, dirty face and clothes far too large for his slender frame.

"Just be having a bit of fun, Miss Kingly," he said with a roguish grin.

"Mmm. I have a good mind to give your peach tart to another."

The lad did not appear particularly concerned by the threat. Indeed, his grin only widened.

"Now, you know I be yer favorite, Miss Kingly."

The maiden gave a chiding click of her tongue,

but there was no mistaking the glint of amusement in her eyes.

"You are a scamp."

"Aye, but an adorable scamp."

Miss Kingly chuckled as she reached into the basket she carried to remove a small bag.

"Are there any injuries?"

"Freddie was roughed up a bit last night," the lad answered, his grin fading.

"Where is he?"

"In the corner."

"Here." Miss Kingly handed the basket to the boy. "Feed the youngest first."

"Aye, Captain," the urchin readily agreed, turning about to hurry from the door.

At the maiden's side Lucien stepped into the dirty, shadowed interior of the warehouse. He briefly halted as the smell of sewage and rotting food threatened to overwhelm his heightened senses. Great Nefri, but the place was a cesspit.

A fierce urge to grasp Miss Kingly in his arms and take her from this awful place rippled through him. No maiden should be exposed to such wretched surroundings. But even as the thought was running through his mind, his gaze caught sight of the mass of children huddled around Thomas and the basket of food.

There were at least twenty of them, ranging in age from sixteen to a few who could not be more than five. His heart faltered at the knowledge that they had been thrown onto the streets as if they were no more than garbage.

It was little wonder that Miss Kingly found it impossible to turn her back on such misery, he thought, turning his head to watch the maiden as she moved toward a small form huddled in a distant corner.

It seemed impossible to believe that any creature with any heart at all could allow such misery to exist.

Uncertain whether to join Miss Kingly and risk frightening the injured child, Lucien was halted as a small hand suddenly clutched his fingers.

Glancing down, he was instantly enchanted by the tiny girl with a heart-shaped face and large brown eyes that were regarding him with absolute trust. With great care not to startle the child, he settled his tall length onto a dusty barrel, indifferent to the knowledge his breeches would be ruined.

She regarded him in silence before calmly climbing onto his lap and polishing off the peach tart she held in her grimy fingers. Lucien instinctively cuddled her close, thoroughly caught off guard by the warm glow that entered his heart at the sensation of her tiny form settling against his chest.

He was uncertain how long they sat there in silence, but sensing someone watching him, Lucien lifted his head to discover Miss Kingly regarding him in surprise.

"Are you finished here?" he asked in low tones.

She gave a slow nod of her head. "Yes."

Gently running his hand over the girl's tangled locks, he reluctantly set her onto her feet and watched as she hurried toward the other children. Only then did he rise to his feet and fall into step beside Miss Kingly as she made her way back to the door and out into the street.

Realizing that she was still regarding him with puzzled surprise, he abruptly came to a halt and met her gaze squarely.

"What is it?"

"Annie."

It took a moment to work out that she was referring to the child he had held on his lap.

"Is that her name? A charming minx."

"She is very wary of adults. Indeed, I have never been allowed even to come close to her," the maiden confessed.

Lucien smiled at her puzzlement. Obviously she did not consider him the sort of gentleman who would naturally be good with children.

"Perhaps she was felled by my charm," he teased lightly. "Females find it quite irresistible, you know."

A reluctant smile curved her lips. "Whatever the reason, I am grateful you coaxed her into eating her dinner. Although the older children do their best, she is easily overlooked."

Lucien reached up to tenderly cup her chin. "It is no hardship to be kind to children."

A faint tremor raced through her at his touch, and his heart quickened as she reached out to tongue and moisten her lips.

"I wish that all shared your sentiment. There are so many I cannot reach."

Stepping closer, he allowed the passions that had been so long suppressed to course through his blood. In the soft night his blood ran hot.

"That is enough for this evening, Miss Kingly," he said in husky tones. "You have done your duty and it is time to consider more enjoyable pastimes."

Sensing the sudden heat in the air, her eyes widened. "What enjoyable pastimes are you referring to?"

He gave a low chuckle. "You shall soon discover, Miss Kingly."

Chapter 4

Jocelyn shifted uneasily on her chair as she cast a covert glance at the elegant gentleman seated across the small chessboard from her. He should appear ludicrously out of place in the shabby room with his expensive clothes and the candlelight shimmering in the tawny strands of his long hair. Even the delicate beauty of his features was a direct contrast to the harsh surroundings. He surely was a creature of Mayfair.

And yet there was no hint of discomfort in the noble countenance or any air of a gentleman who thought himself above such meager entertainment as a game of chess with an aging spinster.

Instead, a wicked smile played about his lips that thoroughly distracted Jocelyn from any hope of strategy.

Perhaps sensing her intense scrutiny, the golden

gaze abruptly lifted to regard her with open amusement.

"Checkmate," he announced in soft tones.

Startled out of her odd distraction, Jocelyn glanced down at the chessboard to discover that she had indeed been properly cornered.

A disgruntled disbelief flared through her at being so easily bested.

"Impossible," she muttered.

He leaned negligently back in his seat, making no effort to hide his satisfaction. "I did warn you that I am quite skilled."

"I am known to possess a certain amount of skill myself," she retorted with a hint of annoyance.

"You have skill," he conceded before allowing his gaze to deliberately drop to her full mouth. "But not enough daring. You play a game of defense, not willing to risk all to capture victory."

It would be impossible to escape the knowledge that he spoke of more than a mere chess game, and Jocelyn struggled to hide that absurd prickle of awareness that raced through her.

"Risk can as easily bring defeat."

If possible, his smile became even more devilish. "That is why it is so thrilling. Anyone can move pieces in a well-plotted routine." The golden gaze returned to pierce deep into her wary eyes. "Ah, but one who is willing to boldly strike out without knowing if he is destined to taste success or falter in failure is truly a master of the game."

She did not doubt that he was a master of such games. He would be bold and daring whether playing chess or facing an enemy or seducing a woman.

And in truth, she had once been very much like him. Confident, brash, and utterly confident that she was impervious to danger.

Life had taught her a bitter lesson in assuming that she could play with fire and not be burned. And burned badly.

"Routine plodding is far more dependable than brash recklessness," she philosophized.

His eyes narrowed as if he sensed she was hiding secrets deep inside. "But where is the fun?"

"The satisfaction of success."

A surprising hint of tenderness softened the beautiful features. "There is little point in achieving success if you did not enjoy the path leading to your purpose."

"There are other things in life beyond fun and enjoyment," she determinedly argued.

"What?"

"Duty, responsibility, and consideration of others."

Slowly he leaned forward, his hand reaching out to lightly touch her cheek.

"All very noble, Miss Kingly, but life is a banquet that should be sampled to the fullest. Duty, joy, love . . . passion."

Although his touch was as gentle as a feather, Jocelyn felt scalded by the fingers that lingered against her skin. She thought she was no stranger to passion. Hadn't she once before tasted of the forbidden fruit?

But her brief experience did not seem to make her any more prepared for the flutters of excitement that sped through her or the sudden racing of her heart.

With an awkward haste she rose to her feet and backed away from his large form.

"It is growing late," she muttered, watching warily as he swiftly gained his feet and moved to stand directly before her.

"Where are you going?"

"To bed."

With deliberate, relentless steps he backed her toward a nearby wall, placing his hands on each side of her head to effectively trap her.

"Not quite yet, I think," he murmured.

She sucked in a sharp breath, then wished she hadn't. The warm scent of male skin and a faint hint of spice threatened to cloud her mind. A potent, undeniable quiver of longing swept through her.

"What do you want?" she demanded in unsteady tones.

Those distracting fingers lifted to stroke the line of her exposed throat, coming to rest upon the frantic beat of her pulse at the base of her neck.

"You lost the match, my dove. Now you must pay your forfeit."

"I . . . there was no mention of a forfeit."

His soft chuckle feathered down her spine, sending a rash of delightful sensations through her stiff body.

"What is the point of winning a game if I cannot collect a prize?"

Jocelyn discovered herself battling to maintain her usual calm demeanor. This man possessed the most shocking ability to slip beneath her defenses and stir sensations she had thought buried forever.

With wide eyes she regarded the delicate features of his countenance.

"What sort of prize?"

He slowly smiled. "Ah, you should have determined the precise nature of the wager before accepting our bargain."

She wanted to be furious at his audacity. To be able to wound him with the sharp edge of her tongue. But it was utterly impossible when she was shivering at the temptation that swirled thickly through the air.

"Mr. Valin, I warn you that I will tolerate no foolishness," she forced herself to mutter.

The golden brows lifted as his fingers daringly stroked the modest neckline of her gown.

"What shall it be, Miss Kingly? I have no need for coin, nor do I care for trinkets, although . . ." His gaze slowly lowered to where the golden amulet lay against her white skin. "I must confess a fascination with the Medallion that you wear about your neck."

Muddled by his proximity, and not at all prepared for his sudden interest in the amulet, she instinctively lifted her hand to clutch the necklace.

Having become accustomed to the strange weight of the amulet, she rarely recalled the encounter with the old gypsy woman. She had been on her way home from visiting the small farm where she placed those women willing to leave the streets, when the gypsy had suddenly stepped before her carriage. Afraid that she had been hurt, Jocelyn hurriedly climbed down to tend to the old woman.

What followed was oddly difficult to recall, although she did clearly remember the gypsy placing the amulet about her neck and telling her that she must never give it to another. She had warned that a gypsy gift was both blessed and cursed, and that she would receive happiness beyond measure if she carefully guarded the necklace from all others.

Jocelyn, of course, was far too sensible to believe in such nonsense. Gypsies were notorious for spreading such tales. Still, she discovered herself unwilling to part with the bauble. It had become almost a part of her now.

"No," she denied with a shake of her head. "It was a gift."

"Ah. From an admirer?"

"Actually it came from a gypsy."

"A gift from a gypsy." His fingers brushed over the amulet and Jocelyn gave a small jerk at the tiny prickles that seemed to come from the warm metal. "Is it blessed?"

Feeling rather foolish, she gave a lift of one shoulder. "If you believe in such things."

He held her gaze for a moment. "Oh, I believe, as should you. Such a blessing can be a powerful force against evil."

There was something in his tone, some dark quality that made Jocelyn feel a shadow fall over her. "Evil?"

His features became stark, the golden eyes darkened with some inner thought.

"It exists, make no mistake about that, my dove," he warned in husky tones. "And it is closer than you ever dreamed possible."

She shuddered at the words. "What on earth do you mean?"

"You must take great care. A shadow moves through London."

Jocelyn briefly thought of poor Molly and the note that had been left in her dead hand. A prick of dread touched deep in her heart.

"Are you attempting to frighten me?"

Easily able to sense her rising anxiety, Mr. Valin allowed his distracting smile to return.

"No, I only offer a warning. Keep the amulet close to you and give it to no one. It might very well save your life."

Jocelyn stilled at his soft words. It seemed impossible that he would echo almost precisely the same warning as the old woman.

"That is what the gypsy told me. Do you know something of this amulet?" she demanded in suspicion.

"Perhaps." His voice lowered and his accent was more noticeable as his fingers stroked over her skin. "But at the moment I am more interested in my prize."

Jocelyn was well aware that he was deliberately attempting to distract her. Unfortunately he was succeeding all too well. She could think of nothing beyond the delicious feel of his touch.

"Mr. Valin . . ."

"Let me see," he teased softly. "We have ruled out money and trinkets. What do you have left to offer?"

"Nothing."

The golden eyes abruptly flared with undisguised desire. "Do not be so certain. There is always this. . . ."

His words trailed away as he slowly lowered his head. Jocelyn knew beyond a doubt he was going to kiss her. Just as she knew that he was giving her ample opportunity to halt him if she so desired. But even as her hands lifted to press against his chest, her lips were parting in an undeniable invitation.

She wanted him to kiss her, she dizzily acknowledged. Despite all logic. Despite all the warnings clamoring in the back of her mind. Despite all the betrayal she had endured. She wanted to know the feel of his mouth against her own.

Keeping her gaze entangled with his own, he continued downward, at last touching her lips in a tender kiss. Jocelyn's breath caught at the soft caress. It was enchanting. Astonishing. Magical.

With gentle care he explored her mouth, urging her to soften against the welcome hardness of his large form.

Warm, sweet pleasure flooded through her, making her knees weak and her head spin. How easy it would be to lose herself in such delicious sensations.

Far too easy.

With a gasp she pulled back to regard him with a guarded unease. "No. Please, do not."

The golden eyes smoldered beneath his lowered lashes. "Do my kisses offend you?"

Offend her? They nearly set her on fire with longing, she reluctantly acknowledged.

"It is not proper," she rasped.

"That was not what I asked. Do you dislike my touch?" he persisted.

"I . . . I wish to go to my chambers."

"Answer me, Jocelyn." He put a finger beneath her chin, forcing her to meet his relentless gaze. "The truth."

"I do not want to feel this," she whispered.

His lips twitched with rueful humor. "I, on the other hand, could not be more delighted." Without warning he swooped down to brush a kiss over her forehead. "Now run along to your chambers, my dove. We will begin our game again tomorrow."

Jocelyn did not hesitate.

The moment he shifted aside she was swiftly crossing the room and rushing out the door. It was not until she was safely in her chambers that she at last took a deep breath.

Dear heavens. She had been right. Mr. Valin was dangerous. Perhaps the most dangerous gentleman she had ever encountered.

Lucien watched Jocelyn's hurried departure with a rueful smile. He had not wished to allow her to escape so easily. He had not wanted to allow her to escape at all. Not when he had felt her shiver with longing beneath his touch.

In the silken night his long-denied passions shimmered with incandescent heat. Even now he could still smell the warm scent of her skin and feel the satin of her lips. A tremor raced through him.

Miss Jocelyn Kingly was proving a temptation that he was finding more and more difficult to resist. Only the memory of the stark loneliness in those beautiful eyes kept him from charging down the hall and carrying her off to his cramped garret.

She needed a friend and a savior, he sternly reminded himself. Her danger was all too real. Not only from Amadeus and his henchmen, but also from the brittle wounds that she harbored deep within.

He sucked in a deep breath.

A friend and savior. His passions would have to wait.

Lucien moved across the room to pour himself a glass of the brandy he had brought from the hotel. He allowed the fiery spirit to slowly slide down his throat as he appreciated the smoky flavor. Perhaps not as satisfying as passions of the flesh, but certainly worthy of enjoyment, he attempted to console himself.

He polished off the last of the brandy as he aimlessly strolled back toward the chessboard. His smile returned as he recalled Jocelyn's astonishment at having been bested. Tomorrow he would challenge her to a game of cribbage, he decided with a flare of anticipation.

And for his prize . . . well, another kiss was

certainly tempting, but so was the thought of nuzzling that slender neck or tasting the inner skin of her arm.

His fingers tightly clenched the glass. The dangerous heat once again threatened to rise. Lucien closed his eyes with a faint sigh. He possessed an unsettling premonition that this restless ache was destined to haunt him for many nights to come.

Deciding that another brandy was definitely in order, Lucien moved back toward the sideboard. Lost in his thoughts, he was unprepared when the peaceful silence was shockingly pierced by a sudden scream. Pausing only long enough to slip the dagger from beneath his coat, he was charging from the room and sweeping up the stairs in a blur of movement.

The upper corridor was shrouded in shadows, but his vampire sight made it easy to detect Jocelyn backing from the open door of her chamber, her hand pressed to her mouth.

He charged forward, reaching her side in a mere beat of a heart.

"Jocelyn, what is it?" he demanded, his gaze swiftly ensuring that she had not been injured.

Wide-eyed, she turned to face him, not seeming to notice he had managed to reach her side far more swiftly than humanly possible.

"In my room," she breathed in unsteady tones. "I saw someone creeping beside the bed."

"Remain here," he commanded, not hesitating as he stepped forward.

He was brought to an abrupt halt as she reached out to firmly grasp his arm.

"No. We should call for the Watch," she said, her expression one of concern.

He could not halt a faint smile. Although he did not sense the presence of Amadeus in the house, he was quite certain that it must be one of his Inscrolled servants. A poor human beneath such a powerful spell would be a dangerous foe. They would fight without concern for their own welfare and to the death if necessary. Far too dangerous for the Watch.

"There is no time, my dove," he said softly.

Her eyes darkened even as her fingers clutched into his arm. "But he might be dangerous."

"Not nearly dangerous as I."

"Mr. Valin . . ." Her words trailed away as she gazed into the grim determination etched onto his countenance. Clearly she sensed that he was not to be swayed.

"Believe in me, Jocelyn," he said, covering her hand with his own. "I shall not fail you."

Their gazes met for a silent moment in the shadows, and then she gave a small nod of his head. Lucien felt his heart swell at her ready faith in him.

"Stay here," he commanded yet again, turning to

swiftly move across the corridor and into the dim room.

Scanning the small chamber, he located the shadowed form crouched beside the bed. He kept the dagger held low as he silently slipped over the rough wooden boards. Even without his heightened senses he would have been able to locate the miserable servant. Locked in the spell of Inscrollment, the man was slowly rotting from the inside. The smell was nearly overwhelming as Lucien neared.

Perhaps sensing he was no longer alone, the servant awkwardly turned to confront the approaching vampire. His eyes were blank and his lips slack as he faced certain death without fear.

"The woman," he spat out in slurred tones. "Pretty necklace. Pretty necklace."

Lucien discovered himself hesitating. What could Amadeus be thinking? Even if the mindless servant managed to force the Medallion from Jocelyn, it would be powerless. Nefri had bound the artifact to the maiden, and it must be given freely. To steal it would forsake all he had hoped to gain.

"The woman." The man moved forward, suddenly revealing the short but deadly sword he clutched in his hand. "Necklace."

Lucien carefully backed out of reach of the sword. He was an Immortal, but that did not mean he could not be injured, or even knocked unconscious, leaving Jocelyn at the mercy of this soulless man.

"Be gone with you," he ordered in stern tones. "You shall not be allowed to have the woman."

"Pretty necklace," he rasped, moving relentlessly forward.

Realizing that he had no choice but to rid the house of the dangerous intruder, Lucien backed toward the center of the room, where he would have more space to maneuver. Thankfully the man eagerly followed his path, not realizing his danger. Keeping his gaze upon the sword, Lucien feinted with his dagger, leaving himself seemingly open to attack. As expected, the intruder lunged forward for the kill, unprepared for Lucien to swiftly vault to one side and come at him from behind.

Locking his powerful arms about the man, Lucien heaved him off his feet. Then, ignoring the muted struggles and offensive smell, he carried him toward the open window and tossed him through. There was a dull thud as the man hit the ground below. Astonishingly, however, he was swiftly upon his feet and scrambling toward the nearby alley.

Lucien was preparing to slip out and follow the servant back to Amadeus, when he heard Jocelyn suddenly cry out.

"Lucien."

As he hesitated, he felt an unexpected pain bite deep into his shoulder.

Cursing his foolish inattention, he spun around to discover yet another servant standing with the sword that had been dropped.

Blast himself for a fool. He had been so intent upon the intruder, he had not suspected that another hovered out of sight. A near-catastrophic assumption. His lack of wits could easily have allowed Jocelyn to be harmed. The mere thought sent an icy chill through his blood.

Ignoring the blood he could feel flowing from his wound, he clutched the dagger and waited for the servant to attack. It took only a moment as the man gave a mindless growl and heedlessly charged forward.

It was a simple matter for Lucien to dip low as the villain reached him, grasping the fool by the legs and neatly tossing him through the window.

On this occasion he managed to keep his wits about him, and rather than watching the servant plunge to the ground, he maintained a close guard on the room.

Against a far wall he could see the frightened form of Jocelyn, but there were no other shadows in the cramped chamber. Slipping toward the bed, he carefully ensured that there was no one hidden beneath and then moved to search the narrow armoire.

At last convinced that they were indeed alone, he slipped the dagger beneath his jacket and heaved a rueful sigh.

"They are gone."

As if some spell had been broken, Jocelyn gave a low cry and abruptly charged forward.

"Oh, Mr. Valin . . . Lucien . . . are you harmed?"

He grimaced as he carefully kept his injured shoulder turned away. This maiden was certain to question how he was capable of receiving a deep sword wound and healing within a few hours.

"Only a trifling scratch, and only because of my own foolishness," he assured her wryly. "I was so intent upon impressing you with my skill that I blundered into forgetting there might be a second villain. Thank goodness he was as inept as his partner."

His light words were greeted by a lingering frown of concern. "You are certain you are not in need of a doctor?"

"Absolutely certain."

"At least it must be cleaned," she persisted.

Although pleased by her obvious concern, Lucien realized he needed a distraction. He could not allow her to examine the wound. Already the bleeding had halted and the flesh was beginning to weave a smooth bond.

"I will tend to it later." Firmly he moved to gaze

out the open window, not at all surprised to discover that the second villain had disappeared as well. The Inscrolled slaves would be indifferent to any injury, no matter how grievous, in an effort to return to their master. His attention moved to the iron pipe that ran close to the window from the gutters above. That no doubt explained how the intruders managed to enter the house undetected.

"They must have crawled through the window," he murmured.

She crossed to join him. "Yes, it was open when I stepped into the room." There was a startled pause. "They have disappeared."

Realizing that she had expected to discover two broken bodies in her garden, he gave a negligent shrug.

"Yes, the drop is not far."

"Still—"

"At least they are gone," he firmly interrupted, reaching out to grasp her shoulders and turn her to meet his reassuring gaze.

"Yes." A sudden shudder raced through her body. "But why were they here?"

He softly stroked the tense muscles of her shoulders, wishing he could assure her that she need never fear again.

"Desperate thieves, no doubt."

She gave a slow shake of her head, her brow

pleated in unease. "They spoke of a necklace. My necklace."

Lucien sternly kept his expression unreadable. He had hoped that she had not overheard the rasping words of the intruders. It would be difficult enough for her to forget the terror of having her home invaded without worry they might return for the Medallion about her neck.

"Perhaps they noted the amulet when you entered the room and presumed it worth stealing."

"I suppose." Her expression remained filled with doubt. "It is still very odd."

Stepping closer, Lucien carefully encircled her in his arms, hoping to surround her with his strength.

"Let us not dwell upon it, my dove. They are gone and I do not believe that they will soon return."

There was a short pause before she slowly lifted her head to regard him with a somber expression.

"I am relieved you were here."

Lucien stilled, caught off guard by her soft words. Then slowly he smiled deep into her darkened eyes.

"So am I," he whispered gently, wanting nothing more than to ease the fear that lingered within her. This maiden should know only joy, he told himself fiercely. And he would do whatever in his power to see it done. "You see, for a frippery fellow, I do have my uses upon occasion."

To his great relief, a measure of her tension eased and her lips even twitched with reluctant humor.

"Upon occasion, I suppose," she conceded.

He lifted his brow with a wicked glint smoldering in his eyes. "I have numerous other uses beyond rescuing damsels in distress, if you would only allow me to demonstrate."

Despite her best attempts, she could not entirely prevent the faint hint of color that touched her cheeks.

"I believe you have demonstrated quite enough for one evening."

"Ah, but that was only a taste."

"Really, Mr. Valin," she protested in breathy tones.

His hand lifted to lightly stroke the soft skin of her countenance. "I believe you called me Lucien earlier. Such formality is surely unnecessary between friends."

He heard her catch her breath as she abruptly spun away, as if to hide her expression from his searching gaze.

"I think it best if we—" Without warning her words came to a halt and she took a step toward the bed. "What is that?"

Lucien frowned as she reached out to pluck a scrap of paper from the heavy quilt. "I haven't the least notion."

Holding the paper in fingers that visibly trembled, Jocelyn moved toward the window, where the moonlight offered a silver glow.

"Miss Kingly," she read aloud. "They are dying. Will you save them? It is in your hands."

Chapter 5

Jocelyn was uncertain how she discovered herself flat against the wall with Lucien standing directly before her and his hands planted on each side of her head.

One moment she had been slipping on her shawl, preparing to leave for her nightly visit to the streets, and the next she had been swiftly maneuvered toward the wall by an angry gentleman who was currently regarding her with smoldering golden eyes.

"No, Jocelyn," he gritted out between clenched teeth.

With an effort Jocelyn gathered her composure. After a restless night, followed by a long day brooding upon the two thieves who had so rudely intruded into her home, she had been determined to shake off the lingering unease.

Certainly she had been unnerved by the strange thieves. And even more so by the mysterious note they had left behind. But she could accomplish nothing by cowering in her house and fearing every small noise.

She had already learned her lesson in attempting to hide from life. After her scandal, she had done her best to disappear. For weeks she had remained in Surrey, rarely leaving her chambers except when she was certain she would be alone. She had wanted only to flee the pain and embarrassment somehow.

But as the long, dark days had passed, she slowly realized that she was being ridiculous. Surely she possessed more courage and worth than to dwindle to an old, bitter spinster with nothing but regret to fill her memories?

Perhaps the future that she had thought would be hers was gone, but that did not mean she could not find a purpose to her days.

She would face the world bravely. She would help others. Her life would be filled with more than shame and fear.

So, ignoring the temptation to remain comfortably at home and forgetting the danger that lurked just outside the door, Jocelyn had finished her dinner and collected her shawl from the foyer. She had not expected Lucien to appear just as she was stepping toward the door, or that he would so neatly trap her.

"I am going, Mr. Valin," she warned, attempting to ignore the proximity of his large form. Not an easy task when she felt cloaked in his fragrant heat.

Or when the astonishingly beautiful countenance was so close that her fingers itched to reach up and test the smooth bronze of his skin. "And there is nothing you can do to halt me."

"Are you so certain?" A dangerous glint entered the golden eyes. "I could lock you in your chambers until you regain your senses. Or better yet . . ." His gaze deliberately lowered toward her mouth. "In my chambers."

Jocelyn struggled to breathe. She had promised herself she would not react to this man's obvious appeal. Heavens above, she had sworn to forbid him even near. Unfortunately, while her mind might readily acknowledge the danger sizzling in the air, her body was not nearly so wise.

"Mr. Valin."

"Lucien," he firmly corrected her. "Or Luce, if you prefer."

"Mr. Valin," she repeated, only to discover her courage faltering as he slowly began to lower his head. "Oh, very well . . . Lucien," she hurriedly amended, not willing to risk another of those disturbing kisses. The very fact that she was finding it difficult not to lean toward that male form warned her that prudence was preferable to pride. "I must discover if any of the women were harmed."

"I can discover any information you might desire."

"No."

"Why?" The elegant features hardened with impatience. "Why are you being so stubborn?"

Her eyes darkened with an unconscious vulnerability. "Because I learned long ago that I cannot hide from unpleasantness. To cower in fear behind closed doors is no life. I would rather confront my fears, and even danger, face-to-face." She reached out to place her hand upon his arm. "Lucien, I will not live in a prison of my own making."

An oddly arrested expression settled upon his countenance. Almost as if her words had reached deep within him. Then he offered her a wry smile.

"I cannot help but desire to protect you, Jocelyn. It is simply in my nature."

Her fingers tightened upon his arm. Surprisingly she discovered that she was far from offended by his confession. Instead, a warm glow threatened to fill her heart.

"Yes, I know," she said softly.

His lips twisted. "You are determined upon this?"

"Yes."

"You will not leave my side?"

Her brows lifted at his commanding tone. Now he was going too far.

"I have been caring for myself a long time, sir. I no longer depend upon others when I am perfectly capable of seeing to my own needs. It is, in fact, how I prefer my life."

Without warning, his hand shifted to cup her chin in a gentle grasp. "Stubborn."

She grimly ignored the flare of pleasure that tingled through her. It would be all too easy to become addicted to his touch.

"Strong-willed," she corrected him.

His soft chuckle filled the foyer. "Is there a difference?"

"Of course."

"If you say," he murmured, his fingers slowly moving to trace the firm line of her jaw.

The danger in the air shimmered with a sudden heat. "I . . . we should be on our way," she whispered.

His eyes swept over her flushed countenance, lingering for a tantalizing moment upon her unsteady lips.

"You are always eager to be hurrying away when things become interesting."

Interesting?

Perilously insane, more likely.

"Interesting for you, perhaps," she forced herself to retort.

"I think for the both of us if you would just lower your guard."

"My guard is staying precisely where it is," she warned in what she hoped were firm tones. "You might as well resign yourself to that fact."

He gave a shake of his head, the tawny hair that

framed his lean countenance shimmering in the candlelight.

"Never," he swore softly. "I will wait all eternity if need be."

"An eternity?"

"Yes."

Her breath once again became elusive. "You are being absurd. Let us go."

His fingers searched along the curve of her neck, slowly testing the softness of her skin.

"You cannot run from me forever, Jocelyn," he warned in husky tones.

It took far more effort than she cared to admit to abruptly thrust away from the wall and step from his tempting nearness. She felt bewitched, and not at all herself.

In an effort to disguise her odd trembling, Jocelyn made a great show of smoothing her plain gray gown and ensuring her expression was calm.

"I can run an eternity if need be," she retorted in thankfully steady tones.

He smiled ruefully at her swift retreat, although a shimmer of determination remained in the golden eyes.

"Ah, no, that I will not allow," he warned as he moved to place her hand upon his arm and escorted her out the door and down the steps to the darkened street. "Where shall we go first?"

"To the warehouse," she said, having made her

decision earlier in the day. "I wish to ensure the children are safe."

Lucien gave an understanding nod before stepping forward and at last hailing a passing hack. They rode in silence as they made their way the handful of blocks to the derelict warehouse. Jocelyn was soon lost in her concern for the children and women who were forced to sell themselves upon the streets. They were unfortunately vulnerable and all too often the victims of violence. A violence they possessed few means to oppose. Her distraction, however, was ruthlessly pierced as they moved closer and closer to the warehouse. A shiver raced through her as she felt an odd prickle of evil crawl over her skin.

It was ridiculous, she attempted to tell herself. One could not feel evil. And yet, her fingers instinctively reached up to touch the amulet around her neck, as if it were offering her a warning she should not ignore.

The sensation only grew stronger as the hack halted in the shadows of the warehouse. With a stiff reluctance she forced herself to accept Lucien's help in alighting, then moved toward the narrow door. Much to her astonishment, she discovered it already open. A frown marred her forehead. The children were wise enough never to leave the door unattended.

"Thomas?" she called softly.

In a heartbeat Lucien had firmly grasped her arm, the moonlight glinting off the dagger he held in his hand.

"Wait here a moment," he commanded, his features oddly grim.

"No, Lucien. I will not be left behind."

Just for a moment he appeared poised to argue. It was obvious that he desired to keep her tucked away from danger. Then, noting her determined expression, he gave a resigned shake of his head.

"Very well," he conceded, "but remain behind me."

With a startling graceful movement Lucien slipped through the door, leaving Jocelyn to follow behind. She was careful to keep close, still bothered by that ominous sense of dread. Ridiculous or not, it could not be shaken.

They had managed to enter the cavernous room and take several steps forward, when the familiar form of Thomas abruptly stepped in their path.

"'Ere, now. It be Miss Kingly's gentleman."

Lucien came to a smooth halt. "Good evening, Thomas. Is all well?"

An unexpected grin split the dirty, angular countenance. "I'd say. A bloke came earlier with a whole cartload of food."

"What bloke?" Jocelyn demanded, stepping from behind Lucien with a startled frown. For months she had been caring for these children, and never to her knowledge had another shown the slightest interest in their welfare.

"Oh, Miss Kingly." Thomas gave a cocky bow. "Evening to you."

Jocelyn's frown did not ease. "Who brought you the food, Thomas?"

The lad lifted a bony shoulder as he waved his hand toward a distant corner.

"He is over with Freddie."

Turning her head, Jocelyn slowly stiffened as she recognized the thin, balding man attired in black.

"Vicar Fallow," she breathed.

Almost as if hearing her soft words, the vicar slowly turned and regarded her from across the room. Even at such a distance the pale eyes seemed to chill her deep within. They glittered in the darkness with an unholy light, sending a rash of prickles over her skin.

Then she was sternly chastising her absurd fancy. This gentleman had revealed nothing but generous kindness. First by chasing off the villains who had attacked her in the street, and now tonight, by offering starving children a much-needed meal.

She should be delighted with his appearance at the warehouse, not shuddering with distaste.

Keeping that thought firmly in mind, Jocelyn managed to conjure a smile as the vicar hurried across the floor to offer her a faint bow.

"Miss Kingly."

"Vicar," she murmured. "It was most kind of you to bring food to the children."

He moved his hands to his bony chest in a modest gesture. "I fear it is not much."

Jocelyn glanced to where the children greedily gorged themselves upon the large platters of food. "It is far more than they had before."

"Perhaps." The vicar waited until Jocelyn returned her gaze to his thin countenance. "I only wish it were possible to take them away from such squalor. They should have homes with loving families."

"We can do only what is in our power."

"That is true, my dear." He heaved a deep sigh. "Still, I worry for their safety. It is said another maiden was killed this evening."

Jocelyn felt the blood drain from her face. No. This could not be happening. Not another poor, wretched maiden.

"Oh, no," she whispered.

"Terrible, is it not?" Vicar Fallow murmured, reaching out to pat her arm lightly. "A beast walks the streets of London. It is said he hunts someone or something."

Something?

Unconsciously stepping away from his distasteful touch, Jocelyn lifted a hand to the amulet about her neck.

What was happening?

And why?

"I . . ."

"Jocelyn." Abruptly appearing at her side, Lucien wrapped a comforting arm around her shoulder. "There is no need to linger. The children are fed this night."

Shaken by the revelation of yet another murder, Jocelyn readily allowed Lucien to lend her support. The familiar scent of his male warmth shrouded her in a sense of well-being.

"Yes."

The gaunt countenance of Vicar Fallow hardened at the arrival of Lucien, but the thin smile remained intact as he regarded the shaken Jocelyn.

"Miss Kingly, do not forget that I stand ready to be of assistance if ever you should need me."

She felt Lucien's arm tighten about her shoulder as she gave a vague nod of her head. Clearly the two gentlemen had taken a swift dislike of each other.

"Thank you, Vicar."

"Come, Jocelyn," Lucien urged, turning her around and leading her from the warehouse.

Jocelyn made no demur. She wanted to be away from the warehouse, and even the dangerous streets of St. Giles.

A beast did, indeed, seem to be walking the streets of London, and she very much feared he was stalking her.

* * *

Lucien cursed himself for a fool as he carefully bundled Jocelyn in the waiting hack and then settled himself close to her side.

He should have insisted that she not enter the warehouse. He had sensed before they had even arrived that Amadeus would be waiting. But he had assured himself that while he was near, the traitor could do nothing to harm the maiden. And that it was important he discover precisely what Amadeus was plotting.

Besides, he had been touched by her plea to face her life without the walls of a prison, he ruefully acknowledged.

Although life behind the Veil offered eternal peace and prosperity for vampires, he had discovered a growing resentment at being confined over the past two centuries. He did not want a tidy existence that provided for his every need. He longed for the unpredictable, for confronting a day with no notion of what might occur. Like Jocelyn, he desired to confront the delights, pains, and passions life had to offer in the fullest.

And so he had ignored his good sense and allowed Jocelyn to accompany him into the dark streets. Now he could only wonder if he had made a dreadful mistake.

Wrapping his arms about her, he leaned his head against her satin hair.

"You are very quiet," he murmured.

"Vicar Fallow said that another maiden was murdered."

He grimaced, wondering if he should confess that it was Vicar Fallow himself who had committed the atrocity. It would certainly ensure that she never trusted the renegade. But it would also raise endless questions that Lucien was not yet prepared to answer.

How could he confess that Amadeus was a vampire without exposing himself?

And how could he possibly protect Jocelyn if she feared him as a monster?

"I am sorry," he said gently.

"What does this have to do with me?"

Lost in the sweet scent and heat of her, Lucien discovered himself caught off guard by her sudden question.

"What do you mean?"

"First there was Molly, who had a paper with my name in her hand, and then, last night, those horrid men left that note warning others would be killed."

Lucien tucked her closer, briefly wishing that Nefri had chosen any other maiden but this one to bind with the Medallion. He did not want Jocelyn in danger. He did not want to hear that edge of fear in her voice. And most of all, he did not want to know that Amadeus was always skulking in the shadows, waiting to do whatever necessary to gain command of the artifact.

"I truly do not know, my dove," he retorted in rueful honesty. If only he knew what Amadeus plotted, he would feel considerably more confident in his skill to protect her.

She gave a shake of her head. "It makes no sense."

"At the moment I fear I must agree. I do promise, however, that I will discover what the demon is plotting."

Without warning she pulled back to regard him with a worried frown.

"You will not put yourself in danger?" she demanded.

He slowly smiled at the genuine anxiety etched upon her beautiful countenance. Jocelyn may not yet accept the fact that an unmistakable affection was growing between them, but it was there whatever her determination to keep him at arm's length.

"No more danger than necessary," he assured her.

In the shadows her magnificent eyes suddenly flashed with an unmistakable fire.

"Lucien."

He laughed softly at her chiding tones, firmly pulling her back into his arms and pressing her head to his chest. It felt astonishingly wonderful to hold her close.

There was a silent pause before she heaved a soft sigh. "Why is this happening?"

He glanced out the window of the carriage to view the filthy streets lined with desperate, hungry people. How easy it would be to whisk Jocelyn away from all of this and provide her with the beauty and luxury she deserved. But that would not keep her safe from the traitors, and he was far from certain that she desired to leave those poor souls who depended upon her.

It appeared for the moment he could only offer support.

"Jocelyn, you are a strong woman. Strong enough to face this danger and survive."

He felt her shiver. "How can you be so certain?"

Determined to lighten the dark mood that was threatening to overwhelm her, Lucien deliberately tilted her chin up so that he could smile deep into her troubled eyes.

"Because I am not only handsome, charming, and witty, I am also quite perceptive. I no doubt already know you better than you know yourself."

Thankfully the tightness of her features lessened and a hint of amusement glinted to life within her eyes.

"You, sir, are impossible."

"And charming and handsome and witty," he added, bending slowly forward to softly brush those tempting lips with his own.

For one delicious heartbeat she allowed his mouth to linger. Then, with a near-tangible reluctance, she pulled back to regard him with a faint frown.

"You can make no claim of winning any kisses on this night, Lucien," she pointed out in unsteady tones. "There were no wagers or forfeits to be paid."

"Shall I admit that I simply could not resist?"

She opened her mouth to deliver a pert retort, but thankfully the hack drew to a shuddering halt and Lucien was swift to slip out of the door and help her onto the street. She did manage a jaundiced glance as she swept past him and toward the house, but it did not entirely hide the color that stained her cheeks.

Ridding himself of the impatient driver, Lucien strolled up the path to join her as she opened the door and entered the foyer. She was clearly eager to be away from his presence, but with a firm motion he reached up to grasp her arm.

"Hold a moment, Jocelyn. I wish to ensure your chamber is safe."

Her lips thinned at his commanding tone, but as if sensing he would not be pressed upon this issue, she gave a slow nod of her head.

"Very well."

"Wait here."

With a last glance toward Jocelyn, Lucien turned and slipped through the dark silence. Although he could feel no threat in the air, he was not about to make any mistakes on this night. Jocelyn had been frightened enough. He was uncertain even her staunch courage could cope with another unpleasant surprise.

It did not take long to search through the upper chambers, and certain that Amadeus had no further traps devised, Lucien returned down the stairs and took Jocelyn's hands in his own.

"All is well," he assured her softly.

In the light of the candle that had been left by Meg, Jocelyn's features appeared remarkably fragile. Lucien caught his breath, mesmerized by her beauty.

"Then I shall wish you a good night," she retorted.

His hands briefly tightened upon her fingers, desperately wanting to prolong this moment. Only the shadows lingering in her dark eyes kept him from pulling her into his arms and covering her lips with his own.

She was far too vulnerable this evening. He would not take advantage while she was defenseless.

"Sweet dreams, my dove," he murmured, reaching down to brush his mouth over her troubled brow before stepping back to allow her to leave.

She hesitated only a moment before she was moving through the foyer and up the stairs. He stood silently until he was certain she was in her chambers, then he turned to make his way down the hall.

He knew precisely what he would discover in the small kitchen at the back of the house.

Stepping into the cramped room, his gaze swiftly fell upon the large, dour-faced woman seated at the table with a heavy frying pan in her hands.

With his lips twitching in amusement, Lucien strolled to stand beside the table. "Ah, Meg. I thought I would find you still awake."

The woman regarded him with an aggressive frown that would have frightened a hapless thief into an early grave.

"I won't be having any more of them villains bothering Miss Jocelyn."

"She is safely in her chambers," he reassured the loyal servant.

"I warned her there would be nothing but trouble living in such a place," Meg muttered in disgust. "Perhaps now she will listen to reason."

Lucien grimaced. "I would not place too much hope in such an occurrence. She is devoted to her work among the poor."

Meg gave a click of her tongue. "Devoted enough to end up with her throat slit, no doubt."

He stiffened. "Oh, no. I will not allow that to happen," he retorted in fierce tones.

The servant regarded him with a disapproving

glance. "And how will you protect her when you are here for only a few weeks? Soon you will be back among your fancy friends and Miss Jocelyn will be alone."

"I will be here for as long as Jocelyn needs me." He met the distrustful gaze squarely, his features as hard as granite. "I will not allow her to be harmed."

"Then you are not like most gentlemen of society," Meg said with a sniff.

Lucien barely swallowed a sudden laugh. He wondered what the older woman would think if he assured her just how different he truly was. Obviously her opinion of London dandies was not entirely pleasant, but he could not imagine that the notion of a vampire beneath her roof would be any easier to bear.

"I can safely assure you that I am utterly unlike any other gentleman of society."

With a small grunt Meg heaved herself out of her chair, the frying pan still clutched in her hand.

"I shall wait and see."

"As you wish." He sent her a kindly smile. "Go to bed, Meg. I will keep watch upon Jocelyn."

She waved the pan in a warning gesture. "Not too close a watch, mind you."

"Believe in me."

He watched as the servant wearily made her way out of the kitchen and toward her own small bed behind the pantry. For a moment he considered whether to return to the warehouse and attempt to track Amadeus to his lair. He was certainly no further along in convincing the traitor into returning to the Veil than he had been when he first arrived in London. Worse, he still did not know exactly when Amadeus might next strike.

Then he gave a slow shake of his head.

He could not leave Jocelyn in the darkness of night. It was the time of vampires. It was when those who had indulged in bloodlust were at their strongest. And, of course, there was always the danger of Amadeus's henchmen.

He would do precisely as he had promised.

He would stand guard over the woman who was rapidly becoming a very necessary part of his life.

A woman who was stirring more than just his passions to life.

Chapter 6

Hidden in the cellars of a local brothel, Amadeus sat beside the man chained to the heavy table. For nearly a week he had patiently tortured the foolish dandy, careful to keep him upon the edge of death without allowing him to tumble into oblivion.

It was tedious, delicate work. Only a master such as himself could possibly maintain such a fine line between life and death.

But even a master could begin to lose patience, Amadeus conceded, reaching up to remove the gag from the pathetic wretch's mouth.

The pudgy face of the dandy was set in rigid fear as Amadeus bent over him.

"No," he choked out in terrified tones.

Smothering his angry impatience, Amadeus forced a comforting smile to his lips.

"Be at ease, my child," he soothed. "I am here to help. Would you like some water?"

"Yes."

Careful to dribble only the smallest amount of water between the gaping lips, Amadeus bent over the nearly delirious gentleman. The fool appeared a sorry sight with his hair matted with sweat and his finery stained with his own blood. Far different from the arrogant pup who had swaggered into the brothel searching for the more exotic sins of the flesh.

"Now, look at me," he commanded in relentless tones. "Look deep into my eyes. Tell me, what do you see?"

Unable to resist the compelling force of Amadeus's voice, the man gazed helplessly into the pale eyes.

"Darkness," he babbled in fear. "Evil. Evil."

"No, you idiot," Amadeus gritted out. "What do you see? What truths do you behold?"

The dandy shook his head from side to side, spittle foaming at his mouth.

"Servant of hell, begone."

"Fah."

Thoroughly disgusted by the ridiculous buffoon, Amadeus leaned downward and sank his fangs deep within the fat throat. In moments the man below him was arched in the throes of death, and the vampire slowly glutted himself in the delights of bloodlust.

And why not?

It had obviously been a vexing waste of time to attempt to learn anything from the wretched human. Like all the rest, he was weak and unable to concentrate when faced with the ultimate wonder. He had provided him nothing. Nothing but the usual babblings.

Wiping the blood from his lips with a handkerchief, Amadeus slowly regained control of his icy fury.

There were endless mortals to experiment upon, he silently consoled himself. And once the Medallion was in his grasp, he would no longer need to conceal himself in such squalid surroundings with only the dregs of humanity to choose from.

The Medallion.

The pale eyes glittered in the thick darkness.

His desire for the powerful amulet was becoming nearly overwhelming. He could feel it in the distance. A shimmering temptation that taunted him by remaining just out of reach.

"Master."

Amadeus turned to discover his most recent servant shuffling into the dark room.

"What is it?"

"I have brought the glove."

"Ah, yes." Moving forward, the vampire plucked the glove from the man's outstretched hand. Earlier in the day he had commanded the servant to slip into Miss Kingly's home and procure a piece of her clothing. He grew weary of the woman's stubborn refusal to accept his generous offer of friendship. And even more weary of Lucien's unwelcome interference. Tomorrow evening he would attempt a more direct means of acquiring the Medallion. But first . . . "I must hunt another mortal for my experiments. Have this body tossed in the river."

Even for a summer day it was hot.

Golden sunshine bathed the remote meadow in a brilliant afternoon light, the faint breeze spiced by the scent of wildflowers.

But it was not the cloudless sky or the unfamiliar heat that was causing the faint moistness that trickled down Jocelyn's back.

Oh, she might adamantly tell herself that the rapid pace of her heart and unmistakable fever in her blood came from the sun overhead. And that her mouth was dry from the heat. Unfortunately she could not quite make the thought ring true.

Instead, she very much feared it was the tall, lean gentleman who was currently pressed behind her with his arms around her. Although he was officially attempting to teach her how to shoot the bow and arrow she currently held in her hands, very little of her mind was upon the lesson. How could she possibly concentrate upon anything beyond the delicious curls of excitement that were running rampant through her?

It was indecent; she attempted to chide her wayward reaction to his proximity. She knew nothing of this gentleman who had so swiftly invaded her home and her life. He was as much a mystery as the day he had first walked into her study.

And yet, with every passing hour she discovered herself more and more drawn to his dazzling presence. In just a few days he had awakened within her all those unpredictable passions and thirst for life she had thought safely put behind her. And worse, she was uncertain whether to curse him or bless him.

All she did know was that when she was with him she forgot all the pain and darkness that had marred her life. She did not think of the scandal that had ruined her future among society. She did not think of her parents, who had turned her out of their home. She did not even think of the danger that suddenly shrouded her in fear.

There was nothing but Lucien and the gentleness of his smile that could reach her very soul.

Seemingly unaware of her growing weakness, Lucien leaned closer, his breath brushing her cheek as he pressed her arms higher.

"Now pull back slowly," he commanded, waiting until she had pulled the bow tight. "Yes. Hold your arm steady."

Glaring toward the target set across the open meadow, Jocelyn grimaced at the low words. She had already attempted to hit the blasted thing on a dozen occasions. Lucien, of course, had proven to be just as efficient an expert with the bow and arrow as he was at everything else. He had managed to hit the bull's-eye with every arrow he sent winging toward the target.

It was decidedly maddening.

"I am trying," she muttered.

"Concentrate upon the target."

His fingers brushed over her arms left bare by her blue muslin gown. Jocelyn gritted her teeth at the sharp pleasure that flowed through her.

Concentrate? When he was so close that she could feel the very heat of him searing her skin?

"I see the target," she retorted in tart tones.

"No, concentrate upon it until there is nothing else," he corrected her in that dark, honey voice. "Now breathe steadily."

Knowing that it was impossible to concentrate upon anything but the gentleman pressed so intimately against her, Jocelyn heaved a sigh.

"Surely it cannot be so difficult to fly an arrow toward a target?"

"Do you wish to learn the proper technique or not?"

"I suppose."

"Then, concentrate." Keeping his hands upon her arms to help her aim, he waited until she had managed to steady her swift breaths. "Now."

At his command, Jocelyn abruptly let the arrow fly, thoroughly astonished when it actually managed to head in the proper direction, and even caught the bottom of the target. It promptly bounced to the ground, but she did not care.

"I hit it." Grinning broadly at her success, Jocelyn spun about to confront Lucien. "Did you see?"

An indulgent expression spread across the delicately chiseled countenance.

"Yes, I did see. But you allowed your arm to dip when you released the arrow. Would you care to try again?"

"Good gads, no," she retorted with sincere weariness. "I shall be stiff for the next fortnight as it is."

The golden eyes sparkled at her blunt confession. "Very well."

Realizing that she was standing much closer than propriety allowed, Jocelyn reluctantly stepped from his tall form. It was far too easy to forget propriety when she was with this gentleman, she acknowledged ruefully.

Not that she particularly cared about the rigid rules of society any longer. She had already lost that battle. But, she was still a lady, and she would not allow herself to behave as a common tart. Her honor was all she had left.

"Perhaps we should return," she forced herself to murmur. "Meg will begin to fret if we are gone too long. She can be rather protective of me."

His smile was rueful at her vast understatement. "So I had noticed. Still, it does seem a pity. It is a beautiful day to be away from the clutter of town."

Jocelyn lifted her face up toward the golden sunshine. It was beautiful. She had nearly forgotten how lovely the English countryside could be. Surrounded by the dark, grim streets of London, it was easy to become lost in its depressing gloom.

Now she allowed herself to breathe deeply of the sweetly scented air.

"Yes, it is," she whispered, allowing the peace to soothe her troubled soul. "I forget how quiet it can be."

His golden gaze lingered upon her upturned countenance. "Quiet enough to hear the beat of a heart."

Jocelyn abruptly stilled at his odd words.

No. It was simply not possible. She could not hear, and certainly she could not feel, the beat of his heart. It was absurd. Mad. And yet . . . there was the oddest sensation within her. As if she were connected with this man in a manner that defied logic.

"I . . ."

"What is it?" he demanded.

"Just for a moment . . . no, nothing. It is ridiculous."

Almost as if sensing her strange confusion, Lucien stepped closer, his fingers reaching up to gently cup her chin.

"Do not turn from the truth, my dove."

She frowned into the countenance that was becoming so terrifyingly familiar. "What truth?"

"That we are becoming entwined in both heart and soul," he said softly.

She should have laughed at his words. Two people did not become entwined. They lusted, they loved, and, on the rare occasion, they even liked each other. But they did not share thoughts and feelings as if they were one.

Still, she did not laugh.

Not when she felt her entire being was consumed by such an intimate awareness of Lucien.

"No," she whispered.

His fingers tightened upon her chin, his expression relentless as he held her wary gaze.

"You can sense it as well as I, Jocelyn," he whispered in mesmerizing tones. "The beat of our hearts, the joining of our minds, the desire that binds us together."

She could sense it. She could sense it pulsing through her blood and seeping deep into her soul.

A flare of near panic struck her heart. This was not supposed to be happening. Her life was meant to be calm, predictable, and devoted to others.

Wetting her dry lips, she gave a shake of her head. "Lucien, I cannot do this."

"Why?" His gaze stabbed deep into her wide eyes. "What do you fear?"

"Betrayal," she said before she could halt the revealing word.

The golden eyes darkened as his fingers tenderly moved to stroke her pale cheek.

"Never, my dove. You can believe in me."

A tremor shook her body. He could not possibly understand. No one understood.

"I think we should go," she breathed.

There was a strained silence, as if he battled the urge to force her to accept his pledge. Then his lips twisted with rueful humor.

"As you wish. Our time will come. Eventually."

Taking the bow from her hands, Lucien moved to retrieve the arrows, and then with exquisite care he helped her to the carriage he had rented for the day.

Jocelyn settled herself on the leather seat with a hint of regret.

When Lucien had first suggested they spend the day out of the city, she had hesitated. She was all too aware of the danger of spending such a vast amount of time alone with this gentleman. He was too achingly handsome, too charming, too sensually compelling not to be a danger to any maiden.

But the desire to be away from the cramped house and dark streets had proved to be irresistible.

She did not want to spend the day brooding on yet another murdered maiden or on the strange fear that she was being ruthlessly hunted. Just for a few hours she wanted to feel young and unfettered and happy.

And she had.

The day had been filled with laughter and the sort of lighthearted teasing that she had not enjoyed in far too long.

Now it was time to return to her home and the ever-present duty of the life she had chosen. A life that until Lucien's arrival had been quite enough to fill her with satisfaction.

Sternly telling herself that she was still quite satisfied with her chosen existence, Jocelyn devotedly attempted to ignore the pleasure of just being seated so closely beside him as they retraced the narrow path to London. She could not, however, entirely prevent her renegade gaze from occasionally straying to admire the purity of his profile.

Blast it all, he was so utterly beautiful. The chiseled perfection of his features. The faint bronze of his skin. The tawny satin of his long hair. The pure gold of his eyes.

And above it all, the shimmering appreciation for life that crackled about him with an irresistible force.

It seemed rather unfair that one gentleman should be so blessed.

Especially for those poor, unsuspecting females who happened to stray across his path.

Intent on her thoughts, Jocelyn paid little heed to the fact that they had reached the outskirts of London, not even when they strayed through the more elegant squares as they lazily made their way back toward her small home. Had she had her wits about her, she would have been properly on guard. As it was, she had no warning when she heard a startled male voice call out her name.

Abruptly turning her head, Jocelyn felt a chill inch down her spine at the sight of the elegantly attired dandy who angled his mount directly toward the carriage.

It had been nearly three years since she had last laid eyes upon Lord Patten. He had not changed. His dark hair was still artfully tousled about his narrow face, and the dark eyes still burned with a restless boredom. With the wisdom of age, however, Jocelyn now could see the faint petulant turn of those full lips and the weakness in the rounded chin. A pity she had not been so observant before, she ruefully acknowledged.

Bracing herself for the inevitable encounter, Jocelyn felt Lucien slow the carriage as Lord Patten bore down upon them. She would not allow this gentleman to know just what it cost her to face him with her chin held high.

"Jocelyn." The dandy brought his flashy mare to a halt as he allowed his gaze to openly survey her modest gown and hair pulled into a stern knot. "Good heavens, it is you."

Somehow she kept her smile intact despite the obvious insult in his tone. She was well aware she no longer resembled the giddy, overly naive debutante he had known. And in truth, she was far more content with the mature woman she had become. At least she was now too wise to be deceived by shallow charm and the lies of a practiced seducer.

"Good afternoon, Lord Patten."

The dark brows lifted at the chill in her tone. "I did not realize you had returned to London. I have not seen you about."

Jocelyn shrugged. "I have been far too occupied to attend the usual events."

Predictably the foul dandy turned his head to glance speculatively at the silent Lucien at her side, a mocking smile abruptly curving his mouth.

"I see. There does not seem to appear a need to explain what, or should I say who, has kept you occupied."

Jocelyn sensed Lucien stiffen. Slowly he leaned forward to stab the nobleman with a dagger glare. "Take care, my lord, I have little patience for fools."

There was no missing the stark warning in his voice, and an ugly color suddenly stained Lord Patten's narrow face.

"Indeed? And who might you be?"

"Mr. Valin, and a friend to Miss Kingly."

"Valin?" The dandy frowned as he attempted to place the name. Suddenly a rather sickly recognition rippled over the thin features. "Are you related to Mr. Ravel?"

"A cousin," Lucien readily admitted, seeming to take pleasure in the obvious unease at the mention of his relative. Jocelyn could only presume that Mr. Ravel possessed a powerful position among society.

"Oh." There was an awkward pause as Lord Patten sought to disguise his sudden embarrassment. At last he turned toward Jocelyn with a strained smile. "Are you staying with your parents?"

A sharp pang tore through her at the offhand words, but thankfully she managed to appear utterly indifferent.

"No."

"Then with a friend?"

"I now possess my own establishment," she retorted in clipped tones.

A genuine flare of shock widened the dark eyes at her abrupt announcement. Young maidens of breeding simply did not possess their own establishment. It was nearly as scandalous as being caught in a grotto, being seduced by a known rake.

"Your own establishment?"

"Yes. And I must be returning home. Please excuse us."

"Wait. Surely I shall see you about town?"

"Highly doubtful."

"But . . ."

"Good day, my lord."

Thankfully sensing her fierce need to be away from the man who had created such pain in her past, Lucien firmly set the horses in motion, nearly running down the dandy who was foolish enough to attempt to delay their departure.

Jocelyn did not even glance backward as they bowled down the street and turned toward the less respectable area of town. Instead, she determinedly sought to battle back the horrid memories that threatened to sweep over her.

It was the past. She had survived and even made a comfortable life for herself. There was no point in dwelling upon what could not be changed.

They traveled in silence for some time before Lucien at last slowed the pace of the horses and slanted a searching gaze over her taut profile.

"An old friend of yours, I presume?"

Friend? She smothered a bitter laugh. Lord Patten would be the last person she would ever choose as a friend.

"An acquaintance," she retorted stiffly.

"Oh, no, there is more than that between the two of you."

She sternly kept her gaze trained upon the shabby houses that now lined the narrow street.

"I do not wish to discuss Lord Patten."

"He is the one who hurt you," he said softly.

Her hands clenched upon her lap. She never wished to discuss the scandal that had ruined her life. Not with anyone. But she especially did not wish to discuss it with this gentleman.

It was all too sordid. Too demeaning. She did not wish to see the tender concern that glowed within those eyes diminish to scorn.

"He was a part of the scandal," she grudgingly conceded.

"And he refused to stand by your side when the situation became messy?"

Her lips twisted with a remembered pain. "Everyone refused to stand by my side. Everyone but Meg."

There was a short pause. "Not even your parents?"

Her nails bit into her palms until she drew blood. "Lucien, I said I do not wish to discuss this."

Without warning he reached out to run his fingers over her cheek in a familiar caress, then with the understanding compassion that could undermine the staunchest of defenses, he gave a slow nod of his head.

"As you wish."

Several hours later Lucien silently slid toward the abandoned warehouse. It had not been a simple decision to leave Jocelyn on her own. Not only did the ever-dangerous Amadeus and his deadly henchmen concern him, he also realized that she was still upset by their brief encounter with Lord Patten. Upset enough to have spent the entire evening in her room, refusing even to come down for dinner.

His features unconsciously hardened at the memory of the foppish nobleman. A desire to track the arrogant pup down and teach him an unforgettable lesson in wounding an innocent maiden was nearly unbearable. He did not doubt it would take only a few moments to make the man sorry he had ever dared to hurt Jocelyn.

Unfortunately he realized that while he might feel better after a midnight confrontation to the dandy, it would do nothing to heal Jocelyn's wounds.

Revenge could not undo the past.

Besides which, he had forced himself to leave the maiden alone so that he could attempt to discover some means of luring Amadeus back to the Veil. It was, after all, the true reason he had been sent to London. He could not waste his precious time upon a spineless worm.

Even if his hands did itch to be around the man's scrawny neck.

Lucien gave a rueful shake of his head. Now was not the time for such thoughts. Not when he was tracking a desperate vampire. If he did not begin concentrating upon his task at hand, he might discover himself blundering into a very nasty surprise.

Sinking even deeper into the shadows, he soundlessly approached the door, coming to an abrupt halt when it swung open without warning and a tiny form stepped into the street to regard him with large eyes.

With his vision he could clearly make out the features of the small child that had so trustingly sought him out the first night he had visited the warehouse. A frown marred his brow as he moved to crouch beside her.

"What are you doing out here, my dear?" he murmured softly enough that he would not startle her.

Astonishingly she reached out to place her small hand against his cheek.

"I knew you were coming."

Lucien regarded her in bemusement. There had always been those special humans able to sense the presence of vampires. Perhaps this child had been born with the gift. If so, it could prove to be a genuine blessing.

"Did you? What a clever minx you are." He carefully watched the tiny countenance. "Has anyone else been near?"

She gave a firm shake of her head. "No, the bad man went away."

"The vicar?"

"Yes."

He let out a slow breath. She did indeed have the gift.

"I want you to listen carefully to me. If the bad man returns, I want you to slip out of the warehouse and hide. Can you do that?" Lucien waited until she gave a nod of agreement. "Good girl. And I want you to warn the other children. The bad man is very dangerous."

The eyes that appeared far too old and wise for such a young child regarded him steadily.

"Will you come back?"

"Yes, I will be back," he promised with a smile.

"I am glad. You are a nice man."

Lucien could not prevent a small chuckle. "And you are a minx." He leaned down to brush a kiss over the tip of her nose. "Now go back inside."

"Good night."

"Good night, my dear."

Lucien waited until the girl had scurried back inside the warehouse before he rose to his feet. He could only hope the child recalled his warning if Amadeus did return. Although the traitor had no reason to harm the poor children, there was no use in taking any chances.

Once assured she was safely inside, Lucien continued past the warehouse and toward the narrow, broken streets beyond. It was destined to be a long night, he acknowledged ruefully. Although he suspected that Amadeus must have his lair somewhere in the labyrinth of destitute buildings, there was only one means of locating him. He would have to explore the entire rookery block by miserable block. Not a pleasant prospect considering the foul odors and filth that was already ruining his glossy boots.

Eventually he would draw close enough to sense the presence of the vampire, he thought in an attempt to ease his smoldering impatience.

And then . . .

Well, he had to admit he was not entirely certain what he would do beyond attempting to frighten some sense into the traitor.

He would simply have to face that difficulty when it arrived. First he had to find Amadeus.

Chapter 7

Jocelyn was floating in that peculiar world between wake and sleep when the shadowy form appeared beside her bed. Oddly she felt no fear as she sat upright to regard the apparition. Not even when a soft glow of illumination suddenly flared about the intruder.

Instead, her eyes widened in bemused wonder.

"Molly," she whispered softly, easily recognizing the freckled countenance and reddish curls.

"Thank goodness I have found you, Miss Kingly," the young maiden said, her expression filled with fear.

A cautious voice in the back of Jocelyn's mind warned her that something was wrong. It whispered that there was something that she should remember about Molly.

But cloudy confusion seemed to fill her thoughts, and it was impossible to think clearly.

"What are you doing here?" she asked instead.

The girl pressed her hands to her bosom as she leaned over the bed. "I need you."

"Are you in trouble?"

"Terrible trouble. I am so afraid. Will you help me?"

"Of course." Jocelyn frowned, shaking her head as she attempted to clear the fog of sleep from her mind. "What can I do?"

"Come with me."

"Come? Come where?" Jocelyn watched the apparition float toward the door, that voice of warning still sounding deep within her. "Molly?"

The woman stood at the door, waving an impatient hand toward the reluctant Jocelyn.

"Come."

With sluggish reluctance Jocelyn forced herself to climb out of the bed. This was all wrong. Why would Molly be in her home at this time of night? And yet, she could not fail Molly. The maiden had come to her for help, and it was her duty to do whatever she could to provide assistance.

"Where are we going?" she demanded as she hurried across the uneven floorboards. Molly did not answer as she slipped into the dark hall and headed for the stairs. "Molly, wait."

The maiden did not halt as she continued over the landing and down the steps. Jocelyn moved to follow the shimmering form, but without warning a hand reached out to grasp her arm in a firm grip.

"No, Jocelyn, you must stop."

Decidedly confused, Jocelyn turned her head to discover an old gypsy woman standing at her side. She gave a vague blink, not certain how her home came to be cluttered with so many unexpected guests.

"Please, I must go," she said in thick tones, realizing that Molly had disappeared from sight. "Molly needs me."

The thin, wrinkled face hardened at her words. "No, it is not Molly."

"Of course it is. I just saw her."

"No, do you not remember? Molly is dead."

A sharp pang abruptly stabbed Jocelyn's heart even through the cloud of confusion.

"Dead? But she was here."

"No, that was not Molly."

"But . . ."

"Jocelyn, there is someone trying to deceive you. You must not follow. Molly is dead."

With a wrenching effort Jocelyn forced herself to battle through the fog. "Yes," she murmured with a furrowed brow, recalling the odd vicar who had told her of Molly's death and then the arrival of Mr. Ryan. "I do not understand."

"Let us go back to bed."

Barely aware she was moving, Jocelyn allowed the strange gypsy to lead her back into her chamber and toward the bed. She regarded her companion with a puzzled expression.

"You are the gypsy who gave me the necklace."

A sudden smile touched the weathered countenance. "Yes, my dear. Do you remember my warning of the necklace?"

Jocelyn reached up to touch the amulet about her neck, rather startled to discover that it was warm beneath her fingers.

"You said that I am never to take it off or to give it to another."

Gently helping Jocelyn climb into bed, the gypsy covered her with the thin blanket.

"That is right, dearest. Never take it off for any reason. Not even if you believe it might help to protect someone you care about."

Jocelyn snuggled into the feather mattress, already slipping back into sleep.

"Why?"

In answer the woman reached out her gnarled hand and brushed it over Jocelyn's forehead.

"Sleep, my dear. Sleep in peace."

On cue the darkness rose up and Jocelyn was tumbling into a deep, dreamless sleep. She was unaware of the danger that lurked just out of sight, or of the powerful vampire who guarded her slumber.

For the first time in years she was at peace.

Brooding frustration smoldered within Lucien as he made his way back to Jocelyn's small home.

Despite his meticulous search, he had been unable to discover any hint of Amadeus. There was no scent of the vampire among the endless clutter of buildings or the numerous prostitutes who plied their wares upon every corner. Not even his henchmen had been upon the streets.

At last he had been forced to concede defeat.

He was not destined to discover Amadeus on this night, he had concluded in disgust.

Or so he had believed.

As he neared Jocelyn's cramped neighborhood, he felt a familiar tingle brush over his skin. Pausing, he allowed himself to consider the sudden sensation. It was the undeniable presence of a vampire.

With a chill in his heart he hurried closer, abruptly realizing that it was the sense of Amadeus that he felt.

Amadeus . . . here.

It was no wonder he had been unable to discover the traitor among the whores and pickpockets, he thought with grim fear. The vampire had used his absence to approach Jocelyn.

Flowing through the darkness with blinding speed, he entered the house and moved up the stairs. In the beat of a heart he was in Jocelyn's chamber. He stepped toward the bed, only to halt when a shadowy form abruptly appeared before him.

His hand instinctively reached for the dagger before realizing that the old gypsy woman was not

Amadeus in disguise, but Nefri, the most powerful of all vampires.

His eyes widened as he offered a bow of respect. Nefri was a legend among vampires and regarded as the most powerful, most blessed of all Immortals.

"Nefri," he murmured.

A smile touched the wrinkled countenance. "Lucien."

His gaze shifted toward the form upon the bed. At any other time he would have been overwhelmed to at last encounter the Great Nefri. It was considered a blessing to merely be in her presence. At the moment, however, he could think of nothing beyond Jocelyn.

He had sensed Amadeus close. He had not been mistaken.

"Miss Kingly?"

"She sleeps peacefully," the older vampire said in soft tones.

"She is well? She had not been harmed?"

"All is well."

The tight knot in his stomach eased, but he remained on rigid guard. He had already failed once this night. He would not fail again.

"Amadeus was here," he said in dark tones.

Nefri gave a nod of her head. "Yes, he assumed the shape of poor Molly and attempted to lure Jocelyn from the house."

"Bloody hell." Lucien closed his eyes in disgust.

He had known it was a risk to leave Jocelyn. And yet, he had allowed his eagerness to end the battle with Amadeus to cloud his wits. He had once again been overly impulsive and far too eager to act rather than remain patient. Only, on this occasion it was not himself he had harmed with his unsteady nature. "I should never have left her alone."

As if sensing his bitter self-recriminations, the older vampire stepped close enough to lay her gnarled hand upon his arm.

"Lucien, you could not have known his plans."

"I allowed Jocelyn to be in danger."

The pale eyes that glittered like jewels in the darkness hardened at his harsh tone.

"You must not be so hard upon yourself," she commanded in tones that brooked no argument. "You have done an admirable job in protecting the Medallion."

Lucien was not so easily reassured. Not while his body still trembled with the lingering fear at the realization that Amadeus had boldly entered this house and attempted to harm Jocelyn.

"I thought to track Amadeus to his lair, and instead I left Jocelyn to his mercy."

The fingers upon his arm tightened. "Listen to me, Lucien. If you wish someone to blame for placing Jocelyn in danger, you can look to me. It was my choice to bind her with the Medallion. But I did so because I sensed she possessed a pure heart and the necessary strength to bear the trials she must endure. We can only do our best to protect her. In the end it will be Jocelyn who will determine who is to win this battle."

He gazed into the wise countenance, battling a renegade stab of anger that Nefri had ever discovered Jocelyn. The poor maiden had endured far more than she ever should have been forced to bear. Surely it was unfair to place her at the mercy of renegade vampires. A danger that had been so willingly thrust upon her.

"How can she fight a battle she does not even realize she has entered?" he charged.

"Is she prepared to learn the truth?" Nefri swiftly countered. "And are you prepared to tell her of yourself?"

Lucien stiffened at the mere thought. Confess to Jocelyn that he was a vampire? To watch her face fill with horror? To know that every time he came near her she would be filled with terror?

"No," he retorted in abrupt tones.

"Then we must wait. We cannot allow her to be frightened into fleeing. She would then certainly be at the mercy of Amadeus."

Lucien glanced toward the slumbering woman upon the bed. His heart twitched in pain. He might wish that Jocelyn had not been involved in the battle between vampires, but now that she was, he had to make certain she was kept safe.

"Yes," he agreed in low tones.

Nefri regarded him with a knowing gaze, easily able to sense his growing bond to the young maiden. "But, Lucien, do not allow your feelings for Jocelyn to conceal the truth too long. There must be honesty between you," she warned.

Lucien took an instinctive step backward, shaking his head in denial. "She will never understand. How could she?"

The smile returned to the old woman's lips. "You will find a way."

So easy for her to say, Lucien acknowledged wryly. This great and powerful vampire had dedicated her life to the ancient lore of the past. She had created the Veil that brought peace and wisdom to her brothers. She had sacrificed herself to bear the burden of the Medallion until the traitors had attempted to steal it from her. She was beloved among all.

While he had devoted his life to pleasure and revelry. He had never had another depend upon him or seek his protection.

It was terrifying to suddenly be thrust into the role of hero. And even more terrifying to hold Jocelyn's safety in his hands.

"I wish I could share your confidence," he said in husky tones.

"Have faith in yourself, Lucien," Nefri retorted. "I do."

He studied the thin countenance, not for the first time wondering how he had ever been chosen for such a dire task.

"Why?" he demanded simply.

Her expression softened as her hand reached up to lightly pat his cheek.

"Because like Jocelyn, you possess a pure heart and a spirit that brings joy to all those about you."

Hardly the stuff of heroes, he thought with a pang. Surely he should be responsible and brave? Able to slay dragons?

His lips twisted as his gaze returned to Jocelyn. "Will it be enough?"

"That is for fate to decide," Nefri said softly. "We can do only what is in our power. Be at peace, Lucien."

With a last smile Nefri stepped back into the shadows and disappeared.

For many moments Lucien pondered the appearance of Nefri.

We can do only what is in our power. . . .

Wise words, no doubt. He was perhaps not a perfect hero. Or even the most suitable vampire to protect Jocelyn. But there was no one else who would be more concerned for her welfare, he acknowledged with a renewed sense of hope. Or more determined that she was kept out of danger.

He would devote his heart, his soul, and his very life to her.

He could offer no more.

Needing to be close to the maiden, he slowly moved to the bed, then, careful not to disturb her slumber, he lay down beside her and pulled her into his arms.

The sweet scent of her wrapped about him, and with a smile Lucien allowed his taut muscles to relax.

At least for the moment she was safe.

Jocelyn knew she was being a coward.

For three days she had virtually hidden herself in the small, stuffy study. She had avoided Meg and Lucien with determined care and even neglected those upon the streets who so depended upon her.

A part of her was embarrassed by her sudden bout of brooding self-pity. It had been years since she had allowed the pain of her scandal to darken her heart. It was the past. Wishing that she had not been such a foolish, headstrong maiden could alter nothing.

But the encounter with Lord Patten had ripped open the wounds that had never fully healed.

She might easily tell herself to forget the gentleman who had been her downfall and concentrate upon the life she had made for herself, but the heavy mood would not lift.

She was standing before the window, gazing

blindly at the narrow street, when she was suddenly aware that Lucien had entered the room.

There had been no sound, no indication of his arrival, but Jocelyn knew beyond a doubt he was standing in the doorway.

It was, in truth, rather frightening to realize just how sensitive she had become to his presence. She knew when he was in the house, and where. She knew when he drew near. Absurdly, it even seemed that she could sense what he was feeling and even at times what thoughts were within him.

At the moment she sensed a tightly bound frustration within him that seemed almost to reach out and stroke over her skin.

With an effort she smoothed her expression and slowly turned to encounter the smoldering golden gaze.

As always she caught her breath at the sight of him. Although plainly attired in a smoke-gray coat and black breeches, there was nothing unassuming about him. Instead, there was a compelling beauty in the lean features and golden eyes that commanded attention.

"Lucien," she breathed softly.

Easily holding her gaze captive, he crossed to stand before her. "This cannot go on, my dove."

Jocelyn shivered as those tingles of awareness washed through her. "Pardon me?"

"I have allowed you to hide from me for days. My patience is wearing thin."

A hint of color touched her cheeks. It was one thing to know she was cowering from the world. It was quite another to be confronted with her cowardice.

"Do not be ridiculous," she attempted to bluff. "I am not hiding."

He arched a dark golden brow. "No?"

"I have been very busy." Her hand absently waved toward the desk that was littered with papers. "It is not a simple matter to run two separate households."

His expression remained stern. "Perhaps not simple, but you are far too competent to be forced to devote every hour of the day to accounts."

It was impossible to deny the truth in his words. No one would believe that she must spend such long hours adding up columns of numbers.

With a frown she wrapped her arms about her waist. "Is there something you need?"

Surprisingly his lips twisted in a rather rueful fashion. "Your company would be a pleasant change."

Her heart gave a sudden leap at his tempting words. There was no denying that the presence of Lucien always managed to lighten her day. Even when she was determined to remain aloof and indifferent to his persuasive charm he lured her into forgetting herself. How could any maiden resist such a potent charm?

But while she was forced to acknowledge that he could provide her with a much-needed comfort, she discovered herself reluctant to press her poor spirits upon him.

It was hardly fair to ruin his day as well.

"You would do better to seek companionship elsewhere," she warned him with a sigh. "I am not in the humor for entertainments."

The golden eyes shimmered wryly at her sad tones. "No, you would rather brood over your encounter with Lord Patten."

Her lips thinned at his taunting. "It is not amusing."

"No." His expression became somber. "Nor is it wise. Brooding upon the past will not change it, Jocelyn. There is no magic that will accomplish such a feat."

It was what she had told herself a hundred times over the past few days. That did not, however, make it any easier.

She abruptly turned about to gaze out the window. "Do you have no regrets?" she demanded in unconsciously bitter tones. "Nothing you would alter if you were able?"

There was a pause before Jocelyn felt warm hands lightly touch her shoulders, offering her an unspoken strength.

"None of us is without regrets," he murmured.

"We have all taken paths that were less than smooth, but they quite often teach us lessons that must be learned."

Jocelyn battled the urge to lean back into the warm comfort of his chest. She was not so lost to reason that she did not sense that every day, every moment, she became more and more entangled with this gentleman.

Not just in the desire that was undeniable between them. But in a far more dangerous manner.

One that might very well break her heart.

"Some lessons are more painful than others," she muttered.

"True enough." The disturbing fingers gently squeezed her shoulders. "Tell me of Lord Patten."

She tensed at the soft question, but for once she did not cringe from the painful memories. Instead, she allowed her thoughts to reluctantly return to those days that seemed to be a lifetime ago.

"I met him during my first Season in London," she slowly confessed. "He was handsome, charming, and I was incredibly naive."

"You fell in love with him?" Lucien demanded in oddly thick tones.

Jocelyn shuddered. Love? Oh, no, there had been nothing pure or beautiful about her feelings for Lord Patten. Instead, they had been too sordid to admit without a sick sensation in the pit of her stomach.

"No," she whispered with a grimace. "I do not even have that excuse. You see, in Surrey I was considered the most beautiful and sought-after debutante in the county. There was no gentleman who did not vie for my attention."

He gave a low chuckle. "Hardly surprising."

Her own expression remained dark. "I was spoiled, willful, and vain. A dangerous combination."

"You are far too hard upon yourself, Jocelyn."

She gave a shake of her head. "No, it is the simple truth. I came to London expecting to dazzle the *ton* with my charms and, of course, to discover a husband who would offer me wealth and position."

His fingers abruptly tightened upon her shoulders. "Of course."

"It did not seem a difficult task." She paused for a moment, shamed by her memories. "I was swiftly toasted as an Incomparable, and within a fortnight I had received a dozen offers of marriage. It was all far too easy . . . even dull."

"Yes," he murmured.

"I began to long for excitement."

"You desired a challenge."

"Yes."

"And you found it in Lord Patten?"

She recalled the giddy excitement she felt when he walked into the room and the petulant annoyance when he seemed indifferent to her charm. He swiftly consumed her every thought.

Now she could only wonder at her vast stupidity. "He was very clever. Of all the gentlemen who fought to gain my favor, he alone remained aloof. No matter how I flirted, he refused to be captivated."

"Which only made you more determined to capture his elusive attention," he swiftly concluded.

"Of course." She gave a short, humorless laugh. "It was all a game to him. A game which he had mastered, while I was a bumbling idiot."

Lucien shifted closer, his breath brushing the bare skin of her neck with delicious warmth.

"What happened?"

Her hands unconsciously clenched in tight fists, the nails biting into her palms. It was only in her nightmares that she ever allowed the haunting memories to return.

"I was attending Lady Glendale's ball. It was absurdly stuffy, and I stepped onto the terrace. Lord Patten joined me there. As usual, he was quite flippant, and I grew annoyed at his mocking disdain." She was forced to pause and take a steadying breath. "I informed him that I was not quite the innocent fool that he thought me to be."

"I presume that he was eager to discover the truth of your words?" he demanded in scathing tones.

"He dared me to join him in a nearby grotto. I quite willingly agreed."

Without warning Lucien was gently but quite firmly turning her to meet his probing gaze. She was startled to discover the grim expression that had hardened his elegant features.

"He attempted to seduce you?"

Embarrassed heat flooded her cheeks at his blunt question. "Yes."

The golden eyes shimmered with a formidable danger. "Did he harm you?"

Jocelyn gave a slow shake of her head. In truth it would be easier to admit if Lord Patten had forced himself upon her. At least then she could lay the blame upon him. But she could not in all honesty deny that she was quite eager to explore the heat of his kisses.

"No. It was all terribly exciting for a brief time. This was the danger I had desired. Then . . . my father came in search of me."

He grimaced. "That was no doubt unpleasant."

A sharp, ruthless pain flared through her as the bitter words of her father echoed through her mind.

"He was furious, of course. He demanded that Lord Patten wed me by special license."

"But the nobleman refused?"

"Yes. He claimed that I had followed him to the grotto and tossed myself upon him."

Disdain rippled over Lucien's countenance. "A coward as well as a rake."

"And a liar," she added for good measure. "In

truth I was relieved I was not to be forced to wed him. I realized at that moment that such a marriage would be a misery."

His hand lifted to cup her cheek. "I am relieved as well. You deserve much better than the likes of Lord Patten. Still, it could not have been easy for you."

"It was horrid," she retorted, her stomach rolling with a queasy regret. "The word of my scandal spread through London by the next morning. My parents . . ."

"What, Jocelyn?" he demanded as her words trailed to silence. "What did they do?"

She struggled to swallow the sudden lump in her throat. Never before had she confessed to anyone the bitter confrontation she had endured with her parents. She was uncertain that she could even speak the words.

"I . . . they informed me that the shame I had brought upon them was insufferable," she at last managed to get out in bleak tones. "As far as they were concerned, I was now dead and would be sent to live with a distant cousin. I would be given a quarterly allowance, but I was never to enter their house or attempt to contact them again. Not ever."

Chapter 8

Lucien smothered the instinctive flare of fury that raced through him. Obviously the Kinglys were pathetic, unworthy fools who cared more for their reputation than their own child. They should be publicly disdained along with the wretched Lord Patten.

Still, his concern was for Jocelyn and the bitterness that lingered within her. A bitterness that would eventually destroy her if she did not discover a means to heal her past.

Once again his vengeance must be held.

Allowing his fingers to gently stroke the skin of her pale cheek, he gazed deep into her troubled eyes.

"Oh, my dove," he murmured softly. "It is no wonder that you carry such wounds."

She shuddered at his words, but she grimly attempted to keep her expression calm.

"I have accepted their decision."

Lucien gave a slow shake of his head. He was too

closely bound to this woman not to sense the pain just below the surface. He could feel it as if it were his own.

A rather frightening realization.

"No, we all seek the love and approval of those we hold dearest. Even if they are undeserving of our need."

"My parents' love and approval was based solely upon my ability to wed a gentleman of prominence." She grimaced. "Once I had destroyed that hope, I was worthless to them."

"Then they are fools," he growled, regarding the delicate features with a glittering gaze. How could anyone hurt this sweet, gentle maiden? It was inconceivable. "You have done great deeds without regard to the sacrifice to yourself. They should take pride in what you do."

"Pride?" She gave a short laugh. "Good heavens. They would be horrified if they knew what I do."

"Because their souls are empty. Do not judge yourself by their worthless values."

She frowned at his soft words. "What?"

His fingers slipped beneath her chin, keeping her puzzled gaze locked with his own.

"You blame yourself for being a disappointment to them."

Her eyes darkened, but she did not glance away. He would not allow her to turn from the truth of his words.

"Perhaps," she at last admitted in low tones.

"And you allow yourself to doubt your own worth because of them."

"No—"

"Jocelyn." He firmly interrupted her instinctive refusal to confront her pain. "Do you truly believe you could have been fulfilled following the path they desired for you? There is much more to you than a shallow desire for wealth and position. You would have been imprisoned in such an existence."

For a moment he feared that she would refuse to even consider his words. Then slowly her features softened. Lucien knew that she was considering the image of herself in one of the numerous elegant homes with nothing more to do with her time than darting from one mindless entertainment to another. She would have soon been miserable in such a dull routine.

She was too intelligent, too driven to achieve a meaning in her life to be content playing the role of social matron.

Still, he could sense that she was not yet prepared to dismiss the scandal that had so altered her life.

"That does not excuse the shame that I brought to my family," she said slowly.

He gave an impatient click of his tongue. "I believe you have been more than adequately punished for any mistakes you made as a very young maiden."

"I fear that my parents would never be so forgiving."

Lucien allowed his disdain to harden his features. Someday soon he would indulge himself in confronting the Kinglys. It would be a great pleasure to reveal just how contemptible he found them to be.

"Their forgiveness is meaningless," he said sternly, his fingers grasping her chin. "It is your own forgiveness that you must seek. Allow the past to heal, Jocelyn. Only then will you find peace."

"I . . . I wish it were that simple."

"It is," he assured her, his expression softening as he stepped closer and smiled into her wide gaze. "The past is done. It no longer determines who you are. It is the future that you must concentrate upon."

A silence fell as Jocelyn allowed herself to consider his persuasive arguments. Lucien forced himself to remain quiet, knowing that this maiden must discover for herself that she no longer need punish herself for mistakes that were long gone. She had created the wounds and she must heal them.

At last a rueful smile curved her lips as she allowed her gaze to roam over his dark countenance.

"Who are you?" she demanded without warning.

Lucien stilled, his expression suddenly wary. "What do you mean?"

"There is something about you. Something . . . different."

"Certainly I am different from Lord Patten," he agreed, suddenly eager to distract her. She was far too shrewd not to eventually realize he was not the usual London dandy. And with the power of the Medallion slowly heightening her senses, she was even more dangerous. "I would never harm you, Jocelyn. Certainly I would never abandon you."

The dark blue eyes shimmered with a brief glow before she sternly gained command of her emotions.

"You will be gone in just a few weeks," she reminded him in cold tones.

Lucien smiled wryly. As much as he might admire this maiden for her stubborn will, there were times when it was decidedly inconvenient.

He would have to battle for every step closer he might take to her.

"I shall be here as long as you have need of me," he swore with unmistakable sincerity. "That I promise you."

Another silence descended before she was pulling free and abruptly turning about to hide her expressive countenance.

"I have built a good life for myself," she muttered, speaking more to herself than to him.

"You have created a life that is devoted to others,"

he corrected her with a hint of frustration. "What of yourself?"

She lifted a slender shoulder. "I find pleasure in saving the women I do from the streets."

"And you are never lonely?"

"I . . . I have Meg."

Lucien gave a loud snort, considering a lifetime filled with no one but the sharp-tongued servant as companionship.

"She is no doubt a fine companion, but she cannot fulfill all your needs."

She turned to regard him with open suspicion. "Needs?"

Readily taking advantage of her proximity, Lucien wrapped his arms about her waist, bringing her close enough so he could hear the very beat of her heart.

"Enjoyment. Desire." He paused. "Love."

Her brow furrowed. "Such desires are dangerous."

He leaned his head down to rest his forehead against her own. Their breaths mingled as he allowed the sweet warmth of her to seep into his body.

"No," he denied in fierce tones. "Allowing life to slip past while you hide in fear is dangerous. There is no more bitter regret than looking back and wondering what might have been had you dared to risk it all."

He felt her shiver even as she gave a soft, rueful chuckle. "You are very persistent, Lucien."

"Only because I know I am right."

"So confident?"

"I live in hope." Unable to resist temptation any longer, he shifted the small distance to gently cover her lips. It was an innocent caress, no more than the briefest of touches. But, as a sharp, hungry pleasure flared through Lucien, he pulled back in sudden awareness. He ached for this woman. Ached for her with a need that was becoming dangerously painful. He was playing with fire to remain so intimately close to her. Reluctantly dropping his arms, he took another step backward, his expression tight with suppressed desire. "Now, I am weary of this house. What shall we do today?"

He had the satisfaction of watching Jocelyn struggle to regain her own composure as she needlessly fussed to straighten the skirts of her peach gown.

"Well, we could go to the market for Meg, and then to the bazaar to search for clothing for the children. . . ."

"No." He adamantly refused her brisk suggestions. The bright sunlight that slanted through the window demanded that he flee the confines of the smothering city. "I desire to leave London. This black air is choking me."

She placed her hands upon her hips as she regarded him with a stern expression. "No more archery. I am still sore."

Lucien considered a moment before offering her a faint smile. "Then, why do you not escort me to the farm you have purchased for your young women?"

She gave a blink of surprise at his sudden request. "It is not really a farm. Only a cottage with a small field."

"I would like to visit it."

"It would hold little interest for you."

He arched his brows in a challenging motion. "I wager I would find it fascinating," he retorted, then, knowing how best to bend her to his will, he touched upon her stern sense of duty. "Besides, you surely need to occasionally visit and ensure that all is well?"

As expected, her thoughts swiftly turned to those women who depended upon her charity.

"It has been some time since I was last there," she admitted.

"Good." Not about to give her time for second thoughts, Lucien smoothly turned and headed toward the door. "I shall brave Meg's wrath and request a supper to be packed. We shall make a day of it."

Feeling surprisingly lighthearted, Jocelyn nibbled upon the delicate mushrooms in cream sauce and fresh peas.

It had been a lovely day.

After renting a carriage, Lucien had happily driven them the short distance to the cottage Jocelyn had requested her father's man of business purchase for her nearly a year ago. The investment had put an end to her small savings and often consumed a fair amount of her allowance, but it had been worth every quid. There were few things more satisfying than visiting the six young maidens who currently lived at the cottage. Not only because they were clearly happier in their new surroundings, but because Jocelyn had also provided the women employment with the local weavers. They were learning skills that would allow them to be independent once they had become strong enough to leave the cottage. They would never again be forced to sell their own bodies to provide food for their tables.

Or that, at least, was her hope.

Covertly glancing from beneath her lashes, Jocelyn regarded the elegant bronze features of Lucien as he sat beside her on the cover he had spread upon the ground in the pretty meadow.

She could not deny that she harbored a reluctance to allow this gentleman to accompany her to the farm. Although Lucien had proven to be generous and kind beyond a fault, she was all too aware that few shared her compassion for fallen women. Most believed that they willingly enjoyed selling their bodies for profit, or even that once having become prostitutes, they were beyond redemption. Gentlemen especially preferred not to consider the notion that only desperation and hunger would lead a woman to such a profession.

She had known that she would be absurdly disappointed if Lucien had treated the women with anything less than respect.

Now she could only smile at her fears.

Lucien had not only revealed a kind consideration for the nervous maidens, he had swiftly charmed them into giddy, rather wide-eyed admirers as he allowed them to show him about the cottage and surrounding gardens. Not one was immune to his potent appeal. Not even Sally, who was as a rule terrified of most men.

Of course, no one could blame the susceptible women. Not even Jocelyn's staunch resolve was enough to battle the persuasive Lucien.

As if sensing her lingering regard, Lucien set aside his empty plate and regarded her with a lazy smile. In the gathering dusk his features took on a shadowed, mysterious beauty.

"More chicken?" he murmured.

She grimaced as she set her plate upon the cover. After three days of barely nibbling at the trays of food Meg had sent to her, she had been suddenly consumed with hunger. For the past half hour she had gorged upon the delicacies that Lucien had removed from the basket.

"Good heavens, no," she groaned. "I am stuffed."

Leaning forward, he refilled her empty glass. "At least have more champagne."

She lifted her brows, her expression teasing. "You are not perhaps attempting to get me foxed?"

The golden eyes abruptly shimmered with that irrepressible humor. "I will admit that it would be quite interesting. I have never seen you cast to the wind."

"Interesting for you, perhaps. I will be the one nursing a thick head tomorrow morning. Not at all a pleasant prospect."

His chuckle echoed through the peaceful meadow. "True enough. Still, I do not believe that you will be overly bosky from two glasses of champagne."

Jocelyn was not nearly so confident. Already there was a giddy glow flowing through her blood, and a decidedly unfamiliar excitement fluttering in the pit of her stomach.

Of course, she did not believe for a moment that the tingling sensations came from the expensive bottle of champagne. Only this gentleman had ever been capable of creating such a dizzying flood of emotion.

At this moment, however, she readily ignored the whispers of warning in the back of her mind. She did not desire to be the sensible, utterly dependable maiden who never accepted risk in her life.

With a small smile she picked up the full glass. "Then I shall be daring."

As if sensing her uncharacteristic mood of care-free joy, Lucien shifted closer to her seated form, his warm scent cloaking about her.

"I desire to propose a toast," he murmured as he held out his glass to touch her own.

Jocelyn regarded him in puzzlement. "A toast? To what?"

"To you, my dove. And all your amazing qualities."

She fought back a sudden rush of embarrass-ment at his soft words. "Absurd."

"No." He captured her gaze with ease. "You are without a doubt the most remarkable woman I have ever encountered."

Unaccustomed to such blatant flattery, Jocelyn shifted uneasily. "Hardly remarkable."

"Do not contradict me," he commanded in arro-gant tones. "Not only do you risk your own well-being each evening when you go onto the streets, you have been the savior to women who had no hope. They have a future because of you."

"I pray you are right," she retorted, her thoughts turning back to the women they had just left behind. They had endured so much. Far more than any maiden should have to bear. Only time would determine if they could overcome the pain in their lives. "They deserve a measure of happiness."

That tender expression that always stole her breath softened the elegant features.

"Happiness that you have given to them. I do not know any other woman who could have accomplished so much." He reached out to remove the forgotten glass of champagne from her hand and placed it upon the grass with his own. "Not only have you taken them from the streets, you have offered them a home and allowed them to learn skills that will keep them provided for the future."

She ducked her head as she felt a childish blush steal into her cheeks. This gentleman managed to make her feel like a gullible schoolgirl.

"Lucien, please. I do only what I can."

"And modest as well," he murmured softly. "A most potent combination."

"You are being a fool," she chided in flustered tones.

There was a moment's pause before Jocelyn felt a warm hand cup her chin and gently press her countenance upward.

"Look at me, Jocelyn," he commanded.

Slowly she lifted her heavy lashes to meet the eyes that glowed with a pure golden light in the falling dusk.

"What?"

"Be proud of what you have accomplished," he

said firmly. "Be proud of who you have become. It is far more worthy than being the neglected wife of some mindless dandy."

She paused as she pondered his words.

It was true that the road she traveled had not been the one she had expected to. Certainly she could never have dreamed as a child she would one day live in the dark streets of St. Giles with only an elderly servant as company.

Still, she could not deny that she found it difficult to think of herself in an elegant town house with nothing to occupy her mind beyond the cut of her dress and the latest gossip.

Could she ever have been satisfied with such an existence?

Could she have found joy in tending to a husband who preferred his life at his club and his mistresses while she chatted over tea and flitted about dance floors?

Her life might not have been of her choosing, but Jocelyn knew in her heart that it provided a sense of accomplishment that she never could have found in the more fashionable world.

"Yes," she at last breathed softly.

A sudden expression of satisfaction rippled over Lucien's countenance before he leaned forward and pressed his lips to her own.

Caught off guard, Jocelyn did not even make a

pretense of resisting the sweet caress. She did not desire to resist, she fuzzily acknowledged.

Tantalizing warmth shimmered through her blood, a burst of excitement exploding within her stomach. Her lips parted in silent invitation, and with a fractured groan Lucien gathered her in his arms.

"You taste of champagne," he murmured against her mouth.

Her hands rose to clutch his shoulders. She struggled to think through the fog of pleasure that clouded her mind.

"Lucien."

"Yes, Jocelyn?"

"It . . . it is growing late."

He gave a soft laugh, his warm breath sweetly brushing over her sensitive lips.

"Yes, it is. I have waited too long to hold you in my arms."

She felt lost in the golden heat of his eyes, longing for nothing more than to remain pressed against the strength of his hard form. This was where she truly belonged, she inanely acknowledged. The only place she desired to be.

Alone with this man who had filled her empty heart with joy.

Nearly overwhelmed by the stark realization, she struggled to break the spell of enchantment.

"You have won no bets," she reminded him in breathless tones.

His brows rose in a teasing fashion. "Ah, you have forgotten. Earlier I wagered that I would discover your small farm fascinating, and I assure you that I did so."

She gave a choked laugh at his absurdity. "That was no genuine wager."

"Of course it was," he argued, his hands stroking the curve of her back. "And now I demand my forfeit."

Jocelyn shivered in delicious anticipation. "I do not believe that you play fair, sir."

"Why, Miss Kingly, surely you do not accuse me of cheating?"

It was decidedly difficult to keep her mind upon the playful conversation when those hands continued to trail up and down her spine and the temptation of his lips were only a breath away.

"You are certainly swift to take advantage of the situation," she accused him.

"I must need be swift with you, my dove. You are far too elusive for my liking."

She searched the dark countenance, wondering why she did not feel the panic or even reluctance that had plagued her since the scandal. Surely she had not forgotten just how dangerous desire could be to a young maiden?

But even as she sought the lingering sense of distrust for such passions, she discovered that she felt nothing but a growing need to give herself utterly to this man.

"Not so elusive," she murmured.

She heard his breath catch in his throat, then, with a low moan, he was pressing her close and kissing her with a barely concealed hunger.

Jocelyn clutched at his shoulders, reveling in the demands of his lips. This was what she ached for. This restless, yearning desire. This consuming passion that must surely be fulfilled.

She leaned closer, sighing softly when the seeking lips left her mouth to trail a scorching path down her jaw and then the curve of her neck. She took no note of the gathering darkness or of the soft call of distant birds that echoed through the air.

There was nothing beyond the magic of Lucien's touch.

After what may have been mere moments or hours, Lucien reluctantly pulled back to regard her with a darkened gaze.

"Ah, my dove, you have firmly captured me in your spell," he said in husky tones.

She gave a dazed shake of her head. "I have no spells."

"Tell that to my heart."

Her eyes widened at his soft words. His heart? Could he possibly mean . . . did he imply that he was in love with her? Could his emotions have become as deeply entwined as her own?

"Lucien, I—"

Without warning he suddenly pressed his fingers to her lips, halting the impulsive confession that she had been about to utter.

"No, say nothing," he said, an oddly regretful expression upon his handsome countenance. Almost as if he knew what she was about to say and was determined to prevent the words. "The time will come when we may freely speak of such things. But not yet."

She frowned at his unusual reserve. Lucien was not a man who deliberately hid his emotions. Quite the opposite, in fact.

"Why?" she demanded, an unwelcome disquiet worming its way into her heart.

Something that might have been pain rippled over his finely chiseled features.

"Because I could not bear to lose you."

Chapter 9

A peaceful silence had descended upon the cramped sitting room. Seated in a chair beside the window, Jocelyn glanced toward the golden-haired gentleman who was settled upon the sofa.

After an evening devoted to ensuring the children in the warehouse were well fed and also seeking out the various prostitutes who had come to depend upon Jocelyn's assistance, they had returned to the quiet house for a light dinner.

Although feeling far too restless to seek her bed, Jocelyn had been determined to avoid yet another of Lucien's dangerous games. She was not a fool. She was well aware that she was but a breath from tossing aside all sense and giving in to the passions simmering within her.

So, collecting her large sewing basket, she had made her way to the sitting room, determined to finish the linen shirt she had been stitching for Thomas.

Much to her amazement, Lucien had swiftly

joined her. She had half expected him to demand that she fulfill her side of their devilish bargain. She had, after all, taken the money he gave her each evening for accompanying her to the streets. But instead, he calmly scooped up a blouse she was altering for Annie from the basket and with needle and thread had moved to the sofa to work upon the unfinished hem.

He should appear the fool, she told herself as she covertly studied the lean profile outlined in the flickering candlelight. Whoever heard of a sophisticated gentleman stitching like a common tailor?

But there was nothing foolish in the beautiful features set into lines of concentration, or the slender, artistic fingers that moved with a supple grace. He appeared perfectly comfortable and not at all embarrassed to be performing such a menial, womanly task.

She tried and failed to think of any other gentleman of her acquaintance who would be so secure within himself.

There was simply no one else to compare with Lucien Valin, she acknowledged with a faint sigh. It was little wonder that he had so easily bewitched his way into her heart.

As if sensing her intense regard, the golden head abruptly lifted and he flashed her that wicked grin that never failed to stop her heart.

"Well?"

Lost in the beauty of his smile, it took a moment for her to realize he was holding up the small blouse for her inspection. Feeling decidedly foolish, she rose from the chair and crossed the floor to take the garment.

Soon she would be one of those witless maidens who could do nothing but giggle and simper when in the company of a handsome gentleman, she chided herself.

"You are very swift," she murmured, hoping to hide her brief flare of embarrassment.

"Will it do?"

Rather absently raising the blouse to glance at the fresh hem, her attention was firmly caught by the tiny, utterly precise stitches.

Not even the most talented dressmaker could have achieved such efficient work.

She gave a slow shake of her head. "I do not believe it."

He rose to his feet, his golden brows raised at her muttered words. "What is it?"

"It is perfect. Absolutely perfect."

He gave a choked laugh. "And that is a bad thing?"

"Everything you do is perfect." She lifted her head to meet his glittering gaze. "Do you have no faults whatsoever?"

"You are being absurd."

"Indeed?" She regarded him steadily. "I have yet

to see you fail at anything. You have mastered chess, hazard, archery, and cribbage. You charm young children, wary women, and even Meg, who is never charmed. And now you sew a perfect hem."

Surprisingly his amusement faded as he reached out to gently remove the blouse from her hands. He tossed it upon the sofa before turning to grasp her shoulders.

"Jocelyn, I can assure you that I am far from perfect," he said, what might have been regret darkening his eyes. "In truth, there are any number of my acquaintances who would assure you that I have more than my fair share of faults."

She frowned, unable to accept his words. Surely all who met Lucien tumbled into love with him. How could they not?

"I do not believe you."

His fingers briefly tightened, his lips twisting in a rueful fashion.

"You should. I can be irresponsible, frivolous, and inclined to infuriate others with my peculiar sense of humor."

She searched his expression, sensing a vulnerability that she would never have expected beneath his smooth assurance. It pierced her heart in a manner that she had never experienced before.

Barely aware of what she did, Jocelyn raised her hand to lay it against the satin softness of his cheek in a comforting motion.

"I enjoy your sense of humor," she said with a fierce sincerity.

The golden eyes abruptly shimmered in the dim light as he reached up to cover the fingers still pressed to his countenance.

"Oh, my dove, you do know best how to touch my heart."

Her breath caught at the fragile, wondrous moment.

The sensations that filled her were not those she had experienced with Lord Patten. This had nothing to do with vanity or a need for adventure or even the desire for physical pleasure.

What she felt now was deeper, more profound. Her heart, even her very soul, knew the truth.

It was perhaps the most important moment in her entire life.

"Do I?" she whispered.

"Can you doubt it?" he demanded in hoarse tones.

"Lucien . . ."

Her lips parted in an open invitation for his kiss, but even as his head began to lower, an unreadable emotion swept over his countenance and he was pulling back.

"Jocelyn, we must speak," he abruptly insisted.

A chill inched down her spine. She reluctantly recalled his manner earlier in the day. She had been so close to confessing her feelings. She had wanted him to know that he had found a place within her heart. But even as the words had trembled upon her lips, he cut her short.

And now, once again, he was holding her at length.

There was clearly something wrong.

"I thought we were speaking," she said in a failed attempt at humor to cover her fear.

His features became unreadable as he drew in a deep breath. "There are secrets you do not know of me, Jocelyn. Secrets that are not easy to confess."

She stiffened, feeling as if her heart were being squeezed with a ruthless force.

"Are you married?"

He appeared momentarily shocked by her question before he gave a sharp shake of his head.

"No. I have never desired to bind myself to another." His hand moved to touch her cheek. "Not until now."

She unwittingly hid a sigh. Surely anything could be overcome as long as he was free to offer her his heart.

"Then, what is it?"

Surprisingly she felt his fingers tremble against her face, as if he were struggling to control his inner emotions. The chill within her became more pronounced.

"You said that I was different. I fear that you were

quite right. I am unlike any other gentleman you have ever encountered."

Her brows drew together in a puzzled frown. "That does not matter to me, Lucien. Considering most gentlemen I have encountered, I can only be relieved that you are different."

He gave a sigh, his fingers compulsively moving down her cheek to stroke the line of her jaw.

"That is because you do not yet comprehend what I mean by different."

"You are not making any sense. I know you. There is nothing—"

Her ardent words were untimely interrupted when the door to the sitting room was rudely thrust open. With a gasp of dismay Jocelyn jumped away from Lucien and turned to meet Meg's speculative gaze.

"Meg." She ridiculously ran her hands over her gown, realizing that the servant was bound to have noticed the intimate familiarity between her and Lucien. There would no doubt be a stern lecture on the morrow at her foolish weakness. "Has something occurred?"

The housekeeper flashed Lucien a jaundiced glare before returning her attention to the flustered Jocelyn.

"That gent is here again."

"Gent?"

"That one who ruined my floors."

With her thoughts still tangled by Lucien, it took a while before Jocelyn at last realized Meg must be referring to the Bow Street Runner who had called before.

"Mr. Ryan?"

"Aye."

Her hand lifted to press to her heart. It was far too late for any callers. What could he possibly desire?

"I see," she murmured. "I suppose you should show him in."

Meg planted her hands upon her hips. "At this hour?"

Jocelyn gave a lift of her shoulders. "I would rather discover what Mr. Ryan has to say than to spend the entire night speculating."

The servant gave a disapproving click of her tongue. "The man should be abed, not out disturbing young ladies."

"He is only doing his job, Meg. Please show him in."

Just for a moment the woman hesitated, as if determined to protect Jocelyn from the intruder. Then with a sniff she turned on her heel and stomped toward the door.

"Indecent," she muttered as she stepped into the hall.

Dismissing the housekeeper's obvious annoyance, Jocelyn slowly turned to meet Lucien's searching gaze. She did not want to be interrupted at this moment. Not when she needed to know what Lucien had to say, and to be reassured that everything was going to be well. Not when she needed to be held in his arms and for this night forget the ugly streets and fear that lurked just outside her door.

But it was impossible.

Mr. Ryan would not have called if he did not have something of importance to reveal. Whatever her reluctance, she knew that she had to see him.

"Lucien, I must meet with Mr. Ryan. Perhaps you—"

Without warning he stepped forward to grasp her upper arms firmly. "No."

She gave a startled blink. "What?"

The elegant features hardened to a determined expression. "He can speak with me present."

"But why? This has nothing to do with you."

"Of course it does. If it affects you, then it affects me. I will not leave."

A ridiculous rush of relief threatened to buckle her knees. She had prided herself on her strength. She depended upon no one, and that was precisely how she desired it to be.

But suddenly she realized that there was something very wonderful in knowing Lucien was near.

Not that she intended to confess her desire for

his company, she wryly acknowledged. He was far too confident as it was.

"Is that a command?"

He grimaced, belatedly realizing how sharply he had spoken. "No, I am not that foolish. But you need not brave your troubles on your own, Jocelyn. I am here to be at your side. Will you allow me to remain?"

She allowed her expression to soften. Really, this was the most remarkable of men.

"If you wish."

With a swift motion he bent downward to brush his lips over her forehead before pulling back and moving discreetly away. She resisted the urge to touch the tingling skin, instead attempting to smooth her countenance to the calm composure she had once found so very easy. It would not do to appear like a giddy schoolgirl in the first throes of love.

It was scandalous enough to be discovered with a gentleman in her sitting room at such an hour.

Squaring her shoulders, Jocelyn was prepared as the burly gentleman entered the room, clutching his hat in his hands. His shrewd gaze briefly rested upon the silent stranger near the empty fireplace before he was offering Jocelyn a small bow.

"Ah, Miss Kingly, forgive me for intruding once again. And at such a late hour."

She managed a small smile. "Not at all. May I

introduce you to Mr. Valin? Mr. Valin, this is Mr. Ryan. He is from Bow Street."

The two gentlemen shared a long, silent gaze before the Runner was giving a nod of his head.

"A pleasure, Mr. Valin."

"Mr. Ryan," Lucien murmured.

"Would you care for tea?" Jocelyn politely offered. "Or perhaps you would prefer brandy?"

"Nothing, I thank you. I will not intrude long."

"Do you have word of Molly's killer?" she hopefully prompted, not at all surprised when he gave a regretful shake of his head.

"I fear not. Despite my numerous nights upon the streets, there does not appear to be anyone willing to admit they were acquainted with Molly or if they noted her upon that specific evening."

Jocelyn knew his words were a gross understatement. Those of the streets were wary of strangers. Any stranger. And if they suspected that Mr. Ryan was a member of Bow Street, they would be as likely to slit his throat as to confess to any knowledge of crimes in the neighborhood.

"No, I do not suppose they would," she murmured in sympathy. "Most have their own secrets to hide."

The large man gave a nod of his head. "As you say."

"Then, what is it you desire of me?"

There was a faint pause before Mr. Ryan grimaced.

"There have been two more prostitutes discovered murdered since Molly's death."

Jocelyn stared at him in stunned disbelief. "Two more?"

"One was discovered floating in the river; the other was left not far from here."

She pressed a hand to her twisted stomach. Had the world gone mad? Who would harm such helpless women? They had nothing to steal. They did not hurt others. They simply were attempting to survive in a harsh world that offered them nothing.

It was all so horribly, wretchedly unfair.

"Dear heavens," she whispered, her heart clenching with pain.

With a silent swiftness Lucien was at her side, his hand coming to rest upon her lower back in a gesture of unspoken sympathy.

"What does this have to do with Miss Kingly?" he demanded of the Runner.

The pleasant features hardened with a surprisingly grim expression. "The last victim had a ribbon tied about her neck with a note that was written to Miss Kingly."

Jocelyn sucked in a shocked breath. "To me?"

"That is what I presume." He gave a lift of one large hand. "It had your name and the words 'the necklace or death' scrawled upon the paper."

Just for a moment she thought she might be physically ill. The dark evil that was stalking her was becoming horribly, horribly tangible. Not only from those strange men who had broken into her bedchamber, but with Molly's murder and now the other poor victims.

She unconsciously reached up to grasp the amulet that lay against her skin.

"I . . . this makes no sense. Why would anyone desire my necklace? It possesses no value."

She thought that Lucien stiffened at her side, but her attention remained upon the frowning Runner.

"Are you certain?" Mr. Ryan demanded.

"No more so than any other bit of gold."

"Has anyone approached you and admired the necklace, or wished to borrow it?"

She paused, briefly considering the men who had broken into her home. They had said something of the necklace, had they not? And there had been those odd dreams of the old gypsy woman warning her to protect the amulet.

Then she gave a small shake of her head. The Runner would think her mad if she began babbling of odd intruders and gypsy dreams. She wasn't certain that she entirely believed the strange happenings herself.

"No," she at last muttered.

Mr. Ryan heaved a weary sigh. "A pity. I had hoped you might have some knowledge of who might be stalking these young women."

She battled the threatening tears. "I wish that I did. I am sorry."

Stepping even closer, Lucien placed his arm protectively around her shoulder. There was a sudden air of danger that crackled about him as he narrowly regarded their guest.

"Miss Kingly had nothing to do with the murders."

Much to his credit, the Runner managed to meet that fierce golden gaze without flinching. A remarkable task, indeed.

"I do not suspect that Miss Kingly is involved, but I cannot ignore the fact that two of the victims carried notes with her name upon them."

Lucien tensed, but before he could speak, Jocelyn turned to offer him a sad shake of her head.

"He is right, Lucien. There must be some reason that this monster has left my name on those wretched maidens." She gave a deep shudder, her stomach once again threatening to revolt. "We must discover why."

"Not tonight," he retorted in icy tones.

Not even the undoubted courage of Mr. Ryan was equal to the dark, looming threat of Lucien Valin.

"No, of course not." He offered her a strained smile. "You will come to me if you discover any information?"

"Certainly."

"Then I will trouble you no further." He gave a bow. "Good evening."

Jocelyn barely noticed as the large man turned and quietly left the room. Her heart felt heavy and her mind clouded with a pained terror.

What was happening?

If someone wished to harm her, why would they kill pathetic women upon the street? And why would they possess such an odd fascination with her amulet?

Why?

"Have a seat, Jocelyn." With tender care Lucien guided her to a nearby chair. Waiting until she had numbly settled upon the threadbare cushion, he briefly disappeared, only to return with a small glass of brandy that he pressed into her hand. "Drink."

She did as she was commanded, giving a choked cough as the fiery spirit slid down her throat. Lifting her head, she met his concerned gaze with a frown.

"Two more girls dead," she said in quavering tones.

He grimaced, kneeling beside the chair to grasp her chilled fingers in a warm grip.

"I am sorry, Jocelyn."

"This is unbearable." She shivered in fear. "Who would do such a thing? And why?"

"As you said . . . a monster," he said quietly.

"A monster who is searching for me," she retorted, no longer able to deny the truth.

There was a faint pause before she heard him heave a sigh. "I fear so."

Something in his dark tone made her search his oddly pale features. He sounded so certain. As if . . . as if he knew.

"Lucien . . . who is this man?"

The bronze features tightened as he studied her wary expression. "He is a very evil man. A dangerous man."

A thick lump threatened to choke her. She did not want to believe that Lucien had anything to do with the darkness that clouded about her. He was her strong shoulder that she desperately desired to lean upon. He was a steady comfort in her growingly unstable world.

But her hapless wishing could not alter the pained regret that was glittering in his golden eyes.

"What does he want from me?" she forced herself to demand.

"The Medallion."

Her fingers lifted to clutch the golden amulet. "My necklace?"

"Yes."

"But . . . why? It surely cannot be of value."

His eyes briefly closed before he lifted his lashes to regard her with a tortured expression.

"It is valuable, my dove. More valuable than you could ever imagine."

She struggled to accept his ragged words. It seemed impossible. What gypsy, no matter how old or mad, would offer a valuable amulet to a complete stranger? Such a woman living in obvious poverty would surely sell the necklace or at least barter for some gain.

And yet, she could not deny that the necklace had become a source of fascination for some villain. A villain willing to kill for it.

She found it suddenly difficult to breathe. "What is it?"

His hand reached up to softly touch the fingers that held the amulet in a deadly grip.

"It is an ancient artifact of the Immortals."

"Immortals?"

His lips twisted in a humorless smile. "Vampires."

Jocelyn was thrusting herself to her feet without realizing that she had moved, nearly toppling Lucien over as she glared down at him with blazing eyes.

"That is not amusing, Lucien."

With a slow, hesitant motion he straightened, warily regarding her sharp frown.

"No one knows that better than I."

She grappled to make sense of his absurd words. "Do you mean that someone is ridiculous enough to believe that this Medallion has the power to make them into a vampire?"

An odd expression rippled over the lean countenance. "Lately I wonder if it is so ridiculous. It has altered you in a very profound manner. I can feel it." He stabbed her with a shimmering glance. "Can you not?"

She stilled in fear. She wanted to laugh hysterically at his obvious insanity.

Vampires?

Magical amulets?

Ludicrous.

Somehow, however, the laughter froze in her throat. In her fingers the Medallion glowed with unnatural warmth, as if to warn her that it was indeed altering her to suit its purpose.

She instinctively backed away, her heart thundering so loud that she thought it might explode.

"Stop this, Lucien, you are frightening me."

"Trust me, that is the last thing I desire." His hands clenched at his sides, a searing pain upon his face. "I need you to listen to me, Jocelyn. The Medallion is a powerful artifact, and it belongs to the vampires."

"There are no such things as vampires," she ridiculously whispered.

"They are very real. And they have returned to the world of mortals. They stalk the streets of London."

Chapter 10

Lucien watched the shocked horror ripple over her face. "Why are you saying this?" she choked out in thick tones.

He heaved a sigh. "Because it is the truth. The truth you claimed you desired to know."

"Vampires killed Molly and those other women?" she demanded.

"Yes."

"Vampires?"

"Yes."

A heavy silence filled the room, allowing Lucien to hear the harsh rasp of her breath.

"And . . . how do you know this?" She at last forced herself to ask the question that Lucien had dreaded.

He stepped forward, holding out his hand in an unconscious plea for understanding. "Jocelyn."

"No," she abruptly cried, backing from him in instinctive fear. "I do not want to hear."

Lucien's heart broke as he regarded Jocelyn's shattered expression.

He had known this moment would be difficult. He had steeled himself for her anger and disbelief. Even her fear. But now that it had arrived, he realized that it was not difficult. It was bloody impossible.

Great Nefri. She had never appeared more vulnerable. Her eyes were darkened with fractured pain and her features pale with the strain. Worse, there was an air of wounded betrayal shrouded about her taut form.

She did not want to believe he was a monster from her worst nightmare. Not when she had opened her home to him. And her heart.

Lucien longed to tug her into his arms and assure her that all would be well. He wanted to soothe her fears and return the enchanting smile to her face.

Unfortunately he realized that he was the last soul in the world who could offer her comfort. Until he could somehow reach past the fear that currently filled her heart, he was the enemy.

Instead, he could only watch in pained frustration as she struggled to accept the unacceptable.

"I attempted to tell you earlier," he said gently. "Before we were interrupted by Mr. Ryan."

She gave a shake of her head. "Dear heavens, you cannot believe that you are a vampire?"

He swallowed a rueful laugh. "This is not a delusion of an unstable mind, Jocelyn. I am a vampire."

"This is insanity," she whispered.

Lucien stepped forward, uncertain how to convince her of the truth without sending her fleeing in terror. He attempted to take heart from the fact that she had not bolted already. Surely he could reach her if only she would give him the opportunity.

"Please, if you would just listen to me—"

"No." She raised a hasty hand, her eyes wide with fright. "Just stay away."

His heart twisted in agony. "I will not harm you. I would never harm you. I was sent here to protect you."

"Protect me? From what?"

Lucien paused, his hands lifting to run through his thick hair. How was he possibly to tell this maiden that she was not only harboring a vampire beneath her roof, but that another was ruthlessly stalking her? And that she currently carried a powerful amulet that could very well decide the fate of all vampires.

She would think him crazed.

Or, worse, blame him for the danger that now haunted her.

"This is very difficult," he muttered. "Will you at least have a seat?"

"No, I—"

"Jocelyn," he interrupted in commanding tones,

his gaze catching and holding her own. "At least hear me out."

Amazingly her face paled an even more shocking shade of white, but she managed to move to a nearby chair and sat stiffly upon the edge of the cushion.

"If you insist."

Lucien briefly closed his eyes and attempted to clear his rattled thoughts. It was utterly imperative that he find the words to warn her of her impending danger without further thrusting her away. A fine balance that he was not at all certain he could discover.

At last he reluctantly opened his eyes and met her dark, accusing gaze.

"Jocelyn, I realize that this is difficult to accept, but vampires are not a myth. We have been here for longer than you could ever imagine. And, in truth, we were once unfortunately the monsters we were portrayed. A vampire that is consumed with bloodlust will kill without mercy or thought for his victim. But in taking a human life we not only are gifted with many powers, we are also cursed with sunbane that prevents us from leaving our lairs except at night."

Her hand slowly crept instinctively to cover her neck. "But you do not fear the sun."

"Since my return I have not indulged my bloodlust. I have not taken a mortal life."

She shuddered in horror. "Dear heavens."

Eager to assure her that vampires were more than just monsters who fed upon humans and stalked the streets at night, Lucien moved toward the chair and bent down beside her. He grimaced as he could feel the fear that raced through her slender form.

Was it possible that less than an hour before, this maiden had been filled with the glorious, dazzling warmth of love? He would give everything he possessed, his very soul, to feel that warmth once again.

"Vampires no longer walk among humans. Two hundred years ago the greatest of all vampires, Great Nefri, used a powerful Medallion to create the Veil."

Her brow pleated in understandable confusion. "The Veil?"

"It is a place of peace for the vampires," he said, a surprisingly reminiscent smile touching his lips. Odd, considering how he had always chafed at the thought of being so firmly imprisoned. And the fact that he was far from certain that he wished to return. "We are no longer bound by mortal forms or weaknesses. Instead, we devote ourselves to study and the ancient philosophies. It is a world quite separate from your own."

Her frown deepened at his soothing words. Obviously she was not about to be easily reassured no matter how peaceful and scholarly he claimed vampires to be.

"Then, what are you doing here?" she demanded.

He reached out to grasp the arm of the chair, careful not to touch her but close enough to halt any hasty urge to retreat.

"Unfortunately not all vampires were willing to give up the power of bloodlust. There are those who feel that they possess a superior dominance over humans. They resented being forced behind the Veil."

"What do they want?"

"To return vampires to the world of mortals," he said simply.

She brooded upon his words, swiftly capable of realizing the dire consequences. Her hands clutched together in her lap.

"How?"

"They seek the Medallion that Nefri used to create the Veil. With such a powerful artifact they could not only destroy the Veil, but it would give them dominion over the other vampires."

She allowed her gaze to meet his own, perhaps seeking the truth deep in his eyes.

"What does this have to do with me?"

Lucien drew in a deep breath. He did not want to deepen her terror. This was all overwhelming enough as it was. But he knew that he could not hold back the truth. Not only because he needed to earn back her trust, but also because he had to warn her of Amadeus. Soon the vampire would become desperate enough to attempt a more direct means to gain command of the Medallion. She must be prepared to resist his dangerous plots.

"When Nefri discovered that there were traitors plotting to steal the Medallion, she very wisely divided it into three amulets." His hands gripped the arm of the chair. "Then she bound the amulets to human maidens."

Perhaps unconsciously, her fingers reached up to touch the necklace that lay against her skin.

"Amulets?"

"Your amulet, Jocelyn."

She gave a frantic shake of her head, then abruptly leapt from the chair. Lucien was swiftly upon his feet, but she did not flee as he had briefly feared. Instead, she turned around to regard him with a glittering gaze.

"No . . . you are wrong. This amulet was given to me by an old gypsy woman."

"The woman was Nefri. She came to you in disguise."

"The vampire?"

"Yes."

Her expression crumpled, her hands rising to press against her temples. Lucien could only watch in helpless concern as she battled to accept his words. Blast, Nefri. Whatever her belief that Jocelyn was strong enough of spirit to bear this burden, he desperately wished Nefri had chosen any other maiden.

She was so alone. And so very vulnerable.

"This is absurd," she at last muttered in harsh tones. "Why would she give such a thing to me?"

Lucien cautiously edged forward, his face filled with sympathy. "Because she was able to bind the Medallion to you as a human, which means that it cannot be taken by force, or even death. It can only be given freely."

Her brows pulled together. "That was why she told me never to remove it or give it to another."

"Yes."

"But . . ." She held the amulet in her hand. "It is not bound to me. I can easily remove it."

"The Medallion itself allows for free will," he explained in soft tones. "If you choose to give it away, then it will not halt you."

"Oh."

He dared another step forward, warily watching her pale features. "A more important reason she chose you was that she understood the strength and purity of your heart. She knew she could find no better guardian."

"Guardian." She uttered a short, near-hysterical laugh. "How can I be a guardian when I did not even realize what I possessed? I might have given away the necklace on a dozen occasions."

"It was a risk, but Nefri had few options."

A sudden anger flared to life in the beautiful blue eyes. "She could have told me the truth."

He grimaced. It was an argument he had used himself. Only now did he fully comprehend Nefri's dilemma. What maiden with any sense at all would willingly place herself in the path of a murderous vampire? Even supposing Nefri could have convinced them that vampires existed at all.

"And what would you have done?" he gently demanded.

Her expression twisted as she realized that she would have turned away Nefri as a crazed old woman.

"I do not know."

"You would have thought her mad."

She wrapped her arms about her waist. "Now I fear that I am the one who is mad."

"You do not believe me?"

"I do not know what I believe." Her head slowly turned as she glanced about the small, shabby room that no doubt had once brought her comfort. It was a place of security. Or at least it had been. Now she was being asked to believe that there was nowhere that was truly safe. He could not blame her for her reluctance. "I cannot think."

Unable to halt himself, Lucien slid forward, allowing his hands to lightly descend upon her shoulders. He ached to pull her close. To surround her with the strength of his own body. Instead, he gazed deeply into her wide, troubled eyes.

"I know it is difficult, my dove—"

"No," she sharply interrupted, pulling away to regard him with a startlingly fierce expression.

Caught off guard, Lucien held out his hands in a pacifying motion. Great Nefri, she was as skittish as a newborn colt.

"What?"

"Do not call me that."

His breath caught at her broken tones. He felt as if he had just been slammed in the stomach. She was so terribly wounded. And he was the cause.

It was not just the unbelievable tale of vampires. Or even the powerful Medallion she wore about her neck. It was the fact that she had allowed him into her heart.

After years of keeping herself aloof from others and avoiding the pain and disappointment she had experienced at the hands of Lord Patten, she had at long last permitted herself to reach out to another.

Now she felt utterly betrayed.

And he had no one to blame but himself, he acknowledged bitterly. Not even Nefri.

It had been his choice to pose as a dandy on the run from his angry cousin. His choice to live beneath Jocelyn's roof. And his choice to seek a closer relationship than necessary to simply protect her.

And all to see her smile.

His expression was pleading as he held out a slender hand. "Jocelyn."

"No." With a shake of her head she backed away, the pain visible upon her face. "I thought you were different. I thought I could believe in you, but you have done nothing but lie to me from the moment you entered my home."

His hand abruptly clenched as it fell to his side. "I came here to protect you."

She gave a sharp, humorless laugh. "And to have a bit of a lark with the poor, scandal-tainted spinster?"

"Stop it, Jocelyn." Indifferent to the flashing danger in her eyes and the stiffness of her frame, Lucien stepped forward and firmly grasped her upper arms. She could insult him to her heart's content. He would readily accept whatever blows she might need to throw. But he would not allow her to belittle herself. "I will admit that I desired to bring a smile to your lips and to ease the bitterness within you. Hardly contemptible motives."

Her mouth curled at his insistent words. "I do not need your pity, Mr. Valin."

"Good, because pity is the last thing you would ever receive from me," he gritted out, careful to keep his fingers from digging into her soft skin in exasperation. He had done enough damage to this innocent maiden. "I admire you more than any other woman I have ever met. Your kindness, your strength, your ability to take adversity and alter it to something so good. Quite frankly, Miss Kingly, you astonish me."

For a breathless, wondrous moment her expression softened at his words. She even began to sway slightly toward his waiting warmth before she abruptly became rigid beneath his hands. A sudden bleakness returned to the pale features.

"How can I trust anything you say?"

Lucien fiercely held on to the small beacon of hope he had just witnessed. Beneath the pain and confusion, she did still care for him. It had been etched upon her pale features. And now that he was near her, he could feel it beat through her very blood.

Over the past few weeks they had become irrevocably linked to each other. The shimmering bonds of love and affection had been established whether either of them desired to acknowledge them or not.

Perhaps he should have taken more care, he chastised himself. Not only for the tender feelings of poor Jocelyn but for his own peace of mind.

In time Jocelyn might very well put him out of her heart and find another to love. It was the way of humans to be able to love and mate more than once during their short life span. For a vampire, however, such a love came only once. And it endured for all eternity.

Such a thought should be terrifying. He had deliberately avoided such entanglements. To be bound to another was a responsibility he was incapable of accepting.

Oddly, however, he felt nothing but a warm flood of joy at the shimmering golden threads of love that firmly tied him to this woman.

"I know, Jocelyn, and you know," he said in tones that defied argument. "Deep within you. You can sense what is in my very soul."

She gave a shake of her head, but there was a hint of uncertainty that flashed through her eyes. He was well aware that the Medallion had given her the power to perceive well beyond her human capabilities.

"That is not possible."

"The Medallion has made it possible," he murmured.

"How?"

He gave careful thought to his words. The last thing he desired was to give her yet another thing to worry over.

"It has altered you," he at last admitted slowly. "You feel things more. You are more sharply aware of your surroundings and able to sense the emotions of others. It is a rare gift for a human."

Thankfully her expression did not tighten with

fear. Instead, her full, tempting lips twisted in a rueful fashion.

"If that is true, then why did it not warn me you were a vampire?"

His hand shifted to lightly cup her soft cheek. "But it did. You just chose to ignore what your heart whispered."

"Yes." She heaved a faint sigh. "So once again I was the fool."

Lucien gave an impatient click of his tongue. Clearly she was determined to hold on to her sense of betrayal. At least for the time. He did not entirely blame her, but he did not possess the luxury of indulging her wounded sensibilities. Not while Amadeus continued to lurk in the shadows.

"Jocelyn, I know that you are angry with me, but you must hear what I have to tell you," he said in stern tones.

With a shake of her head she was pulling from his grasp. "I cannot. Not tonight."

He frowned in concern. "You are in danger. The traitors will do whatever they must to gain command of the Medallion."

"Please, Lucien." She held up a hand that visibly trembled. "I can bear no more."

She spoke the truth. Even from a distance he could sense she was holding on by a fragile thread. If he pressed any further, she might shatter beneath the strain and panic. He could not allow her to lose her reason. Not when he had no notion what she might do.

"I am sorry," he said in low tones. "My last desire was to have you hurt by me."

She pressed her hands to her bosom, her eyes shimmering with unshed tears. "We will talk in the morning."

"Yes." He gave a slow nod. "Good night, my dove."

"Good night."

Lucien watched in silence as she unsteadily made her way from the room. His hands clenched at his sides as he battled his instinctive urge to keep her close to him. He did not want her out of his sight. Not when she was so clearly upset.

What if she bolted during the night?

What if she decided that he was crazed and called for help from Bow Street?

What if she decided to rid herself of the troublesome Medallion and bring an end to her danger?

What if . . .

The potential for disaster swirled through his mind, but he made no move to follow Jocelyn. She had promised that they would speak in the morning, and he had to trust her. He owed her that at least.

Instead, he moved to pour himself a measure of the fine brandy. The past half hour had proven to be the most difficult he had ever endured. Not only the realization that he had deeply wounded

Jocelyn, but the knowledge that he might have irretrievably destroyed any hope of a future.

With a jerky motion he sipped the smoky spirit, his features stark. Great Nefri. When had he started considering a future with Jocelyn?

Was it when she had confessed her painful rift from her parents? When she had taken him to meet the young maidens she had helped to leave the streets? When he had witnessed her kindness to the poor children in the warehouse? When his lips had first touched her own?

Perhaps it had been the moment he had first entered the house and caught sight of those proud, wounded blue eyes of hers.

Whenever it had occurred, he was a fool.

He had come here to protect her. And more important, to ensure that the traitors did not lay claim to the Medallion.

Those should be his only thoughts until Amadeus was returned behind the Veil and Jocelyn was safe. Everything else would be a distraction that might very well prove to be disastrous.

For all vampires.

Polishing off the last of the brandy, he set the glass aside and moved to extinguish the candles. He had no need of light to keep careful watch through the night, and he knew that Meg would remain awake until she was certain that both he and Jocelyn had sought their beds. She was a servant from the old school, and no one could convince her that a nobly born person could possibly recall locking the door or properly putting out the fires.

Moving silently into the hall, he crossed to climb the narrow stairs that would lead to the small garret. He had discovered that his window offered a fine view of the streets, and it was the most reasonable spot to keep guard over the household. And it also allowed him to give some rest to his earthly form.

With his wits distracted by thoughts of Jocelyn, he had reached the door to his chamber, when he belatedly realized there was a faint scent in the air that could come from only one source.

Instantly on the alert, Lucien slipped the dagger from beneath his coat and held it firmly in his hand. A vampire was near. And he could think of only one vampire who would be awaiting him in the garret.

With caution he pushed the door to his rooms open and stepped within. Although the narrow chamber was cloaked in darkness, his sight was easily able to penetrate the shadows. His brows tugged together as he realized that there was nothing to be seen.

"Amadeus," he growled in low tones, moving farther into the room. "I know that you are here. Show yourself."

A faint shimmer of mist suddenly appeared in a

distant corner, and Lucien carefully hid the dagger behind his back. He did not trust the traitor. If Amadeus had become desperate, Lucien did not doubt for a moment Amadeus would do whatever necessary to rid himself of Lucien's unwelcome presence.

"Show your black soul," he commanded roughly, watching the mist advance.

There was no response, and an odd premonition sent a trickle of ice down his spine. Amadeus possessed the power of mist-walking, but there was something wrong. This mist was thickening as it approached, and darkening to charcoal color.

Lucien slowly backed away, remaining before the door to ensure whatever was within the mist was not allowed to leave the chamber. He could not let this threat reach Jocelyn. No matter what he had to do.

Coming to a halt, Lucien held the dagger before him. The mist began to spread, becoming a wall of thick fog. He sought to peer through the heavy shroud, but it was impossible. That sense of impending doom deepened as the mist neared, and Lucien fought the urge to rush back through the door.

Whatever this was, he must somehow halt it.

Jocelyn must be kept safe.

That was all that mattered.

Like a thick, icy blanket, the fog slipped about

him, and Lucien discovered himself firmly trapped. The dagger fell from his hand as the chill cut straight to his heart and a moan of pain was wrenched from his throat.

Bloody hell.

It was a mist wraith. A spell that had once been in the command of the vampires but had been banished from the world centuries before. It was far too dangerous to all vampires.

At the moment it merely held him in its tentacles. Once it had gained command of him, however, it would feed upon his spirit until he was nothing more than an empty shell.

Lucien closed his eyes and battled to fight the panic that threatened to overwhelm him. To struggle would only hasten his demise. The creature would feast upon his heightened emotions. Only by remaining calm could he hope to discover a means of escape.

Calm . . . Great Nefri.

Chapter 11

Jocelyn paced the cramped quarters of her bed-chamber with uneven steps. Perhaps absurdly, she had hoped that being away from the disturbing presence of Lucien would ease her troubled heart.

Instead, it had only darkened her already black mood.

Vampires? Magical Medallions? Old gypsies who weren't gypsies at all?

It was enough to drive any poor maiden mad.

But while her mind reeled with the effort to accept that vampires were not simply creatures of the imagination but real and living beneath her roof, in her mind it was Lucien's betrayal that lingered.

Dear heavens, she had shared dinner with him, laughed with him, played games with him . . . shared passion with him.

She had opened her past and revealed all the betrayal she had endured. She had opened her heart.

And she had given her trust.

And that was what hurt the most.

She closed her eyes and sucked in a shaky breath. What was the matter with her?

A man was in her home, claiming to be a mythological vampire. There was a deranged killer out on the streets, attempting to force her to hand over a Medallion that supposedly held the fate of the vampires. A Medallion that was altering her in a manner she could not even comprehend.

And all she could think of was her disappointment that Lucien was not the gentleman she had thought him to be.

Her near-hysterical laugh echoed through the room, and she pressed her hands to her face. Perhaps she was going mad. It would certainly be the preferable explanation for the horrid day.

Preferable certainly to the thought that the man she loved was a vampire.

Reaching the narrow window, she pressed her cheek to the cool pane and closed her eyes. She should be thinking of what she intended to do. All too soon it would be morning, and she would be forced to face Lucien once again. She needed to consider whether she intended to demand that he leave her home or to accept his claim that he must be near to protect her.

At the moment neither option seemed bearable.

Having him near and yet knowing deep within

that everything about him had been a lie was bound to be painful. Then again, if there were a traitorous vampire stalking her, did she truly desire to face him on her own?

She heaved a sigh, wishing only to lie upon the narrow bed and put all of her troubles behind her. Come the morning, she might even manage to convince herself that this was all no more than a ghastly nightmare.

"Miss Kingly."

The muffled sound of her name being called had Jocelyn abruptly opening her eyes. Dazed by the unexpected intrusion into her thoughts, she scanned the empty garden. There was nothing to be seen for a moment, and then, unbelievably, the slender shape of a young lad stepped from behind a bush.

"Thomas," she breathed as she hurriedly fumbled with the latch and threw up the sash. "What is it?"

The urchin stepped forward into a shaft of moonlight to reveal a heavy bandage around his hand. "There was trouble at the warehouse. I need your help."

"Dear heavens. Do not move," she commanded in urgent tones. "I will be down in a moment."

"Please, you must hurry," he called.

There was no need for his urging as she hastily turned to rush from her chamber and down the narrow flight of stairs. Poor Thomas. He always seemed so swaggeringly confident. So invincible. So very wise. It was quite easy to forget he was just a little boy. And now he had been harmed. It was insupportable.

She moved to the back of the house and used the kitchen door to lead her into the garden. She nearly tumbled over her skirts in her haste, until at last she gave a hiss of impatience and hauled them well above her ankles to rid herself of their annoying tendency to cling.

Only when she had actually left the house and entered the dark shadows of the night did she take note of the odd chill in the air. Only moments before she had been smothering in the unusual summer heat; now she could not ignore the prickles that raced over her skin.

It was very strange, but she did not allow herself to be distracted. Thomas was in need of her help and she could not fret over a sudden coldness in the air.

Coming to a halt beside the waiting lad, she gently took his arm in her hands.

"Oh, Thomas, what has occurred?"

He gave a faint sniff as he attempted to be brave. "A horrid man forced his way into the warehouse. I could not halt him, Miss Kingly. I am sorry."

Jocelyn caught her breath in horror. Was it the traitorous vampire that Lucien had warned her of? Had he concluded that slaying poor prostitutes was not as desirable as harming innocent children? The thought was enough to make her heart stop in fear.

"No, Thomas, you should not even have attempted such a thing," she said in appalled tones. "I cannot see to your injuries here. We must go inside."

Without warning he pulled his arm from her grasp, his grimy face set in lines of determination.

"No."

"Thomas, do not be stubborn. You must have those wounds cleaned or they will fester."

"Not yet." His eyes appeared feverishly bright in the silver moonlight. "The man is still at the warehouse."

"What?" she breathed in shock.

"He has Annie."

"No." Her eyes widened in disbelief. "Is she harmed?"

"No, but the bugger has threatened to kill her."

Jocelyn struggled to think through the sudden cloud of terror that filled her mind. Not an easy task with the image of the tiny, fragile child in the hands of a bloodthirsty monster burning before her eyes.

Every instinct urged her to rush to the warehouse and save the little girl. It was her nature to attempt to protect those who depended upon her.

Only that sternly practical part of her nature that

had saved her upon so many occasions kept her feet from mindlessly fleeing down the street. She could not face this monster on her own. Regardless if he were merely crazed or a vampire, she needed help.

"We must go to Mr. Ryan," she abruptly decided. Surely he was the logical choice. He was the only one in the position to put a final end to this villain. "He will be able to take this monster away."

Thomas gave a violent shake of his head, his expression fearful. "No, you cannot. The man said as you was to come alone."

Jocelyn froze at the unexpected words. She had presumed that Thomas had come to her because he realized she would be willing to help. It had never entered her mind that the man had actually sent the lad to fetch her.

The chill in the air thickened, making her shudder with the sense of impending doom.

"What do you mean?" she demanded in cautious tones.

Thomas seemed to hesitate before he swallowed heavily. "He sent me to fetch you. He said you were to come alone and to bring the necklace."

"My necklace?"

"That is what he said. We must hurry."

The necklace. So that was it. She gave an unconscious shake of her head. Lucien had been right. He had warned her the traitors would do whatever necessary to gain command of her Medallion. Now they had revealed precisely how desperate they had become.

She may not desire to believe in vampires or magical Medallions, but she was left with no choice. She had to save Annie. No matter who or what might be threatening her.

"What did this man look like?" she demanded in rasping tones.

Thomas reached out to tug on her arm in impatience. It was obvious he did not approve of her wary caution.

"A big man. With a knife. Annie is in terrible danger. Come on."

Jocelyn grimly held her ground. No one was more eager to rescue the poor girl than herself. But she was wise enough to realize that she could not do so alone.

If it was a vampire holding Annie captive, then there was only one person who could be of help.

"Hold a moment, Thomas. I must fetch Mr. Valin."

A surprising flare of fury rippled over the thin countenance. "No. He said alone."

Feeling a pang of sympathy at the boy's desire to be on their way, she gave a faint sigh. No doubt Thomas was blaming himself for not being able to protect the other children.

"This man is very, very dangerous, Thomas," she

explained in gentle tones. "We cannot face him without the help of Mr. Valin. I will be only a moment."

Reaching out to lightly pat his shoulder in a comforting motion, Jocelyn turned on her heel to return to the house. Despite her earlier feelings of betrayal toward Lucien, she could no longer hesitate to turn to him for assistance. Whatever had occurred between them, he was the one person she knew that she could depend upon in times of danger.

He was the only one she desired at her side.

She had taken only a step, however, when there was a sudden rush of wind behind her. The sharp breeze nearly knocked her to her knees, and she hurriedly turned to discover Thomas surrounded in mist.

Unthinkingly she reached out, attempting to reach the boy before he was entirely hidden by the strange fog. But even as she did so, the mist was thinning and Thomas was gone. In his stead stood Vicar Fallow with an unpleasant smile twisting his lips.

Her heart halted as she gazed at the familiar countenance in disbelief.

It was not possible. It had been Thomas who had been standing before her. She would know his thin face and oversize ears anywhere. Indeed, she would have sworn on her grandmother's Bible that it had been her young friend. People did not shift from one form to another.

People did not, but vampires who possessed the powers of bloodlust might very well, a dark voice whispered in the back of her mind.

Suddenly she understood her instinctive revulsion toward the man who had pretended such a kindly interest in her. And the reason that he had so determinedly appeared whenever she happened to leave her home.

Her heart resumed beating at a frantic pace. So frantic it nearly smothered her. Lucien had done his best to convince her of the truth of his words. And the danger that surrounded her. She simply had not wanted to listen.

Watching the sudden panic that fluttered over her pale features, Vicar Fallow allowed a cruel chuckle to fill the air.

"I fear that Lucien is otherwise occupied at the moment, Miss Kingly."

"Vicar Fallow," she breathed, still reeling with disbelief.

He offered a mocking bow. "At your service."

"You . . . you are the traitor."

"Traitor?" His features seemed to tighten at her insult. "Such an ugly word, my dear. I am a simple scholar."

Her hands pressed together. A thick, icy danger cloaked the air, making it difficult to think. She knew she should flee, but stark terror held her captive.

"You are attempting to steal my amulet," she blurted out, hoping to distract him long enough that Lucien might notice their presence in the garden and come to rescue her.

A rather feeble plan, but the only one she possessed.

He shrugged with indifference at her accusation. "A necessary inconvenience, I fear. My studies must continue, and for that I need the power of the Medallion."

"Studies?" She gave a blink of surprise. He had claimed to be a scholar, but it made no sense. He was a ruthless killer, was he not? "What studies?"

"The search for the truth."

"How can the Medallion offer you truth?"

His smile was edged with cruelty as he took a deliberate step toward her. "I do not believe you would care to know the precise details of my experiments. You have a peculiar fondness for even the lowest vermin that haunt the streets of London."

She shuddered at his evil words, but a welcome flare of anger rushed through her, awakening the courage that had briefly deserted her.

She would not cower before this monster. Not after all the wickedness he had done.

"It was you," she stated in flat tones.

He arched an arrogant brow. "Me?"

"You are the one who killed Molly and those other women."

"Ah, but I cannot take full credit, my dear," he drawled in a taunting fashion. "There would have been no need for such senseless slaughter if you had not proven so lacking in trust. I had hoped for a far more peaceful means of acquiring the Medallion."

She gave a fierce shake of her head. She had never desired anything but happiness for those women. It had been this horrid fiend who had harmed them.

"No, I do not believe you. You are a monster."

The eyes abruptly glittered with a spark of anger. Clearly he did not like having the truth spoken so bluntly.

"There is no need for insults," he spat out in warning. "Indeed, I would suggest you take great care in how you address me. Your position at the moment is precarious at best."

Jocelyn had no need of the warning. Every instinct within her screamed with alarm. Never had she faced such menace. Such tangible evil.

Still, she forced herself to meet that malignant gaze without flinching.

"You cannot force me to give you the Medallion."

His thin lips twisted with annoyance at her daring claim. "No. Someday Nefri will pay for that bit of impertinence. But there are other means of acquiring what I desire."

Jocelyn swallowed the lump in her throat. She did not like the sound of that. Not the tiniest bit.

"Other means?"

"I have devoted my life to the finer arts of torture, my dear." His eyes narrowed as her face paled at the unspoken threat. "As much as I might admire your spirit, there is little hope you will be capable of denying what I wish. At least not for long. You are, after all, a mere mortal."

She could not halt her instinctive step backward. Torture? Dear heavens. Did she possess enough courage? Could she face pain and maintain her honor?

With a wrenching effort she banished the heavy sense of doom that threatened to shroud her. She could not allow herself to give in to despair.

"I may be a mortal, but Lucien is not. He will never allow you to harm me," she forced herself to retort boldly.

Without warning the man gave a dark laugh. The harsh sound sent a distinct chill down her spine.

"I did warn you that he was otherwise occupied. He will not be able to join us, I fear. At least for the next century or so."

Her hands fell to her sides at his mocking words. "What have you done to him?"

A smug expression descended upon his countenance. "During the course of my studies I have discovered several forbidden powers of the vampires. It was, of course, difficult to choose which would be the best for Lucien. He had to be punished for daring to interfere, and for causing me to remain in this stinking pit of a city while he protected you. I decided at last to be a trifle exotic. I called forth a spell that has been banned for centuries. No doubt it will be quite a shock for poor Lucien."

"No." She regarded the vile man in horror. She knew nothing of vampire spells or what they might do, but she realized that Lucien was in terrible danger. The thought was enough to make her stomach tighten in agonizing knots. "Is he injured?"

The man briefly closed his eyes, as if sending out his thoughts through the darkness.

"He lives for now," he retorted in indifferent tones. "But the mist wraith holds him in his clutches. It will not be long."

She barely prevented herself from launching herself at the smirking Vicar Fallow as her heart squeezed with grief. No. She could not bear for Lucien to die. It would be far worse than losing her own life. In truth, she did not know if she could bear the loss. She had to remain hopeful that he could somehow escape. It was that or go mad.

"You are a beast," she spat out in disgusted tones.

"Perhaps." He moved forward, his countenance cold with determination. "Now, I weary of your attempts to keep me distracted long enough for your rescue. A worthy ploy, but the night is passing. I am certain you understand my desire to be at our destination before dawn."

She barely noted his easy ability to read her pathetic ruse. Instead, she struggled with the implication that he was about to force her away from her home and any hope of salvation.

"What destination?"

His hand reached out to clutch her arm. She gasped as an icy pain flared through her muscles to the very bone.

"You will soon discover."

"No. I . . . I will scream."

"And what will that accomplish?" Suddenly his face was far too close. His eyes seemed to sear into her very soul. "Lucien will not hear you, and any mortal that happens to rush to your rescue will be swiftly put to death. Do you truly desire another murder upon your hands?"

"They are not upon my hands, they are upon yours," she dared to say.

"It is your decision. Do you come along quietly or do you desire to call for your housekeeper? I would no doubt find her a tasty morsel."

The thought of Meg halted the scream that threatened to rip from her throat. No matter what her terror, she could not risk the innocent woman. Poor Meg had sacrificed enough to stand beside her. Jocelyn would not allow her to be harmed any further.

"I will come."

"I knew I could depend upon you." A thin white hand lifted to lightly stroke her hair, the oddly feverish eyes studying her as if she were a peculiar animal. "Such a remarkable young maiden. I intend to enjoy exploring you."

The caress was a repulsive mockery of Lucien's soft touch, and without even thinking she abruptly turned her head to spit in the vampire's face.

"You are contemptible."

The hand tightened in her hair, forcing her head back until her neck was readily exposed. Her breath caught as she watched the narrow face approach, the moonlight glinting on the fangs that could suddenly be seen. This was it. She possessed no defense for the teeth that were poised to sink deep into her neck.

She sent up a prayer as she prepared for the inevitable death, then, without warning, she was abruptly set free.

The vampire regarded her with a twisted sneer. "Ah, you tempt me to forget the Medallion and slay you here and now. But I have plans for you, my beauty. Plans that I will not allow to be disrupted. Come."

His fingers dug into her arm and she was being roughly hauled toward the shadows. Suddenly realizing that she was not about to be murdered in her garden, she stumbled forward. She should no doubt be terrified that her death was not to be a swift, mindless affair. The horrid man had threatened to torture her without mercy. And to kill anyone who attempted to interfere.

But oddly a numb fog had descended within her heart.

She could feel no pain, no terror, and no thought of what was to come.

Instead, the vision of an elegant bronze countenance with tender golden eyes filled her mind. It was almost as if he were reaching out to offer the strength she so desperately needed.

Warmed by the vision, she kept it firmly in her thoughts as she was roughly hauled into the vampire's arms and then tossed into the dark confines of a carriage. Landing upon her knees, she gritted her teeth.

"Lucien," she softly whispered.

Lucien had known the moment Jocelyn had encountered Amadeus. It had not been a sense of the vampire, but, rather, the maiden's sudden terror that had reached even through the thick mist that surrounded him and pierced his heart.

At first he had struggled mindlessly to free himself from the clutches of the mist wraith. He had to halt Amadeus. He had to save Jocelyn before the desperate traitor could harm her. But even as he had struggled he realized that he was only ensuring that he would never survive long enough to reach her.

With a grim effort he had forced himself to calm his frantic fear. He would not be able to help Jocelyn if he did not survive his encounter with the wraith. Until then he could only hope to calm her fears and send out what strength he could to bolster her courage.

Ignoring the pain that wrenched his body, Lucien forced the image of Jocelyn into his mind. Then, slowing his rapid breath, he sent his thoughts outward. It took but a moment before he could sense Jocelyn, and he silently called her name.

"Jocelyn."

"Lucien," she whispered, clearly unaware that he was more than a figment of her dazed fear.

"Jocelyn, I am here." He paused for a moment, allowing her time to accept that he was truly able to speak with her. "What has occurred?"

"I . . . I am with Vicar Fallow. He has forced me into a carriage and we are leaving the city."

Lucien's heart twisted with agony. Even then she was being taken farther from him. Great Nefri, he had to win his way free swiftly if he was to rescue her.

"Has he harmed you?"

"No."

He briefly closed his eyes in relief. "Be strong, my dove. I will come for you."

"Lucien, he said that you are trapped by some spell."

He grimaced, wishing she did not realize he was not already in pursuit of them. The last thing he desired was for her to lose heart at the thought he would fail her.

"I fear so," he grudgingly conceded. "I bumbled into the trap laid for me like the veriest fool."

"Are you injured?"

"Only my pride."

"He said . . . he said that it would kill you."

"I am not so easy to be rid of," he swiftly retorted. "As you well know."

Even across the distance he could sense a brief flare of rueful humor at his teasing words. Then, just as swiftly, that dark fear returned.

"You must take care. Do not do anything . . . impulsive."

He smiled wryly. She knew him all too well. "I will be careful. It is you who must be on your guard."

"I will try."

The uncertainty in her voice nearly sent him mad with terror. It was only with an effort that he did not scream out his frustration. Instead, he forced himself to keep himself grimly under control. Until he could manage to reach her, Jocelyn would be forced to keep herself alive.

"Jocelyn."

"Yes?"

"You must not give him the Medallion. As long as you possess it, he must keep you alive."

There was a long pause, during which Lucien could physically feel the panic she barely held in check.

"I do not believe it will be so simple."

Neither did he. He could not forget the twisted, brutal delight that Amadeus took in killing his victims. He might have once been a genuine scholar, but he long ago lost all reason. His obsessive search for some mythical truth had turned him into a monster. A dangerous monster that had learned any number of unpleasant methods of hurting Jocelyn while still keeping her a breath away from death.

"Just hold on, my dove," he whispered, forcing the ghastly thoughts from his mind. He could not allow himself to be overcome with dread. Not when cold logic was the only thing that would save the both of them. "I am coming for you."

"Please hurry, Lucien."

"I will." Knowing that he must end his contact with Jocelyn and concentrate upon freeing himself, Lucien allowed himself one last moment with the woman who had become a part of his very soul. "Jocelyn, I love you."

"I love you too."

A sharp welcome warmth flared through his frozen heart. He had not destroyed it all. There was hope left.

"Then all will be well."

Chapter 12

The pain was near unbearable.

Battling to remain conscious, Lucien could feel Jocelyn traveling ever farther away.

He had to escape, he frantically told himself, pressing against the misty tendrils despite the biting wounds the wraith was inflicting. He could not fail. Not on this occasion. Jocelyn depended upon him. And even if it cost him his very soul, he would save her.

It seemed a more likely prospect with every agonizing moment. The wrenching pain was sapping his strength even as the mist fed upon his spirit. His movements were slowing as the ruthless chill continued to clutch at his body. And worse, without the dagger he had no means of battling the encroaching darkness.

Then quite unexpectedly there was the sound of loud footsteps upon the stairs.

"Mr. Valin," Meg called in her gruff tone.

"No." The word came out as a faint groan.

"Mr. Valin, have you seen Miss Kingly? I cannot find hide nor hair of her."

"Return to your rooms," he managed to croak. "Do not enter."

"What?" There was an impatient rap upon the door. "Are you in there?"

"Go away," he warned.

"Not until you tell me what has happened to Miss Kingly."

There was a rattle of the doorknob, and Lucien attempted to press his weak form to the wooden panels. He would not have the poor housekeeper made into fodder for the wretched wraith.

His efforts, however, were for naught as the mist sensed the warmth of a living being within his grasp. Lessening its grasp upon Lucien, it began to slip through the cracks in the door.

It was all the opportunity that Lucien needed.

Allowing his battered body to sink to the floor, he fumbled to find the dagger he had dropped. For a horrid moment he thought perhaps it had tumbled out of reach, then his seeking fingers closed around the smooth hilt. Without hesitation he struck out.

The vampire-blessed blade easily slid through the misty form, making it cringe backward. Not about to lose his chance, Lucien struck again and again, his ears painfully pierced by the high inhuman screech of the wraith.

With a last desperate attempt the wraith struck out, knocking Lucien's head fiercely against the door. Darkness threatened, but with grim determination he held on, striking out with more haste than skill.

At last there was a high wail and then in the blink of an eye the mist wraith was reluctantly retreating.

For moments Lucien lay gasping upon the floor. His entire body trembled from the lingering wounds and his last desperate effort to rid himself of the wraith. In the hall he could still hear the calls of Meg but he was unable to move enough to allow her in.

At last he dragged himself to his knees and sucked in deep, shuddering breaths. There was no time. He had to act. And he had to act swiftly.

Using the doorknob he forced himself shakily to his feet and then wrenched the door open. The housekeeper tumbled into the room, her round face gray with fear.

"What the devil is going on up here?" she demanded in weak anger. "There was some sort of smoke coming through the door."

"I have no time to explain. I must go after Miss Kingly."

"Go after? Where has she gone?"

"She has been kidnapped."

There was a loud gasp. "Dear God."

"Do not fear, I shall soon have her home," he swore in low tones.

Meg regarded him with narrowed eyes, seemingly noticing for the first time his rumpled appearance and unnaturally pale countenance.

"You do not appear well yourself, Mr. Valin. Perhaps we should call for the authorities."

He gave a firm shake of his head. "No. I must do this on my own. But you might wish to have a hot bath and warm supper prepared for when we return."

"And a nice bottle of brandy," she added in firm tones.

"Yes." He gave a weak smile before pushing himself from the door and making his way down the steps.

He paused only long enough to collect the necessary money to rent a mount before he was out of the house and on his way to the nearby stables. He did not allow himself to contemplate what Amadeus might even now be doing to Jocelyn, or even what he would do when he eventually caught up with them. His only concern was catching up to them as swiftly as possible.

In less than half an hour he had his horse and was on the faint trail of the carriage. It came as no surprise when he discovered himself being led out of London and down a narrow trail that appeared rarely used. Amadeus would have shrewdly discovered a place of privacy to attempt to coerce the Medallion from Jocelyn. He would never act in a hasty or impulsive manner.

Dawn was not far off when at last he turned from the trail and crossed through a heavy copse of trees. Carefully making his way through the underbrush, he abruptly stumbled into a clearing. In the very center was an abandoned castle that had long ago fallen into disrepair. It would have been easy to presume that the ruin was empty, except that someone had quite recently taken the effort to board over the narrow windows.

And, of course, the unmistakable tingle of awareness that assured Lucien that a vampire was nearby.

Returning his mount to the cover of the trees, he tied off the reins and carefully turned to make his way to the castle. He was relieved to discover that Amadeus had not thought to bring any of his henchmen to act as guards, and he easily gained entrance through the heavy door.

With silent steps he made his way through the small vestibule and moved to the nearby steps that led to the cellars below. With dagger in hand he inched his way downward, the sense of both Amadeus and Jocelyn growing stronger with every step.

At last entering the cellars, he was abruptly halted as a loud scratch echoed through the air and a light bloomed to life. Standing in the center of the room, Amadeus glared at him in undisguised hatred.

"Lucien," the vampire rasped, the eyes glittering with a dangerous desperation. "What an unpleasant surprise. I thought you would be nicely disposed of by now."

Nonchalantly strolling forward, Lucien cast a covert glance about the clammy chamber. Along one wall were several dusty barrels and a rack that once held wine bottles. Farther away he could see an array of manacles, chains, whips, and more exotic instruments of torture that he could not even begin to name. His stomach tightened as his gaze at last discovered the narrow wooden table in a dark alcove where Jocelyn lay stretched on the surface with her arms tied above her head and her legs tightly bound together.

Although disheveled, she did not appear to be harmed, and allowing himself only a brief glance at her terrified countenance, he ruthlessly forced his attention back to the furious Amadeus.

There was no time to assure himself that she was well and unharmed, he reminded himself grimly.

Not until she was free of Amadeus's clutches.

"You have crossed all boundaries, Amadeus," he growled in disgust. "Mist wraiths have been forbidden by all vampires. Do you possess no shame?"

The vampire offered Lucien an oddly haunted smile at the accusation. "Very little, I have discovered."

Lucien could conjure no sympathy. Amadeus had brought this wicked compulsion upon himself. He had long ago turned his back on decency and integrity. It was too late to realize his desires had cost him his soul.

"Release Miss Kingly," he commanded in cold tones.

"Unfortunately she has not yet given me what I need," Amadeus retorted.

With a smooth motion Lucien reached beneath his jacket to reveal the deadly dagger. The blade glinted with a dangerous fire in the flickering light.

"Release her. Now."

Amadeus gave a rasping laugh as he crossed his arms over his chest. "Really, Lucien, I must say I am rather surprised. I would have thought you would have lost interest in the chit long ago. You have never been very constant in your attentions." He paused, his expression mocking. "How did you escape?"

Lucien hid a shudder at the icy pain that still lingered. "It is a long and rather tedious story."

"No matter." The vampire stepped forward. "I shall attend to your death myself. It will no doubt be far more satisfying."

With slow, steady motions Lucien backed toward the woman stretched upon the table, careful to keep his attention upon the dangerous Amadeus.

He had to release Jocelyn before the vampire could attack him.

He was far from certain that he was strong enough to fend him off for long.

"I fear that I cannot accommodate you. I have rather pressing business to attend to."

Amadeus merely smiled with cruel amusement. "So it would seem."

"It is not too late." Lucien continued, desperate to keep the vampire off guard long enough to give Jocelyn a chance for freedom. "We can return to the Veil together."

"Fool. I am beyond the petty rules of the Council. I will never return."

"You will return or die."

Amadeus moved toward him, his expression one of icy determination. "One of us will certainly die."

Lucien backed into the table and heard Jocelyn stir. "Lucien?" she whispered.

Clutching the dagger, he struggled to clear his throbbing fear. It took a moment before he was able to at last reach out and touch her mind with his own.

"Jocelyn, lay still," he urged as he carefully shifted so that he could use the dagger to slice through the ropes that bound her. Still keeping his gaze upon the vampire moving ever closer, he helped her to sit upright. "Can you move?"

"I think so."

"Then get behind me."

With awkward stiffness she half tumbled off the table and scurried behind his form. At the same moment Amadeus gave a grating laugh.

"You surely do not believe I will allow the Medallion to leave, do you, Lucien? I will kill her before I allow that to happen."

Lucien once again reached out with his thoughts. "Jocelyn, listen to me carefully."

"What?" she replied in the same manner.

"I want you to run from here as fast as you can. There is a horse waiting in the trees. Return to London and find Gideon Ravel. He will protect you."

"No. I will not leave you."

He gritted his teeth as the vampire neared. "Then we both will die. I cannot protect you and fight Amadeus at the same moment."

"No."

"Jocelyn, do as I say. The Medallion must be protected."

"I do not care."

"You will do this, Jocelyn."

"I cannot."

"Please, Jocelyn, I need you to be strong. You will do this for me."

"I—" There was a reluctant pause. "Very well."

Easily realizing that Lucien was plotting Jocelyn's escape, Amadeus narrowed his gaze.

"Do not be a fool, Lucien. If you do not want the wench to die, then return her to the table."

"If . . . if you insist." Lucien slumped his shoulders as he turned toward Jocelyn, then with swift motions he was violently pushing her toward the door. "Run, Jocelyn. And don't look back."

She stumbled and nearly fell, but thankfully she managed to regain her balance and was hurriedly charging from the room and up the stairs.

"No," Amadeus snarled, moving to follow her.

Lucien was just as swift. Leaping over the table, he placed himself in the vampire's path with the dagger pointed straight at his heart.

"I do not think so, Amadeus."

Coming to a reluctant halt, the vampire trembled with fury. "You have interfered for the last time, Lucien. I will kill you and then that stubborn whore."

"You may try."

A sneer twisted the thin lips. "You believe you can halt me? You remain weak from your life behind the Veil. You are no match for me."

At the moment Lucien could not argue the truth of his words. He was still weakened from his earlier battle, and his wounds had not completely healed. To face a vampire filled with the power of bloodlust was no doubt foolish beyond measure.

Still, he knew that every moment he could keep

Amadeus trapped in the cellar was precious. It meant that Jocelyn was one step closer to safety.

"Not so weak, Amadeus," he softly taunted, shifting to ensure he blocked the door. "I managed to best the mist wraith."

"Ah, yes. A pity I do not have the time to hear your remarkable story."

Lucien shrugged. "We have all the time you desire. Perhaps we could have a nice chat over a fine bottle of wine."

Amadeus lifted his brows at Lucien's gracious words. "While Miss Kingly flees to the protection of Gideon and Sebastian? I think not."

"Not even one drink to toast my soon-to-be demise?" Lucien prodded with a smile. "I have a very fine spirit in London if you would care to wait here while I retrieve it."

As expected, the morose vampire gave a sniff of disdain at his levity. He had always condemned Lucien for his lack of proper dignity, seemingly offended by anyone who did not share his sullen darkness.

"Frivolous to the end, eh, Lucien?" he snarled.

Lucien smiled. "It is preferable to your grim lack of humor."

Spreading his arms wide, Amadeus called upon his powers and began slowly to change into mist.

"We shall see if you are still laughing when I have finished with you," he mocked in hollow tones.

Lucien tightly gripped the dagger and called upon his fading strength.

"We will, indeed," he muttered, wincing as the mist struck out to cut deeply into his arm.

Jocelyn's hands were raw and bleeding as she struggled to pull open the shutters that had been firmly nailed shut.

When she had fled the cellars, she had made it outside the gloomy castle and halfway to the nearby trees, when she staggered to a halt. She wanted to run. To hasten to the trees and find the awaiting horse so that she could return to the sanity of London.

Quite frankly she was terrified.

She had never been so agonizingly frightened in her life.

The ghastly Amadeus had devoted the past hour to revealing precisely how he would torture her. He had spoken of horrors beyond her imagination and pain she could never endure. For a time she had thought she might actually go mad from sheer fear.

Who could possibly blame her for seeking safety? She was no match for a vampire. And as Lucien had said, the Medallion must be kept out of the traitor's hands. Nothing was more important.

This was not her battle. She should do as

Lucien demanded and seek out Gideon Ravel to protect her.

But even as she had stumbled out the door, she had known she could not leave Lucien behind.

How could she? Whatever he was, whatever falsehood he had told her, she loved him. She loved him with a force that nearly consumed her.

If he were to die, then her own life would be meaningless.

And beyond that there was a rebellious part of her heart that condemned her cowardly flight.

No.

She would not be forced into walking away.

Not on this occasion, she suddenly told herself.

She had allowed herself to be humiliated out of society. To be condemned by her parents and thrown out of their lives.

Had she been older and wiser, she would never have given them such power over her. Nor would she have wasted so much of her life regretting what was no more than a mistaken trust in another.

She would prove to herself that she had changed. That she was now a woman who could face bravely whatever life chose to throw at her.

And so she had forced her reluctant feet to carry her back into the cramped vestibule.

That was when she had suddenly been struck with a dangerous plan.

She could not hope to match the vampire's

strength, but she could match his cunning. If only she could wrench free the shutters, then she would have the perfect weapon to battle a creature of the dark.

With a last jerk, the heavy shutter flung open. Jocelyn ignored her throbbing hands and glanced out the broken panes of the narrow window. Although darkness still shrouded the nearby woods, there was an undeniable glow of dawn upon the horizon.

From the stairs she could hear the unmistakable sounds of a battle being waged, and her heart clenched in fear.

"Oh, Lucien, hold on," she muttered in low tones, silently willing the sun to rise.

For what seemed to be an eternity she stood there trembling as she desperately watched for the first rays of sunlight to filter over the trees. And then, at long last, a bright glow washed over her and tumbled into the shadowed room.

Hurriedly turning about, Jocelyn moved through the slender beam of sunlight, bending down to make a distinct mark in the thick dust upon the flagstones. Then, just as swiftly, she pulled the shutter closed, careful to ensure that it appeared firmly nailed in place.

Only then did she turn toward the stairs and call out in a loud voice, "Amadeus. I have the Medallion. It is yours if you still desire it."

There was a thick pause before she heard Lucien moan in dismay. "Jocelyn, no."

"Yes, Lucien." She did not need to feign the decided quaver in her voice. "I will not allow you to be harmed."

"Bring me the Medallion," Amadeus commanded.

"No." Jocelyn sucked in a steadying breath, her nerves so raw that she could barely think straight. "You must first assure me that Lucien is able to leave without harm."

"Of course." The oily voice of the traitor moved closer to the stairs. "You have my word. Now bring me the Medallion."

Jocelyn grimaced, wondering if the evil man truly thought she would accept his word. For heaven's sake, he had kidnapped, tortured, and murdered without compunction. Why would he not lie?

"Not until Lucien is here beside me."

She could hear a rasp of anger float through the air before the vampire was regaining command of his composure.

"Very well." There was a faint rustling, and then Jocelyn could see Lucien making his way up the stairs, closely followed by Amadeus. Her breath caught at the bronze countenance that was cut and battered almost out of recognition. His lean body had fared no better, and his coat was tattered to reveal several wounds that were bleeding in an alarming manner. Smiling cruelly at her horrified expression, Amadeus held out his skeleton hand. "Now. The Medallion."

Jocelyn licked her suddenly dry lips, her heart painfully trapped in her throat. If her plot failed, then Lucien would be killed and she would once again be at the mercy of this horrid monster.

No, she firmly thrust the traitorous thoughts aside.

She would not fail.

Straightening her shoulders, she met the feverish gaze with a stubborn determination.

"Not until you have allowed Lucien to pass."

Amadeus snarled at her bravado. "I will endure no tricks."

"No tricks." Slowly she reached up to remove the Medallion from her neck and held it out.

"No, Jocelyn," Lucien gasped.

She ignored his outburst as her gaze remained on the wary vampire. "Send him to me."

There was a long pause before Amadeus reached out to push Lucien toward her. "Go to her."

She forced herself to remain in place as Lucien painfully staggered forward, his hand covering a gaping wound that spilled blood over his fingers.

"Jocelyn," he gasped weakly, his eyes glazed with agony, "do not do this."

"I must, Lucien," she said softly. "Forgive me."

"No. . . ."

"Enough," the vampire growled, moving forward with an icy fury. "I will have the Medallion."

Jocelyn gave a nod of her head. "Very well. Take it."

Sending up a desperate prayer, she tossed the Medallion toward the spot she had marked upon the floor. It arched through the dim shadows before landing upon the dust. At the same time Lucien gave a wrenching moan.

"No."

With a gloating laugh, the vampire was already scurrying toward his prize.

"Too late, Lucien. Your foolish slut has already given the Medallion of her free will. It is now mine."

"Amadeus," Lucien choked.

Sinking to his knees, Amadeus reached his fingers toward the amulet that glowed with a golden light.

"Already I can feel the power. Glorious power . . ."

Lost in his haze of lust, the vampire did not notice as Jocelyn suddenly turned and reached for the shutter. He did not even realize his danger until a rosy shaft of morning sunlight angled through the window to land directly upon his crouched form.

For a heartbeat the world seemed to halt, then to Jocelyn's amazement a tendril of smoke rose from the vampire. It was swiftly followed by a sudden flare of fire that engulfed Amadeus even as he struggled to his feet.

"No," the tortured vampire screamed, futilely attempting to bat out the flames that were consuming him.

In horror Jocelyn watched Amadeus stumble about the room, his shrieks sending shivers down her spine. He was being burned alive, his body turning to ash as he fell to the flagstones and gave one last scream of fury.

Silence descended, and with agonizing slowness the flames flickered out one by one. Jocelyn remained locked in sick disbelief until at last there was nothing left but the gruesome darkness upon the dust.

Heavens above, she had done it.

She had killed a vampire and saved Lucien.

Chapter 13

With her horrified gaze still upon the black marks on the flagstones, Jocelyn was at last shaken out of her shocked disbelief as Lucien gave a low groan and sank to his knees.

Shaking off the odd fog that clouded her mind, Jocelyn hastily lowered herself beside his weak form.

She had not gone through all of this only to have Lucien die on her now, she silently swore, her hands reaching out to stroke the satin of his hair.

"Lucien, you are wounded."

"Give me a moment," he murmured, his voice so low she could barely discern his words.

"Shall I go for a doctor?"

With an effort he lifted his head to regard her with a strained smile. "A doctor would be of little use to me, I fear."

She bit her lip at his teasing words. "Oh . . . of course."

"Do not fear. I heal very quickly."

Hoping that he was not merely attempting to disguise how injured he truly was, Jocelyn shifted so that she could wrap her arms about him and pull him against her. She needed to have him close. She needed to feel the beat of his heart and his sweet breath against her cheek.

Instantly she was surrounded by his warm strength, and she could at last draw in a deep breath. There was a great comfort in simply having him near.

"I am not hurting you, am I?" she demanded in concern.

"No." He shifted so that they were both leaning against the hard stone wall and released a faint sigh. "This is much better."

Jocelyn buried her face in his shoulder, breathing deeply of his masculine scent. She was still reeling from her horrifying experience, and while she had never allowed herself to doubt that Lucien would come to her rescue, she could not deny that the past few hours had tried her nerves to the very limit.

Confronting a crazed vampire would have terrified the bravest of souls.

"Lucien, I was so frightened," she whispered in broken tones.

Surprisingly he placed his fingers beneath her chin to tilt her countenance upward. The golden eyes glittered with a smoldering fire.

"Unfortunately you were not frightened enough."

"What?"

"Why did you not flee when I commanded you to?"

She wrinkled her nose at his stern tone. To her relief, she could already sense him regaining much of his strength.

"Because I do not take commands from you, Mr. Valin," she reminded him in crisp tones.

He smiled wryly, his thumb absently stroking the line of her lower lip.

"Eventually I will manage to recall that pertinent fact, Miss Kingly."

Her own smile was weak, but a new warmth was beginning to battle the chill that had filled her.

"I do hope so."

His expression became somber as he allowed his gaze to roam openly over her pale countenance and tumbled curls.

"Still, you should not have taken such a risk."

"I could not leave you."

"It was too dangerous—"

"Lucien," she interrupted firmly. "Would you have left me behind?"

His lips thinned at her logic. "It is not at all the same."

"Of course it is." She met his gaze squarely. "I have enough regrets in my life. Would you have me add hating myself for fleeing like a coward?"

He let out a resigned sigh at her adamant expression. "Of course not. But you are forbidden ever to do such a thing again. My heart could not bear the strain."

Despite the welcome warmth that surrounded her, Jocelyn gave a violent shudder. It would be years before she would recall this day without a flare of fear.

"I hope there shall be no need. Unless there are any other vampires stalking me?"

He shifted so that his arms were locked firmly about her. "Not to my knowledge."

"Thank goodness."

With obvious reluctance Lucien turned to glance toward the faint remains of the powerful vampire. A brief anger flared over his elegant features before they softened with regret.

"How did you conjure such a clever scheme?" he demanded softly.

Jocelyn grimaced, pressing even closer to his hard body. She might feel deeply relieved that Amadeus was no longer a threat, but it was utterly unnerving to consider that she had brought death to anyone, even a vampire.

"Not clever, only desperate. I recalled you saying that a vampire who had taken the life of a human could not bear sunlight."

"The bane of bloodlust," he murmured.

"But I had to lure him up here without alerting him to the trap," she continued in uneven tones. "The Medallion was all I could think of."

"Yes." Lucien gave a slow nod of his head. "He was so obsessed, he did not even consider his danger. Not until to was too late."

The memory of those pale, fevered eyes made her stomach clench in disgust. He had been obsessed. Even mad. He would have done anything to claim the Medallion as his own.

"He is dead?" she demanded, needing to be reassured that it was truly at an end.

"Quite dead."

She heaved a faint sigh. "I suppose that I should feel guilty. I have never deliberately harmed another before."

"No." His gaze returned to her darkened eyes, his features suddenly grim. "He would have killed the both of us without thought and ravaged his way through England. He had to be halted."

Jocelyn winced as she recalled poor Molly and the other women who had been ruthlessly murdered by the vampire. Lucien was correct. She could not have allowed further innocents to be brutally tortured by Amadeus. He might even have attacked the children.

The thought was enough to harden her heart.

"Yes," she said.

He grimaced as he studied her shadowed eyes and the pain that still lingered.

"I am sorry, however, that you were forced into

such a position. I should have confronted him the moment I arrived in London."

Jocelyn frowned at the self-contempt that laced through his dark voice. She would not allow Lucien to blame himself. Not when he had nearly died attempting to save her.

"Lucien." She lifted her hand and pressed it to the side of his face. Her skin tingled as it encountered the satin warmth of his cheek. "You could not have known what he would do."

His own hand rose to cover her fingers, his golden eyes haunted with remembered pain.

"I knew he was dangerous."

"Enough," she said sharply.

His brows lifted at the stubborn jut of her chin. "What?"

"It is the past. We cannot change what has occurred. All we can do now is consider the future."

There was a long pause, almost as if he battled the urge to argue with her sensible words. Then the grimness of his features softened and the golden eyes were lit with that warm, rich light that so touched her heart.

"When did you become so very wise?"

Wise? Jocelyn gave a soft chuckle. No one could ever accuse her of being wise in the past. Not when she had so recklessly played the flirt with Lord Patten. Not when she had meekly allowed her parents to force her from her rightful place in their life. Nor even when she had determinedly set upon a new path without first accepting and forgiving the mistakes that she had made.

But now . . . now she realized she possessed a wonderful clarity. She knew precisely what she desired from her life and whom she desired to share it with.

Devoting her life to others was all well and good, but at the moment she wanted to think only of herself.

And this wonderful, glorious gentleman at her side.

"When you walked into my home and rented my garret," she said with a smile.

"Ah." He reached down to softly brush his lips over her forehead before pulling back to regard her with a teasing expression. "I thought you were going to toss me back onto the streets."

"I desired to. I knew you were a dangerous gentleman the moment you entered the room. Only my need for your coin forced me to allow you to remain."

"Do not tell me that you love me only for my fortune," he chided gently.

"And your laughter. And your kindness. And your amazing ability to know my heart better than I know it myself."

He stilled, his fingers moving to trail over her cheek and down the length of jaw. Jocelyn could not halt the tiny shiver of response to his light caress.

"And my kisses?" he prodded.

Jocelyn forced herself to pretend to consider his words. "They are bearable, I suppose."

"Bearable?"

With a low growl he slowly bent his head to touch his lips softly to her own. Jocelyn readily arched toward him. It was not a kiss of passion or physical need. Instead, it was a tender reassurance that they had survived the nightmare and managed to escape with their lives intact.

For moments they clung to each other, drawing strength from the warm emotions that bonded them together.

Then with obvious reluctance Lucien at last pulled back to carefully tuck a stray curl behind her ear.

"Well?"

"Mmm. Perhaps they are wondrous."

"That is considerably better." His smile faded as he drew in a deep breath. "Ah, Jocelyn. I feared that you would never forgive me."

Her gaze dropped as she recalled her horror at discovering the truth that he was a vampire. It was not, after all, every day that a maiden discovered the gentleman she had tumbled into love with was not human, she acknowledged wryly.

And, of course, there had been the fear that she

had been played the fool once again. Echoes of the betrayal she had felt at the hands of Lord Patten had made her lash out with an instinctive need to protect herself from further pain.

But Lucien had nothing in common with the shallow, absurdly idiotic Lord Patten.

He had not been attempting to use her for his own pleasure. He did not consider her a mere object that was to be gained and then tossed aside when he grew weary of her.

He had wanted only to protect her.

And to bring a smile to her face.

Realizing that he was regarding her with a growingly concerned expression, she offered him a smile.

"I will admit that I was rather shocked to discover that you were not a simple rogue but a vampire in disguise."

His expression cleared at her light tone, his brows wiggling in a ridiculous fashion.

"I prefer a roguish vampire."

"Indeed," she said dryly.

"I did not know how else to approach you, my sweet," he confessed in rueful tones. "And in truth, I presumed that I would have returned to the Veil long before you would ever discover the truth. I did not consider the danger that you would steal my heart."

"I believe you were the thief," she promptly

corrected him. "I was quite content with my quiet, uneventful life."

"Perhaps content, but not happy," he murmured.

"No. Not happy."

"And now?"

Jocelyn paused. Wrapped snuggly in his arms, she felt warm and safe and utterly content. She loved this gentleman. And more than anything in the world, she wanted to know he would be at her side for the rest of her life.

But even as she wanted to weep for joy at the thought that he loved her, there was that annoyingly sensible part of her that forced her to recall that it was not so simple.

This was not the usual sort of flirtation. And Lucien was not another London gentleman.

For goodness' sake, he was not even mortal.

There were any number of difficulties that had to be confronted.

"I do not know," she said slowly.

He furrowed his brow as he shifted, better to view her pale countenance. His movements were still awkward, and he could not entirely prevent his wince of pain. Jocelyn's heart cringed at the savage attack she knew he must have endured.

"What is it, Jocelyn?"

"I—" She came to a helpless halt, uncertain how to put her vague concern into words.

"Jocelyn?"

"Amadeus is now dead," she at last blurted out.

His confusion only deepened. "Thank goodness."

"I am no longer in danger," she continued in brittle tones. "There is nothing now to keep you in London."

"Ah." His brow cleared as he realized the direction of her fears. "You are not attempting to get rid of me, are you, my sweet?"

"Will you return to the Veil?" she abruptly demanded.

His hands moved to tenderly cup her face. "No."

"But you said that the vampires now live—"

"This is where I belong," he interrupted in husky tones. "At your side."

She searched the handsome, elegant countenance that had become so dear to her. She was uncertain that she could bear the thought of him walking away and never returning. It would be as if she were losing a part of herself.

And yet, was it fair to ask him to leave his home and his people to be with her? How much would he be forced to sacrifice for their love?

"Is it allowed?" she hesitantly demanded.

He smiled deep into her eyes. "I will demand that it be allowed."

"Does that mean you will become a mortal like me?"

His low chuckle suddenly echoed through the

dusty room, banishing at least a few of the heavy shadows.

"I fear not. I shall always be a vampire. There is no cure." He eyed her closely. "Does that trouble you?"

It should have. It seemed utterly mad even to believe in vampires, let alone to consider offering him her heart.

But as she gazed into those glorious golden eyes, she could see only the gentleman who had teased her to laughter, who had broken through her painful shell of isolation, and who had taught her that the past need not destroy her future.

The gentleman she loved.

"Not as long as it does not trouble you that I am a mere human," she murmured with a faint smile.

"A very lovely and desirable human," he corrected her, his hands sweeping down her neck and moving over her tense shoulders.

She shivered in pleasure, but even as she considered the audacious notion of leaning forward and tasting the sweetness of his lips, she was halted by a sudden thought.

Lucien was a vampire. An Immortal, he had called himself. Eventually she would grow old and die, while he remained precisely the same.

The thought made her heart grow cold.

"But not forever, Lucien," she said with a frown. "I am not an Immortal as you are. I will soon begin to age."

His countenance became a stern mask at her faltering words. "It does not matter, my sweet. I will love you regardless of your age."

"Are you certain?"

"Jocelyn." The golden eyes blazed in the gloom. "A vampire bonds but once. And for all eternity. What I feel for you today I will feel for all the ages."

He had no doubt intended to comfort her with his stark revelation. To ensure that she would never doubt his commitment to her. But instead, her eyes widened with distress.

She could not claim to understand the mysterious ways of vampires, but she did comprehend the knowledge that she could never burden Lucien with a love that would be fleeting at best.

If he bonded himself to her, then he would spend an eternity grieving for her loss. It was unthinkable.

"No, Lucien." Pulling from his grasp, she regarded him with a stubborn expression. She would rather lose him than ask him to sacrifice himself in such a fashion. At least her pain would come to an end someday. "You cannot do this."

His brows lifted at her fierce tone. "What?"

"I will not allow you to love me when I shall be with you for such a short time. It is not fair to you."

There was a moment of startled silence before

Lucien tilted back his head to laugh with rich amusement.

"You will not allow me to love you?" he teased. "It is far too late for such a warning, my sweet."

Jocelyn gave a shake of her head, wishing that he would for once not regard the world as a joke. This was a very serious matter.

"But I will soon die and—"

Her words were interrupted as the door to the castle was shoved open and an old woman attired as a gypsy stepped into the shadows.

"Do not be so certain what the future might hold, Jocelyn," she warned with a gentle smile. "It has yet to be written."

Utterly startled by the unexpected appearance of the old woman, Lucien struggled to gain his feet, only to discover he was far too weak.

"Nefri," he breathed.

"Lucien, do not move," the great vampire commanded, her numerous bracelets clicking in the musty air as she moved to retrieve the Medallion that had been nearly forgotten on the flagstones. Holding out the amulet, she moved to where Lucien was leaning heavily against the wall and gently pressed it to his cheek.

At first Lucien felt no more than a gentle warmth flood through his body at the touch of the powerful artifact. Then the soothing sense of peace became a fiery flood as his numerous wounds began to knit together and his damaged muscles healed. He gritted his teeth, feeling as if he had been shoved roughly into a furnace that burned from within.

At last he gave a shake of his head. "That is enough."

Nefri pulled the Medallion away, her wrinkled countenance filled with concern.

"You are healed?"

Lucien gingerly tested his arms and legs, discovering that the most grievous of his wounds had indeed been mended.

"I believe so."

Nefri smiled, but there was a warning in her eyes. "You will still be weak for several days."

He gave a slow nod, already realizing that his strength was tenuous at best. Not surprising considering the wounds Amadeus had inflicted. He had been certain down in that dank cellar that he was about to face what no vampire should ever face.

Death.

A shudder raced through his body before he was sternly suppressing the dark memories. Jocelyn was right. The past was over and done. The future was all that mattered.

A future with the woman he loved.

"How did you follow us?" he demanded of the vampire.

Nefri heaved a sad sigh, her gaze turning toward the darkened flagstones.

"I felt the passing of Amadeus."

"Yes." Lucien grimaced with regret. No matter what Amadeus had become in his madness, he was still a brother. It would take time to heal from his tragic loss. All vampires would mourn his passing. "He refused to return to the Veil."

Nefri turned back to lay a comforting hand upon his shoulder. "You did only what you had to do, Lucien. There was no choice."

He smiled wryly. "In truth it was Jocelyn who managed to bring an end to his madness."

"Ah." The vampire turned to smile kindly at the silent woman at his side. "I did tell you that she possessed the strength necessary to wear the Medallion."

Lucien watched the rosy glow touch Jocelyn's pale cheeks. It never failed to amaze him that she did not seem to realize just how special she was.

That was something he intended to correct. Even if it took him an eternity.

"So you did," he murmured.

"Here, my dear." Before Jocelyn could predict what the old woman was about to do, Nefri had swiftly slipped the Medallion back around her neck and fastened the clasp. "This belongs to you."

The blue eyes widened even as her fingers unconsciously rose to lightly stroke the amulet.

"Oh, but surely there is no longer any need."

Surprisingly Nefri turned to glance about the

shadows that still shrouded the room. Lucien could almost sense the puzzled wariness that filled the great vampire's heart.

"Although Amadeus is gone, there are still others who would claim the Medallion," she at last admitted slowly, her expression troubled.

Lucien could not ignore the chill that inched down his spine. He had wanted to believe that with the passing of Amadeus, Jocelyn was now safe. She had surely endured enough.

But deep within him had been a lingering sense of unease.

Amadeus may have been mad and obsessed with his studies, but he had never possessed the sort of courage necessary to defy the Great Council and Nefri herself. What had prompted him to believe he could succeed in such a foolish scheme? Or who?

"There is still danger," he at last said in flat tones.

Nefri gave a slow nod of her head. "I fear so. I have come to believe there is more to these traitors than I initially suspected."

Lucien felt Jocelyn stiffen at his side, and he placed a comforting arm about her shoulders.

"What would you have me do?" he demanded.

Without warning a sudden smile touched the lined countenance. "For the moment, nothing more than to remain with Jocelyn."

"I intend to remain at her side for an eternity," he vowed in low tones.

His words hung defiantly in the shadowed air, and half expecting an argument, Lucien was caught off guard as Nefri instead reached out to touch both of their heads in a silent blessing.

"Then all will be well," she retorted in soft tones. "Now, we should be away from here. I have brought you a carriage. It awaits outside."

Lucien struggled to his feet, pleased to discover that he could at least stand.

"You will call upon me if there is a need?" he demanded.

Nefri bent her head in agreement. "If there is a need."

He glanced down at the woman who filled his heart with joy. "You will know where to find me."

The great vampire gave a soft chuckle as Jocelyn blushed a fiery red. "Indeed, I do. May peace be with you."

"And love," Lucien murmured.

"And most certainly love," Nefri repeated in benediction.

Chapter 14

The dawn had just brushed the sky with a shimmer of pale rose when Lucien silently slipped down the steps from his garret toward the bedchamber directly below his own.

It had been two days since they had fled the castle with Nefri. Two days when both Lucien and Jocelyn had been forced to battle the weariness of both mind and spirit that had haunted them. In near silence they had allowed the fretful Meg to pamper them with warm food and clucking concern. Neither desired to discuss the ghastly nightmare they had endured, instead simply sitting close one to the other and taking comfort in the fact that they were together.

This morning, however, Lucien had awakened with a refreshed sense of purpose. The dull ache had left his body, and his mind was clear and focused.

It was time to grasp the future in his hands.

A future that was entirely wrapped around Jocelyn Kingly.

With flowing steps he slipped toward the closed door and silently pressed it open. A soft glow from the window was banishing the shadows as he crossed the worn floorboards and perched upon the edge of the mattress. For a breathless moment he merely regarded Jocelyn's soft profile that lay against the pillow.

In sleep the delicate features were relaxed and the long black lashes brushed her cheeks. She appeared young and utterly vulnerable, making his heart skip with tender emotion.

How utterly and deeply he loved this woman. She completed him in a manner that stilled his restless spirit and brought joy to his soul.

Slowly his gaze lowered, halting upon the full rosy lips.

Hot, glorious passion swept through him as he reached out to lightly stroke the sweet softness of that mouth. Surely he had been patient long enough. Was it not, at long last, the time to claim her as his own?

Beneath his touch she stirred, and rolling onto her back, she slowly lifted her lashes to regard him with a bemused gaze.

"Lucien."

"Good morning, my sweet."

With an effort she pulled herself to a seated position, unaware that the thin linen of her nightrail revealed a delectable outline of the lush form beneath. Lucien, on the other hand, was delightfully conscious of the lovely view. It was only with a stern effort that he managed to suppress the urge to toss off his brocade robe and join her beneath the covers.

She was a human, he grimly reminded himself, and bound by human morals. Until she was his wife she would not be able to give herself to him freely. She had endured enough shame in her life without him adding to her burden.

"What are you doing here?" she demanded, her voice still thick with sleep.

He smiled as he lowered his hand to catch her fingers in a firm grip.

"I desired to discover if you are as beautiful in the morning as I imagined in my dreams," he lightly teased. "After all, if I am to spend an eternity awakening with you in my arms, I do not wish to be unpleasantly surprised with the knowledge your teeth are false and your mood foul."

The blue eyes abruptly sparkled at his words. It was a welcome change from the shadows that had lingered over the past few days.

"Indeed? And pray who mentioned anything of you spending the night in my bed?" she demanded.

His thumb stroked over her knuckles. "Is that not where your husband belongs?"

She stilled, her breath suddenly rasping in the quiet air. "Husband?"

Lucien regarded her closely, well aware this was the most important moment in his Immortal life.

"You said that you loved me."

"Yes."

"Is it not the custom for humans who care for each other to wed?"

"But . . . you are not human," she pointed out in weak tones.

Lucien could not prevent his soft chuckle. "Yes, I know. Still, I intend to live as one and I wish to indulge in your rituals."

There was a long, unnerving silence, and Lucien briefly feared that Jocelyn might have reconsidered over the past two days. It could not be easy to accept that he was not a mortal as she. That he was, indeed, a monster from ancient myth.

His fears were not appeased when her beautiful eyes abruptly filled with tears.

"Oh."

His heart faltered as he leaned toward her with an anxious expression.

"What is it, Jocelyn?"

"I . . . After the scandal I presumed that I would never wed. After all, what gentleman would ever forgive my ruined reputation?" she at last said in choked tones. "Eventually I convinced myself that I no longer cared. What did I need with an overbearing husband? Or even children who could never take their place in society? I told myself that I was better off on my own."

He gazed deep into her shimmering eyes. "And now? Do you wish to be my wife?"

"Oh, Lucien." She reached up to cup his face in her hands. "With all my heart."

He sucked in a ragged breath, relief surging through him with the heady potency of a fine brandy.

"Then it is settled."

"Yes," she murmured softly.

With exquisite care Lucien lowered his head to gently brush her lips. It was a kiss to seal their fate. A pledge of their future together. Lightly he tasted of her sweetness before reluctantly pulling back to absently toy with a dark curl that lay against her cheek.

"My wife," he murmured softly.

Appearing flushed and utterly desirable, she regarded him with a quizzical smile.

"Lucien."

"Yes, my dear?"

"You said that you wished to indulge in my rituals. Do vampires not wed?"

Lucien paused. There was nothing more he desired than to truly bond with this woman. To share the Immortal Kiss so that they were one. But Jocelyn was mortal. She could not possibly comprehend the sheer intimacy that would come of the sharing of blood.

"It is rather a different sort of ceremony," he offered in vague tones.

Predictably her curiosity was instantly aroused. "What do you mean?"

He gave a slow shake of his head. "I am uncertain that you are prepared, my sweet."

"Why?"

Clearly she would not be satisfied until he had revealed all, Lucien acknowledged wryly. Thankfully he loved her as much for her stubborn spirit as for her kind heart.

"Because our bonding is not of pretty words and pledges but of our very souls," he explained in low tones. "We become one with each other, sharing our hearts and emotions and even our thoughts. It can be far too intimate for mortals."

She considered his words for a moment, and then astonishingly raised her hands to touch the amulet that glowed about her neck.

"But I am not just another mortal. I have the Medallion."

Lucien briefly considered the powerful artifact. It was true that the Medallion was subtly changing the maiden. And Nefri had implied that her future would not be that of a mere human. Perhaps it would be possible.

"Yes," he murmured.

She gazed deep into his eyes. "I want to be one with you, Lucien."

"There is no turning back," he warned.

"Good." She reached out to touch his cheek. "Tell me how."

"We must drink of each other's blood."

Despite her best intentions, Jocelyn could not entirely disguise her brief flare of shock.

"I see."

Lucien smiled, covering her hand with his own. "Jocelyn, we will know when the time is proper. For now we have a wedding to plan."

A hint of relief lightened her beautiful features. "Yes."

"And swiftly." He deliberately allowed his gaze to lower toward the thin fabric of her gown. That ready heat flowed swiftly through his veins. Two centuries of suppressed passion were not easily ignored. "I grow weary of that cramped bed in the garret."

A faint color stained her cheeks, but her own eyes darkened with a smoldering need. The air in the bedchamber was suddenly thick with awareness.

"So you are wedding me for a more comfortable bed?" she attempted to tease.

"And what is in it," he growled softly.

She shivered. "Lucien."

He could take her. All he need do was pull her into his arms and she would readily give him all the pleasure his body ached to receive. One kiss, one touch, and she would forget all but the desire that blazed between them.

But even as the realization flared through his mind, his heart could feel the lingering hint of disquiet deep within her.

She had been branded a scarlet woman despite her innocence. And while she would never admit it, the scars still lingered. To give herself without the blessing of marriage would make her question the strength of her honor.

Swallowing a groan, Lucien was again struggling to restrain his unruly passions. Great Nefri, give me strength, he silently pleaded.

"But first there is something we must do," he said in ragged tones.

She blinked, as if startled to discover she was not being thoroughly ravaged. And he hoped a trifle disappointed.

"Oh. And what is that?"

Lucien drew in a deep breath, knowing that he was about to destroy the magic of this moment. Unfortunate, of course. But after devoting hours to thinking of joining his life with this woman, he had realized that she was not yet prepared to put her past completely behind her.

He wanted her unburdened and able to concentrate upon their future together. A future with no barriers.

"We must speak with your parents."

Her eyes widened as she abruptly sank back into the pillows. It was obvious that she was not overly delighted with the thought of confronting the mother and father who had turned their back upon her. Lucien did not blame her for her pained reluctance, but he could not waver. He did this for Jocelyn.

"My parents? Why?"

"My sweet, you cannot make peace with your future while you still harbor anger in your past," he said softly. "It will haunt you until it has been resolved."

Her lips flared at the truth she could not deny. "You desire me to beg for their forgiveness?"

"Certainly not. But neither do I desire you to continue hiding from those who shamed you."

His heart faltered as her face became pale, and the eyes darkened with distress at his stern words.

"That is absurd."

"Jocelyn." His hand lifted, only to fall as she flinched from his touch. "It is one thing to willingly turn your back upon society, and even your parents. It is quite another to be forced away."

"I have told you that it no longer matters."

"It matters to you," he said huskily. "You must confront them bravely and with your head lifted high. You must prove to yourself that you no longer fear them."

She unconsciously wet her dry lips as she reluctantly considered his persuasive argument.

"Lucien . . ."

"Trust me in this, my dear," he pleaded softly. "I shall be at your side."

Their gazes tangled as she battled the inner dread of confronting those who had harmed her. Silently Lucien allowed her stormy emotions to wash through him and offered her back the strength of his unwavering love.

At last she heaved a small sigh. "Very well."

The tall, elegant town house built in the Palladian style was the largest and the most beautiful in the square.

It would have to be, Jocelyn wryly conceded, as she studied the Portland stone building standing proudly behind the wrought iron railing.

The Kinglys demanded the best in everything. From their outlandishly expensive French chef to Mrs. Kingly's ivory and gold carriage to the imported Chinese roses that graced the conservatory, they would accept nothing that was not envied by others in society.

Especially their daughter.

Jocelyn had often wondered if it was her father's

lack of an aristocratic title that made them so compulsive in their need to appear superior among the *ton*. They often complained bitterly enough at being seated too far down the table at a dinner and forced to mix with encroaching mushrooms. And more than once her mother had refused to attend a society function when she suspected that her sister, who had married an earl, would be invited.

Their overweening pride was all-important, and nothing was allowed to tarnish the Kingly name.

Whatever the cause, Jocelyn knew they would not readily welcome home their scandal-tainted daughter. And only the steady warmth of the gentleman at her side kept her from bolting down the quiet Mayfair street.

"I am here," he whispered softly as the door to the house was opened, and a starched butler regarded her with barely concealed amazement.

Drawing in a deep breath, she forced herself to climb the stairs to enter the marble foyer.

She had lived among the most desperate thieves and murderers in all of London. She had walked paths at night that the Watch would not dare tread. She had been stalked by a crazed vampire and managed to kill him.

Surely to goodness she could face her parents.

Unconsciously squaring her shoulders, she turned to face the servant she had known since she was a child.

"Good afternoon, Scowly. I trust you are well?"

Although harshly trained by Mrs. Kingly, the butler allowed a faint smile to curve his lips. He had always been fond of Jocelyn when she was young and had often slipped her treats that were forbidden by her parents.

"Quite well. It is good to see you again, Miss Kingly."

"Thank you." She glanced toward the ponderous staircase that boasted a finely carved balustrade. "Are my parents at home?"

The silver-haired butler gave a slight nod. "Yes, they are in the front salon."

The rather cowardly hope that her parents were dashing about London with their usual need to see and be seen was abruptly crushed. Thankfully, however, her smile never faltered as she felt Lucien place his hand on the small of her back.

She would not be facing her parents alone.

This wonderful, glorious man was at her side.

For an eternity.

"I will show myself in, Scowly," she managed to say in firm tones.

"I . . ." A gleam of approval entered the old servant's gaze. "Very good."

With her head held as high as Lucien had commanded, Jocelyn swept her way up the stairs, rather absurdly relieved that she had allowed her fiancé to convince her to purchase a new gown in a lovely shade of pale blue. It would be difficult enough to confront her parents without concerning herself that she appeared a ragamuffin.

Reaching the open landing that offered a stunning view of the foyer below and the landing above, Jocelyn turned to enter the front salon.

As was her mother's custom, the long, narrow chamber was entirely decorated in ivory. Along the walls were numerous niches that supported large Greek statues that regarded visitors with frozen disapproval. And from above, a painting of Zeus floated arrogantly in clouds. Even the furnishings were in an ivory satin with a collection of rare Greek urns upon the various tables.

It was a lovely, elegant room but cold and utterly impersonal.

Much like her own parents, she acknowledged wryly.

Stepping forward, she nearly faltered as the tall handsome gentleman with silver hair and piercing, blue eyes rose to his feet. At his side a dark-haired woman still beautiful in an aloof fashion also rose.

There was no missing their matching expressions of shocked disdain as they realized that their daughter had dared to defy their stern command never to return.

Then once again Lucien reached out to touch her softly, filling her with the warmth of his love.

"Good afternoon, Father. Mother."

There was a sharp silence before Mr. Kingly stepped forward. "Jocelyn," he rasped. "What are you doing here?"

She smiled wryly. It was obvious that the years had not softened her father's icy anger.

"Do not fear, this is only a passing visit. I wished you to know that I am soon to wed Mr. Valin."

"Wed?" her mother demanded in shrill shock. Together the older couple turned their attention to the tall, handsome gentleman standing at Jocelyn's side. In silence they considered the expensive cut of his bottle-green coat and luster of his Hessians. There could be no doubt that he was a gentleman of both means and consequence. It was in the set of his broad shoulders and upon the proud countenance. Then her father's eyes abruptly widened in amazement. "Mr. Valin? But . . . I know you. You are a cousin to Mr. Ravel."

Lucien offered a faint bow of his golden head. "Yes."

"Well. Well, I say. What a remarkable thing." Pondering the astonishing fact that a gentleman of Mr. Valin's standing would consider marrying the tainted daughter whom he had evicted from his home, Mr. Kingly glanced toward his wife. "Did you hear, Mrs. Kingly? Our daughter is to wed Mr. Valin."

The cold expression faded as Mrs. Kingly swiftly considered the meaning of such a marriage. Clearly deciding that her lofty place in society could only be enhanced by such a fortunate connection, she determinedly forced a smile to her lips as she turned toward Jocelyn.

"Why, you sly minx, what an extraordinary thing," she twittered in playful tones. "However did you manage to capture such an eligible bachelor?"

Jocelyn smiled wryly, reaching out to allow Lucien to engulf her cold fingers in his own.

"Luck, I suppose."

"No," Lucien denied, lifting her hand to boldly brush her fingers with his lips. "The luck was all mine. Your daughter is quite simply the most amazing woman it has ever been my privilege to know."

Mrs. Kingly widened her eyes at the open display of affection. An affection that was quite foreign to her cold heart.

"Ah . . . yes," she muttered.

"Never have I encountered a woman with a kinder heart and a more generous nature."

The older woman smiled weakly. She might not comprehend why a gentleman of society would be concerned with a kind heart and generous nature, but she was cunning enough to realize she desired to win his favor.

To have her daughter wed to such a prominent gentleman would not only cleanse the stain upon Jocelyn's reputation, it would also enhance her own power.

"Indeed."

Lucien smiled into Jocelyn's eyes. "It shall be the happiest moment in my life when I can call her wife."

"A wedding." With an expression of anticipation Mrs. Kingly turned toward her silent husband. "We must begin making plans at once. The ceremony will be at St. George's, of course. Mr. Kingly, you must speak with the prince. His presence will be vital to ensure that the wedding will be considered a success."

Jocelyn abruptly stepped forward. She was not about to allow her parents to turn her wedding into a carnival.

"No, Mother."

Mrs. Kingly turned to regard her with an expression of arrogant disapproval. "No?"

The familiar fear of not measuring up to this woman's impossible standards threatened to rise, only to be fiercely dismissed.

Jocelyn tilted her chin. No. She was a child no longer. If her parents could not accept the woman she had become, then so be it. She would not allow them to force her into a life she did not desire.

"My marriage will not be a social event. I desire a simple private ceremony."

"Do not be ridiculous, Jocelyn," her mother snapped in annoyance. "After your . . . unfortunate incident, it is vastly important to gain the support of the prince. If he attends the wedding, then no one else will dare stay away."

"No." Jocelyn faced her mother bravely. "I am marrying Lucien because I love him, not to secure my place in society."

The older woman blinked, as if startled to discover that her daughter would dare defy her. An icy warning chilled her gaze.

"As stubborn as ever, I see. You are determined to make a mockery of your father and me."

Jocelyn smiled sadly. Her parents would never change. They would always remain utterly shallow and incapable of sharing the love she had discovered with Lucien.

The lingering sense of betrayal she had harbored for years slowly faded, to be replaced by an unexpected pity.

How terribly lonely they must be in this cold mausoleum with nothing to warm their hearts but hollow pride, she acknowledged.

They would never know the joy or the passion she shared with Lucien. They would grow old and die all alone.

"Actually this has nothing to do with you, Mother," she said in soft but firm tones.

"You could at least consider our feelings." Mrs. Kingly gave a loud sniff. "It has been very difficult for us."

Without warning Lucien moved to stand beside Jocelyn, his face set in grim lines.

"This is Jocelyn's decision. You will respect her wishes."

There was a shocked pause before Mrs. Kingly opened her mouth to argue. She would not easily give up her dream of a lavish wedding complete with the prince at her side. But placing a warning hand upon his wife's arm, Mr. Kingly gave a reluctant nod of his head. He easily sensed the danger that cloaked the tall, golden-haired gentleman. A danger that he was unwilling to confront.

"Very well."

"We will advise you when the plans have been completed," Lucien continued, placing his hand upon Jocelyn's back. "Now we must be on our way."

Mrs. Kingly pressed a hand to her heart. "But surely you are not leaving so soon? We are, after all, destined to become family. We should become better acquainted before the wedding. If you will have a seat, I will call for tea."

Jocelyn hid a wry smile. No doubt her mother must be expecting callers. She would certainly want to flaunt the elusive Mr. Valin before her cronies.

"We cannot," she said in tones that defied argument. "There are a great number of details I must attend to. We will send a message when we have a date settled for the ceremony."

Without allowing her parents an opportunity to

respond, Jocelyn turned and headed for the door. An unconscious smile curved her lips.

For the first time in years her heart felt as light as a feather.

Lucien had been right.

She had needed to confront the shadows of her past and banish them. She had needed to discover that she could hold her head up proudly and with no apology.

And that was precisely what she had done.

Now she could face the future.

Her smile widened as she glanced at the handsome bronze face of her beloved vampire.

Chapter 15

The moonlight bathed the small bedchamber in a pool of soft silver. Lying entwined with his wife on the bed, Lucien heaved a deep sigh of contentment.

The earlier wedding had been just as Jocelyn had demanded. The simple ceremony had included only a vicar, and her parents as witnesses. But there had been nothing simple in the shimmering love that filled the air as the two were joined together. Or the soft words that came from their very hearts.

Of course, the day had not been without its share of surprises, he ruefully acknowledged.

They had returned to Jocelyn's small home to discover that the residents of St. Giles had been determined to have a share of the celebration. They had left food and drink and even fresh flowers as a token of their appreciation. Mr. Ryan had also called to leave a fine bottle of brandy that Lucien was swift to claim as his own.

The display of affection meant far more to Jocelyn than her parents' cold presence at her wedding, and his heart nearly burst at the tears of happiness that filled his wife's eyes.

Wife . . .

He tightened his grasp around the slumbering woman as he savored the memories of making her his own.

She was just as delightfully passionate as he had dreamed she would be.

Perhaps even more so.

There had been no fear, no hesitancy as she followed his lead. Only an anxious desire to at last satisfy the need that had built to a near-fever pitch.

A fever that still coursed through his blood, he acknowledged ruefully. He suspected he would never tire of this woman who had bewitched his mind and stolen his heart.

As if sensing the sudden hardening of his renegade body, Jocelyn stirred in his arms. The heavy lashes lifted as she regarded him with a sleepy smile.

"Lucien."

"Shhh, my beloved," he murmured, gently stroking her hair from the pale countenance. "It is very late. You should be asleep."

"This is very nice," she said shyly. "I think I shall enjoy sharing a bed with my husband."

Lucien swallowed a groan. Great Nefri. Did she

not realize what she was doing to his poor, tortured body?

"Yes, my sweet. Now go back to sleep."

Pulling back, she regarded him with a puzzled expression. "What is it, Lucien? Is something the matter?"

He heaved another sigh. She would not be satisfied until he revealed the truth.

"Nothing is the matter. It is merely difficult for me to hold you so closely and not wish to make love to you again."

A delightful color stained her cheeks. "Oh." There was a long pause before she slowly lifted herself onto her elbow. "Lucien?"

"Yes?"

"I am prepared."

"No." He reached out to cup her cheek. "We have an eternity to be together, my sweet. There is no need to rush on this night."

She gave a shake of her head, an oddly resolute expression upon her countenance.

"I mean that I am prepared to bond with you. As a vampire."

Lucien caught his breath. "Jocelyn."

"Please do not argue with me, Lucien." An odd smile curved her lips. "You said that we would know when the time was right. And I do know. I cannot say how, but something within me is telling me that this is the moment."

As if on cue, the Medallion about her neck suddenly began to glow in the silver shadows.

Lucien regarded the powerful amulet before giving a slow nod of his head. He, too, felt the anticipation that tingled in the night.

It was the moment.

The perfect moment to entwine his soul with his true mate's.

Allowing his fangs to lengthen, he held the shimmering blue gaze as he lowered his head toward her neck. He took but a taste of her blood, his entire body trembling as the sense of her filled his mind and his heart.

"My love," he whispered softly, raising his arm to draw blood from his wrist and placed it against her waiting lips.

Sighing, Jocelyn readily completed the ritual, allowing them to become one.

"My eternal love," she pledged as the Medallion flared to golden life.

Hello from the desk of Alexandra Ivy!

I wanted to take this opportunity to update my fabulous readers on what they can expect in the upcoming months.

It's going to be a busy time with the release of the last book in my *Immortal Rogues* trilogy, MY LORD IMMORTALITY, that will hit the shelves in January 2013. Coming in June 2013 will be the tenth book in the *Guardians of Eternity* series, *Darkness Avenged.* Wow. I can't believe it's number ten! This will be Santiago and Nefri's book and I can't wait to discover what you think of their passionate adventure. I've had so many wonderful fans asking for Santiago's story that I wanted to make sure it was special.

I also have a new series that I'm really excited to tell you about. The series is tentatively called *The Sentinels* and will start off in a short story collection coming May 2013. These novels will be different from my Guardians, with the stories revolving around people who are "gifted" with special abilities. They're known as high-bloods and will include witches and psychics and necromancers, as well as the Sentinels. The Sentinels are men and women who are trained warriors who protect the high-bloods when they travel away from their safe-house called Valhalla, or track those high-bloods who are a danger to the mortal population.

In the short story you'll meet Angela Brown, a young graduate student who is a genius in genetics and Niko, the hunter who is sent to protect her from a high-blood who is convinced that Angela can rid her of her mutations. I hope you'll enjoy the Sentinels; they've been such a pleasure to create!

Lastly, I wanted to thank my readers! As always you're the reason I continue to write. Your encouragement and loyalty is truly a source of inspiration. You rock!

Happy Reading!
Alex

In this mesmerizing tale from the author of the Guardians of Eternity *series, a traitorous vampire is determined to destroy the Veil that has long separated vampires from human blood—and the passions it ignites. Only the Immortal Rogues, three vampires charged to protect their kind, can hope to stop his deadly rampage. . . .*

Amelia Hadwell has no time for London's nightlife. Not when her beloved brother's odd ways have their family threatening to institutionalize him. And not when she is questioning her own sanity after being confronted by a murderous shadow creature—then being saved by a captivating stranger, a man who belongs to a world she cannot imagine.

Reserved and scholarly, Sebastian St. Ives has been content without human desires—until they are reawakened by the delicate, brave Amelia, whom he is meant to protect. For the young woman has no idea she possesses the key to a ravenous vampire's dark victory. Now Sebastian must shield her from both a killer and his own growing attraction—or bond with her completely, and forever. . . .

Please turn the page for an exciting sneak peek of MY LORD IMMORTALITY, coming in January 2013!

Prologue

The cottage set in the thick copse of trees was a dark, cramped affair. Abandoned years before, it had been forgotten by all but the spiders and an occasional rat. Even the air was stale with a thick dust that threatened to choke the unwary.

On this moonless night, however, the rats and spiders had been driven from the darkness. Not even those shadowy creatures could dare the cold mist of fog that slowly, ruthlessly seeped through the door.

Drake Ramone suppressed a delicate shudder as he watched the mist swirl ever closer. As a vampire of considerable power, he feared nothing. Why should he?

He was destined for greatness. Both upon this dreary mortal plane and behind the Veil that currently protected the vampires from his wrath. It was his undoubted birthright.

Still, he discovered a vague sense of unease as the

fog thickened. His power was not as formidable as this ancient vampire. Not yet. Until he held the Medallion in his hands he would have to remain an unwilling servant to his master.

"Drake," the mist whispered in steely tones.

"Welcome, Master," he murmured with a low bow. "You honor me with your presence."

There was a grating laugh that echoed eerily through the barren cottage. "Honor? Do you believe me a fool? You honor no one, Drake," the vampire sneered.

"Perhaps not." Drake gave an indifferent shrug. "But I have always honored power."

"No, you lust after power."

"Surely it is one and the same?"

"To honor implies you possess a measure of principles. A tedious weakness that has never troubled you."

Drake offered a tight smile. "Certainly not."

"Which is precisely why you were chosen. Only one with your arrogant ambition would be willing to steal the Medallion and bring an end to the Veil."

"It is our mutual ambition, I believe."

"Yes." There was a pause, as if the elder were searching Drake's black heart. And perhaps he was, as he gave a dry rasp. "But do not allow that ambition to be your downfall. I sense your burning desires. If you betray me I will crush you beneath my heel."

Drake restrained his temper with an effort. When the vampire had first approached him behind the Veil he had been reluctant to agree to his scheme. He was an Immortal. A true blood. He took commands from no one. But as he pondered the rewards that could be his, his reluctance had faded.

It had been nearly two hundred years ago that the greatest of all vampires, Nefri, had created the Veil. She had commanded that the vampires live apart from humans. It was for the good of all, she had claimed, that the vampires exist in seclusion to ponder the great truths and philosophies. They were abruptly separated from the mortal world. The bloodlust that had once made them vulnerable to sunlight and fire had been wrenched from their souls.

Without human blood, however, they had also lost the desire, the lust and hungers, of humans. They forgot their fierce need to hunt.

For Drake it was an unbearable existence. He was no cold, passionless scholar who desired to devote an eternity to seeking a higher existence. He did not wish the knowledge of the elders.

What he wanted was to compel others to his command. He wanted to crush and enslave the humans, and to feast upon their blood. He wanted the other vampires to bend to his will.

An impossible task as long as Nefri held the ancient Medallion that kept the Veil in place.

So, along with Tristan and Amadeus, he had allowed himself to be secretly slipped through the Veil. They had returned to the world of mortals to discover Nefri and take the Medallion from her grasp.

None of them could have suspected that the wily old vampire would choose to separate the Medallion into three amulets, or that she would soul-bind them to mortal women.

Suddenly the Medallion could not be taken by force or even death. The mortals must give the amulets of their free will, or the power within them would be destroyed.

It had been a clever ploy. Even Drake had to admit that much. But that did not halt his seething determination. He would have the Medallion. No matter what he must do.

And once he did, all would suffer beneath his power.

Including this arrogant, treacherous vampire who chided him as if he were a hapless minion.

"I seek only to retrieve the Medallion as you requested, Master," he forced himself to retort, his thin countenance wreathed with a chilled smile. "No more."

The mist swirled. "We shall see. Have you discovered the wench?"

"Yes. I managed to rent a town house within the same block as Miss Hadwell. I have even managed to make contact with her brother, a rather pathetic half-wit. I hope to use the boy to get closer to the maiden."

"And Sebastian?"

Drake curled his lips at the mention of the vampire who had been sent by the Great Council to force him to return to the Veil.

"The fool has taken a house a few blocks away. He poses no threat, however. As usual, he is impervious to all but his musty books and ancient studies. He has not even made an attempt to seek me out. When he does, I shall kill him and be done."

There was a dry hiss of disapproval at his flippant tone. "He is there because I swayed the Council to choose him. Just as I chose that tediously noble Gideon and that vain fool Lucien. I presumed that they would easily be defeated. Just as I chose my servants because I presumed they possessed the necessary intelligence and lust to conquer. A miscalculation that I now must rue."

Drake frowned. "What are you implying?"

"Tristan has been destroyed, along with Amadeus. You alone are left."

Drake felt the chill seep to his bones. While he considered the two vampires who had joined him in the battle to destroy the Veil beneath contempt, he could not deny a vague sense of shock.

"How?"

"In their arrogance they thought they could not

be defeated. The same arrogance that you carry about you, Drake."

The handsome features surrounded by a short crop of golden curls hardened at the insult. Tristan and Amadeus were pathetic idiots when compared to him.

"Sebastian is no match for me."

"He possesses the dagger."

Drake shrugged. Although the dagger given to Sebastian had been blessed with ancient power to destroy a vampire, he remained unimpressed. The reclusive scholar was no threat. Not to a vampire destined to rule all.

"Sebastian will soon be at an end. And once I have the amulet from Miss Hadwell, I will seek out the others. Soon enough, the Medallion will be mine."

"I believe you mean *ours,*" that rasping voice reminded him.

"Ah, yes. Of course."

Without warning, the mist struck out, cutting a thin wound along Drake's cheek. Just as swiftly, it wrapped about the vampire's feet and with a thrust had him tumbling to the dust-covered floor.

"You seek to rise above yourself, Drake. A deadly mistake," the elder warned. "I will have the Medallion. You can rule beneath me or join Tristan and Amadeus in oblivion. The choice is yours."

Wisely remaining upon the hard floor despite the fury that raged through him, Drake patiently waited for the mist to slowly swirl toward the door. It was only then that he raised a hand to touch the blood freely flowing down his face.

Soon, he reassured his savaged pride. Soon he would have the Medallion. Then he would crush all those who had dared to stand in his way.

Beginning with Sebastian St. Ives.

Chapter 1

The old Gypsy was huddled upon the filthy street like a bundle of forgotten rags. Amelia had nearly passed her by when the woman had abruptly held out her hand in a desperate motion.

"Please, kind lady, will you help me?"

Amelia hesitated. The streets near St. Giles were littered with such pathetic outcasts. Thieves, whores, and the dredges of society waged a daily battle with survival. It was an impossible task to help them all.

The sensible choice was to be about her business so she could return to the comfort of her home. To linger would only invite danger. Especially to a young woman on her own.

Amelia's heart, however, was never sensible. Reaching into her basket, she pulled out the apples and cheese that she had so recently purchased and gently placed them beside the old woman.

"Here you are. Fresh from the market."

"Bless you," the Gypsy murmured. "Bless you."

"And here is a guinea. Sleep well tonight, my dear."

"Ah, so kind." The woman reached for the coin, and then, without warning, she pressed a heavy object into Amelia's hand. "Such generosity must be rewarded."

"Oh . . ." Startled, Amelia regarded the golden amulet that sparkled in the palm of her hand. It was oddly designed with faint words scratched upon the metal. "No, you cannot part with such a lovely piece of jewelry. It must be worth a great deal."

The Gypsy slowly smiled. "It is beyond price. As is the blessing that has been placed upon it."

"Then certainly you must keep it. You have more need than I."

"No." A sadness touched the wrinkled countenance. "Darkness will soon stalk you, my dear. A terrible darkness. This amulet will protect you and bring a Guardian to your side. Wear it always and, above all, never give it to another."

Amelia gave a shake of her head. The poor woman was obviously daft. "I cannot keep such a gift."

A gnarled hand reached out to firmly fold Amelia's fingers over the amulet. At the same moment, a strange warmth flared between them.

"It is now bound to you. Protect it well. Only you can halt the danger that threatens all of London. A danger that is drawing ever closer."

Amelia frowned as a chill spread through her body. Daft or not, the old woman was beginning to frighten her. "Danger? What danger?"

"Keep the amulet close. And trust in your heart. Love is always the light that will hold back the darkness."

"I do not understand." Amelia stepped closer, but even as she did, the old woman was fading into a shimmering mist. A sense of panic clutched at Amelia's heart. "Wait. You must tell me. What danger? Tell me. . . ."

A sharp noise echoed through the silent house.

With a sudden wrench, Amelia sat upright in her bed and glanced about the dark chamber. What was it?

Something had awakened her, she realized, as her hand instinctively went to the Medallion on a chain about her neck. Something other than the dream. A dream that had plagued her since the peculiar encounter with the old Gypsy nearly a month ago.

For a moment she hesitated. It was late. Very late. Then, with a resigned sigh she slipped from the bed and pulled a wrap over her nightrail. There was little use in giving in to the desire to lie back and curl up beneath her covers. She would not be able to sleep until she had assured herself that all was well. It was her duty now that she was mistress of her own household.

A faint smile touched her delicate features as she left the bedchamber and moved down the narrow hall. It was not much of a household to boast of.

The house was a modest establishment perched upon the shabby fringes of London's more elegant neighborhoods. The rooms were cramped with well-worn furnishings and the garden so small that the handful of roses she had planted threatened to overwhelm it.

Still, it was ample for her and her younger brother, William. Together with their housekeeper, Mrs. Benson, they rubbed along reasonably well.

Pausing at the end of the hall, Amelia fumbled to light a candle before continuing down the stairs and toward the back of the house. A heavy silence shrouded her as she peered into the shadows. In the flickering candlelight everything appeared to be in order, but she instinctively continued her search into the kitchen.

Something had awakened her. A noise that had warned her that someone was stirring despite the late hour.

Refusing to consider the notion that the noise might have been a rat or some other vile creature, she skirted the large table and moved toward the laundry room. It was then that a movement outside the window suddenly caught her attention. William, she realized as she watched the shadowed form crossing the garden. With a hurried movement she rushed toward the door and threw it open.

As swift as she was, however, she was too late to halt her brother as he dashed from the back of the garden in obvious pursuit of his recently acquired cat.

"Bloody hell," Amelia muttered beneath her breath.

What the devil was William thinking? She had specifically warned him not to leave the house without her or Mrs. Benson at his side. She had even made him pledge in words that not even he could fail to understand.

Certainly he knew better than to go out in the middle of the night.

Amelia pushed her hands impatiently through the heavy strands of her raven hair. Calm yourself, she commanded as she sucked in a deep breath. Becoming rattled would serve nothing. William was not attempting to defy her wishes; he simply did not understand.

And why should he? Since she had taken the small house, she had allowed her brother to come and go as he pleased. For the first time in his eighteen years he was not hidden in his chamber nor treated as a source of embarrassment to be tucked away. She had encouraged him to seek out friends among the neighbors and to spend his days among those unfortunate children in the stews who had swiftly learned to love his simple kindness and, perhaps more important, the numerous treats he would bring with him.

It was little wonder he found it difficult to return

to his life of being treated as a prisoner. He could not comprehend the danger that suddenly stalked the streets of St. Giles. To him the sudden deaths of the prostitutes were a source of deep sadness, but not a direct threat. His heart was far too tender and without guile to ever consider the notion of someone desiring to harm him.

Once again in command of her nerves, Amelia reached for a cloak that hung by the door and wrapped it tightly about her. There was simply nothing to do but go after William. She certainly could not allow him to wander the streets when there was a madman on the loose.

Ignoring the stones that dug into her bare feet, she stepped into the garden and hurried toward the back gate. The heaviness in the air warned that soon a thick fog would be rolling in, and she grimaced. There were few things more unpleasant than London streets at night.

Wrapping the cloak tighter, she heaved a small sigh. It was not that she regretted leaving her parents' grand town house in the center of Mayfair. Nor giving up the lavish lifestyle that had been her birthright. Oh, granted she enjoyed frivolous entertainments and the flirtations of handsome dandies as much as the next young maiden, but it was a shallow pleasure when placed next to the happiness of her brother. And after learning of her mother's determination to have poor William secretly placed in

Bedlam, she had known she had to take matters into her own hands.

No one would be allowed to put William in that horrid place. Perhaps he was dull-witted, and at times rather odd. And there could be no doubt he was inclined to wander off without regard to himself or those who fretted over him. But he was not daft. Nor was he a danger to others.

Still, she had to admit that there were times when she felt the burden of caring for William more heavily than others. Times such as this.

She held the candle high as she entered the small lane that lay beyond her garden, careful to avoid the inevitable rubbish that was carelessly tossed about. Ahead she could hear the shuffle of footsteps and she hurried her pace. The sooner she caught up to William, the sooner she could return to her bed.

Unfortunately, no matter how swiftly she attempted to make her way through the shadows, she could not catch her brother's far longer strides. Muttering a curse, she passed by the darkened houses, her poor feet protesting her maltreatment. On and on she went. Past one street and then another. It was not until she was near the derelict stables that had been left abandoned years ago that she heard a sound of scuffling and came to an abrupt halt.

At last.

Peering through an overgrown hedge, Amelia was able to faintly make out a shadowed shape. It had to be William. Who else would be skulking in the alley at this time of night? But then the shadow shifted and her relief was swiftly smothered. There was a fluid stealth to the shadow that was nothing at all like William's clumsy movements.

She leaned forward, attempting to determine the exact nature of the shadow, only to feel her heart come to a halt.

There was something wrong. Something terribly wrong.

Even from a distance she could sense a dark, smoldering malice. It was in the unnatural chill in the air. In the thick silence that was nearly choking.

And there was a smell . . . a smell of cold steel shared with something far more foul.

Prickles of alarm raced down her spine as she heedlessly dropped the candle. She should flee, a voice warned from the back of her mind. Whatever was in the shadows was evil. And dangerous. She had to leave before it could turn the malignant attention in her direction.

A wise decision, no doubt. Unfortunately, it had barely formed in her mind when the shadow stilled and then slowly shifted toward her frozen form.

"Who is there?" a voice hissed.

Amelia bit her bottom lip to keep herself from squeaking in startled alarm. Through the hedge it appeared that the shadow was . . . formless. As though it flowed and shifted like mercury upon water. It had to be a trick of the moonlight, she tried to reassure herself. Shapeless shadows did not exist except in children's nightmares. Not even on the narrow, mean streets of London.

Then the shadow once again shifted and, unbelievably, Amelia's horror only deepened. There was something on the ground. A body, she slowly realized. A body that was not moving and that was covered in a dark, ghastly dampness that she very much feared was blood.

Dear heavens, she had to get away.

"I feel you," the shadow rasped in a hollow voice. "I smell your lovely, warm blood. Come to me. Come and offer yourself to me."

A faint tingle raced through Amelia at the command. Almost as if the words held a strange power. But even as her mind seemed to cloud, there was a sharp stab of warmth that seared against her skin. Her trembling fingers lifted to touch the amulet about her neck. It was hot to the touch, and strangely comforting.

The shadow, however, appeared to shrink as she grimly held onto the Medallion, a steely hiss echoing through the air.

"You." Slowly, steadily the shadow grew larger, leeching its way toward the hedge. "Come to me."

"No," Amelia whispered, forcing her shaky legs to take a step backward.

"Do not fear. I will not harm you. Come."

Amelia froze. What was this thing? Nothing human, surely? A thing of nightmares. Of horror stories.

A sob was wrenched from her throat, but even as the shadow neared, there was a sudden flurry of movement from behind the shadow. In less than the beat of a heart, a large, utterly solid form had blocked the path between her and the advancing danger.

A form that thankfully appeared to be human.

"Halt." The new form held up an arm and Amelia could see the glint of a sharp blade in the silver moonlight. "I will not allow this."

A dark, grating laugh echoed through the silence. "*You?* You will not allow?"

Amelia's rescuer never wavered. "No."

"Do not be more of a fool than you need to be. Return to your books and pathetic studies. You do not possess the courage nor the will to confront me."

"Shall we see? Shall we test the strength of my dagger? I do not fear you."

Lost in a thick fog of terror, Amelia nevertheless managed to notice that the gentleman now standing between her and the shadow was surprisingly large. Not only tall, but broad through the shoulders and possessing the type of chiseled muscles not often seen in society.

She also realized that his rich, smoky tones held a trace of an accent that was impossible to trace.

Not that she particularly cared if he were a foreigner or not, she acknowledged with a near-hysterical urge to laugh. At the moment she would have welcomed the devil himself if he were here to protect her.

The shadow seemed to swirl, then, with a sudden hiss, it slowly began to retreat toward the nearby stables.

"We will settle this later, fool. I must think how best to punish you for your insolence," the shadow warned before it disappeared entirely.

For a breathless moment there was nothing but the thick silence; then, with a flowing swiftness that was oddly similar to that of the deadly shadow, the gentleman turned and threaded his way through the thick hedge. Amelia regarded him with a sense of lingering shock, not even flinching when he reached out to gently touch her hair.

"Are you harmed?" he demanded in soft tones.

Amelia struggled to breathe as she pressed a hand to her painfully racing heart. "No. I . . . what was that thing?"

He seemed to hesitate. "A creature. A creature of the dark."

"Creature?" Amelia gave a sudden shudder. Did he mean an animal? No. She had seen what she had seen. That had been something other than human or animal. "What sort of creature?"

Without warning, he reached out to grasp her arm in a firm grip. "Come, we must not linger here."

Before she even knew what was happening, Amelia discovered herself being tugged away from the hedge and turned back down the alley toward her home. Just for a moment, she allowed herself to follow his lead, wanting nothing more than to be back in the comforting familiarity of her tiny home. Then she abruptly dug her bare heels into the dirt.

"Wait. I must find my brother. I was following him when that shadow appeared."

His grip tightened, almost as if he considered physically dragging her away from danger. Then he drew in a deep breath.

"Very well, but we must be swift," he said. Without waiting for her approval, the man turned and began searching the high hedges for a sign of her missing brother. He had taken only half a dozen steps when he softly called out, "He is here."

Attempting to still the shaking that still clutched at her body, Amelia moved to stand beside her unknown savior, her gaze searching the hedge until she discovered William happily seated on the filthy ground.

Her brief flare of relief was swiftly replaced by a bout of annoyance. As always, her brother was utterly indifferent to the world, and dangers, about him.

"William, what in heaven's name are you doing?" she demanded in sharp tones.

Glancing upward, her brother offered her that sweet, heart-melting smile that never failed to touch her.

"Cats," he said, pointing at his lap.

Amelia prayed for patience as she noted the numerous kittens that had crawled into a tight ball upon his legs, along with his own stray. Well, she at least now knew where that demon-spawned cat of William's had been disappearing to at night. And precisely what he had been doing during his midnight excursions.

"Cats," William repeated with a wide smile.

"Yes, I see."

"Cats and cats."

"Yes, there are many cats, William, but it is very late. You should be in your bed. A bed you should never have left, as you well know."

William simply smiled, but at her side the shadowed gentleman stirred with growing impatience.

"We must be away from here," he said in low tones. "There is still danger."

She was not about to argue. Not when she fully agreed with his impeccable logic. She did not yet know enough of this shadow creature to be certain that it might not suddenly decide to reappear.

"Come along, William. It is time we return home."

William heaved a sad sigh, but thankfully began

to replace the kittens in the hedge before clutching his renegade black cat in his arms and rising to his feet.

"Cats."

"Yes, yes. We shall visit them later."

Taking her brother's hand, Amelia joined the impatient gentleman as he turned back down the alley. In silence the three moved down the cramped lane, their footsteps echoing eerily. For a time, Amelia was simply relieved to be moving away from the nightmare that had haunted the abandoned stables. But as they continued onward, she discovered her gaze covertly studying the large male form at her side.

"Will you tell me of that creature?" she demanded in tones soft enough not to attract her brother's wandering attention.

"Perhaps. But not tonight. For now we must concentrate on returning you safely home."

She grimaced. She had expected no less. He appeared decidedly reluctant to reveal what he knew of the evil shadow.

"Then at least give me your name so I can properly thank you for rescuing me," she persisted.

"No thanks are necessary. I but did my duty."

Amelia frowned at the odd choice of words. "Duty? Surely it is not your duty to roam the darkness and rescue maidens in danger?"

Rather than answering her question, the man

raised a sudden hand, bringing all three of them to a halt.

"Hold a moment."

"What is it?" she demanded in sudden fear. Dear heavens, she was not prepared for another encounter with unnatural spirits.

"Someone approaches," he answered, pointing toward the unmistakable glow of a lantern.

Peering through the darkness, Amelia breathed a sigh of relief. "Oh. It is the Watch."

"We must not be seen," the man at her side commanded in low tones.

She stiffened in surprise. "Why? We should tell them of the shadow." She gave a shiver as she recalled the recent encounter. "And there was a body on the ground . . . I think that creature murdered some poor soul."

He moved closer, the rich scent of his warm skin a welcome exchange from the stench of the alley.

"Someone was murdered, indeed. Do you wish to be the one who claims that it was a mere shadow?"

"But we both saw it. . . ."

"It would not matter if the entire neighborhood witnessed the murder," he insisted, his head deliberately turning toward the silent William, who stood behind them. "The Watch cannot arrest and hang a shadow. They will desire a more tangible suspect to haul before the magistrate."

Amelia's breath caught at his horrid implication. "You cannot mean William? He has done nothing."

"Are you so certain that the authorities will believe in his innocence?"

She itched to reach up and slap him for even daring to imply someone could possibly think so ill of William. He was sweet and kind and utterly incapable of harming another soul. But even as the fury raced through her, a sensible voice urged her to consider the danger.

It was true that William was completely without guile. And that he would never lift a hand toward another. But she could not entirely deny that there were always those willing to believe the worst of her brother.

Because of his simple nature and large size, it was easy to presume that he could pose a danger. Few would take the time to discover his soft heart beneath his odd demeanor.

She gnawed her lower lip as she watched the lantern come ever closer. "Perhaps you are right."

"Follow me," he urged, stepping out of the alley and into the garden of one of the town houses.

Regaining her brother's hand, Amelia hurriedly set out after the swiftly moving form. In martyred silence, she ignored the brambles and stones that cut into her feet, and even the realization that they were blatantly trespassing from one garden to another. But as he actually angled up a path to one of the darkened houses and pulled open the kitchen door, she came to an uncertain halt.

"What are you doing?" she demanded in breathless tones.

"Leading you into my house," he retorted before he disappeared into the darkness within.

Feeling rather foolish, Amelia tugged her brother forward and stepped over the threshold. Once inside, however, she was forced to come to a halt as the darkness shrouded about her.

"A moment," the disembodied voice of her rescuer whispered through the air, sending an odd chill down her spine.

Not fear, she rather inanely realized. Instead, a stirring fascination with this man who had appeared from the darkness to save her.

There was a faint rasp of a flint before soft candlelight bathed the room.

Amelia blinked as her eyes adjusted to the sudden light. A moment later her breath tangled in her throat as she regarded the stranger.

Good heavens. He was . . . beautiful.

Fiercely, hauntingly beautiful, from his long, lustrous bronze hair that flowed past his broad shoulders to the powerful thrust of his legs. Even his unadorned black coat and breeches only served to reveal the fluid elegance of his body. Bemused, her gaze slowly lifted, tracing the crisply tied cravat to at last reach the lean countenance.

In the candlelight his features were shadowed, but there was no mistaking the startling perfection of his smooth, alabaster skin and finely sculpted features. Almost absently, she noticed that his nose was long and slender, his lips surprisingly full, and his brows the same shade as the bronze hair.

But in the end, it was his eyes that captured and held her attention.

Never had she seen eyes that were such a pure, molten silver. Eyes that glowed with a fierce intelligence. Eyes that seemed to hold her with a force she could feel to her very soul.

She should say something, a dry voice whispered in the back of her mind. Something that would bring an end to the thick, prickling silence that sent a rash of excitement over her skin.

"Oh," was all she could manage.

Thankfully unaware of her predicament, the gentleman lifted an elegant hand to wave it toward the nearby stairs.

"If you take these stairs, they will lead you to the front of the house. You may leave through the main door. Take care not to be seen."

Leave? Alone?

Amelia struggled to clear her foggy wits. "But, what of you?"

The pale countenance was grim as he glanced toward the open door. "I will ensure that the danger does not attempt to follow you. And also distract the Watch if need be."

"But . . ."

He stepped forward, those silver eyes glowing with a determined light. "See to your brother. No one must suspect that he was out of his home on this night. That is all that need concern you for now."

Her mouth opened to argue. She was unaccustomed to taking orders from anyone. Even those gentlemen who had saved her life. But before she could utter even a word, he was moving with that uncanny swiftness to press the candle into her hand and had disappeared through the open door.

She drew in a shaky breath.

Well. So far, it had been quite an evening.

She had lost her brother. Been confronted by a monstrous shadow that had ruthlessly murdered some poor soul. Been saved by a stranger. Run from the Watch. And now was abandoned in a strange house.

Oh, yes. Quite an evening.

Please turn the page for an exciting sneak peek of
the next book in Alexandra Ivy's
Guardians of Eternity series,

DARKNESS AVENGED,

coming in June 2013!

Prologue
The Legend of the Veil

The myths surrounding the creation of the Veil were a dime a dozen, and worth even less.

Some said it was the work of angels who had become lost in the mists of time.

Others said that it was a rip in space made during the big bang.

The current favorite was that Nefri, an ancient vampire with a mystical medallion, created the Veil to provide a little slice of paradise for her clan, the Immortal Ones. According to this particular rumor, it was whispered that on the other side there was no hunger, no bloodlust, and no passion. Only an endless peace.

It was a myth that Nefri, as well as the Oracles

that sat on the Commission (rulers of the demon-world) were happy to encourage.

The truth of the Veil was far less romantic.

It was nothing more or less than a prison.

A creation of the Oracles to contain an ancient mistake that could destroy them all . . .

Chapter 1

Viper's Vampire Club
On the banks of the Mississippi River south of Chicago

The music throbbed with a heavy, death metal bass that would have toppled the nearby buildings if the demon club hadn't been wrapped in spells of protection. The imp magic not only made the large building appear like an abandoned warehouse to the local humans of the small Midwest town, but it captured any sound.

A damned good thing since the blasting music wasn't the only noise that would freak out the mortal neighbors.

Granted, the first floor looked normal enough. The vast lobby was decorated in a neoclassical style with floors made of polished wood, and walls painted a pale green with silver engravings. Even the ceiling was covered with some fancy-assed painting of Apollo on his chariot dashing through the clouds.

Upstairs was the same. The private apartments were elegantly appointed and designed with comfort in mind for those guests willing to pay the exorbitant fees for a few hours of privacy.

But once admitted past the heavy double doors that led to the lower levels all pretense of civilization came to an end.

Down in the darkness the demons were encouraged to come out and play with wild abandon.

And no one, absolutely no one, could play as rough and wild and downright nasty as demons.

Standing in the shadows, Santiago, a tall exquisitely handsome vampire with long, raven hair, dark eyes, and distinctly Spanish features allowed his gaze to skim over his domain.

The circular room was the size of a large auditorium and made of black marble with a series of tiers that terraced downward. On each tier were a number of steel tables and stools that were bolted to the marble. Narrow staircases led to a pit built in the middle of the lowest floor and filled with sand.

The overhead chandeliers spilled small pools of light near the tables, while keeping enough darkness for those guests who preferred to remain concealed.

Not that there was a need for secrecy in the club.

The crowd was made up of vamps, Weres, and fairies, along with several trolls, an orc, and the rare Sylvermysts (the dark fey who'd recently revealed their presence in the world). They came to fight in the pit for a chance at fleeting glory. Or to indulge in the pleasures his various hosts and hostesses offered, whether it was feeding or sex.

None of them were known for their modesty.

Especially when they were in the mood to celebrate.

Santiago grimaced, his frigid power lashing through the air to send several young Weres scurrying across the crowded room.

He understood their jubilation.

It wasn't every day that an evil deity was destroyed, the hordes of hell turned away, and Armageddon averted.

But after a month of enduring the endless happy, happy, joy, joy his own mood was tilting toward homicidal.

Well, perhaps it was more than just tilting he grimly conceded as a tableful of trolls broke into a violent brawl, knocking each other over the railing and onto the Weres seated below.

The domino effect was instantaneous.

With infuriated growls the Weres shifted, tearing into the trolls. At the same time the nearby Sylvermysts leaped into the growing fight, the herb-scent of their blood swiftly filling the air.

His massive fangs ached with the need to join in the melee. Perhaps a good, old-fashioned beatdown would ease his choking frustration.

Unfortunately, his clan chief, Viper, had trusted him to manage the popular club. Which meant no extracurricular bloodbaths. No matter what the temptation.

Buzz kill.

Watching his well-trained bouncers move to put an end to the fight, Santiago turned his head as the smell of blood was replaced by the rich aroma of plums.

His lips curled as the violence choking the air was abruptly replaced by a heated lust.

Understandable.

Tonya could make a man drool at a hundred paces.

Stunningly beautiful with pale skin and slanted emerald eyes, the imp could also claim perfect curves and a stunning mane of red hair. But Santiago hadn't chosen her as his most trusted assistant because of her outrageous sex appeal.

Like all imps, she possessed a talent for business and the ability to create powerful illusions. She could also hex objects, although Santiago made sure that particular talent was only used on the humans who patronized the tea shop next door. Most demons were immune to fey magic, but Tonya had royal blood and her powers were far more addictive than most.

His loyal customers would never return if they

suspected he allowed them to be enthralled by the beautiful imp.

Wearing a silver dress that was designed to tempt rather than cover, she came to a halt at his side, a smile curving her lush lips even as her shrewd gaze monitored the hosts and hostesses that strolled through the room offering their services.

"A nice crowd," she murmured.

Santiago grimaced. Unlike his assistant he was wearing plain black jeans and a dark T-shirt that clung to his wide chest. And, of course, he'd accessorized the casual attire with a massive sword strapped to his back and handgun holstered at his hip.

Never let it be said he went to a party underdressed.

"Nice isn't a word I'd associate with this mob."

Tonya glanced toward the tribe of Sylvermysts who were reluctantly returning to their table. The warriors possessed the striking features of all fey with long hair in various shades of gold to chestnut. But their eyes blazed with a strange metallic sheen.

"Oh I don't know," she purred. "There's one or two I'd consider edible."

"Your definition of edible is appallingly indiscriminate."

She turned her head to study him with an all too knowing gaze. "Yeah well, at least I haven't been neutered."

Santiago curled his hands into tight fists, fury jolting through him. Oh no, she didn't just go there.

"Careful, Tonya."

"When was the last time you got laid?"

The air temperature dropped by several degrees.

"We're so not going to discuss this," he snarled, his voice pitched low enough it wouldn't carry. Despite the earsplitting music, there were demons who could hear a freaking pin drop a mile away. "Especially not in front of an audience."

Foolishly ignoring his don't-fuck-with-me vibes, Tonya planted her hands on her full hips.

"I've tried to discuss it in private, but you keep shutting me down."

"Because it's none of your damned business."

"It is when your foul mood begins affecting the club."

His fangs throbbed. "Don't press me."

"If I don't, who will?" The female refused to back down, the words she clearly longed to fling at him for days at last bursting past her lips. "You prowl through the halls snapping at everyone who is stupid enough to cross your path. I've had six waitresses and two bouncers quit in the past month."

His jaw hardened with a stubborn refusal to admit she was right.

If he did . . .

Well that would mean he'd have to admit he *had* been neutered.

Not only sexually, although that was god awful enough to admit. After all, he was a vampire. His appetite for sex was supposed to be insatiable.

But his general lust for life.

Suddenly his enjoyment in pursuing beautiful women and spending time with his clan brothers was replaced by a gnawing frustration. And his pride in running a club that was infamous throughout the demon world was replaced by an itch that he couldn't scratch.

It was something he was trying to ignore under the theory that it was like a bad hangover; something you suffered through and forgot as soon as the next party came along.

"Hire more," he growled.

Her eyes narrowed. "Easy for you to say."

"Hey, you know where the door . . ."

"I'm not done," she interrupted.

His dark brows pulled together in a warning scowl. "Imp, you're pissing on my last nerve."

"And that's my point." She pointed a finger toward the belligerent crowd that continued to eyeball one another with the threat of violence. "This mood of yours is not only infecting the employees, but the patrons as well. Every night we're a breath away from a riot."

He snorted, folding his arms over his wide chest.

"I run a demon club that caters to blood, sex, and violence. What do you expect? Line dancing, gin fizzes, and karaoke?"

"The atmosphere is always aggressive, but in the past few weeks it's been explosive. We've had more fights just tonight than we've had in the past two years."

"Haven't you heard the news? We're celebrating the defeat of the Dark Lord?" he tried to bluster. "A new beginning . . . blah, blah, blah."

Like a dog with a bone, Tonya refused to let it go.

"Does that look like celebrating?" Once again she stabbed her finger toward the seething crowd. "Your frustration is contaminating everyone."

Santiago couldn't argue.

The club wasn't Disneyland, but it wasn't usually a bloodbath.

At least not unless you were stupid enough to join in the cage matches.

"So what are you suggesting?"

"You have two options." Tonya offered a tight smile. "Go kill something, or fuck it. Hell, do both."

He snorted. "Are you offering?"

"I would if I thought it would do any good," she admitted bluntly. "As it is . . ." her words trailed away as she gave a lift of her hand, gesturing toward a distant corner.

"What?"

"I have something more suitable to your current taste in females."

Santiago wasn't sure what he expected.

Maybe twin imps. He'd always had a weakness for matched sets. *Twinning . . .*

Or maybe a harpy in heat.

Nothing was more certain to distract a man than a week of incessant, no-holds-barred, balls-aching sex.

Instead a female vampire stepped from the shadows.

"*Mierde,*" he hissed in shock.

Not because the woman was stunning. That was a given. All vampire females were drop-dead gorgeous.

But this one had an eerie familiarity with her long, black hair and dark eyes that contrasted so sharply with her pale skin.

Nefri.

No, not Nefri, a voice whispered in the back of his mind.

The face was more angular and the approaching female was lacking the regal aloofness that shrouded the real Nefri.

Not to mention a lack of kick-ass power that would have all of them reeling beneath the impact of her presence.

But she was close enough to make his gut twist into painful knots.

"Will she do?" Tonya murmured.

"Get rid of her," he commanded, his voice thick.

Tonya frowned in confusion. "What?"

"Get rid of her. Now."

Spinning on his heel, he headed toward the stairs leading out of the lower levels.

He had to get out.

"Santiago," Tonya called behind him. "Goddammit."

The crowd parted beneath the force of his icy power, most of them scrambling out of his way with a gratifying haste as he climbed the stairs and entered the lobby.

Not that he noticed.

He was way too busy convincing himself that his retreat was nothing more than anger at Tonya's interference.

As if he needed the fey prying into his sex life. She was supposed to be his assistant, not his pimp. If he wanted a damned female he could get one himself. Hell, he could get a dozen.

And not one of them would be some pitiful substitute for the aggravating, infuriating, impossible female who had simply abandoned him to return behind the Veil. . . .

"Trouble in paradise, *mi amigo*?"

It was a testament to just how distracted he was that he was nearly across the marble floor of the lobby and he hadn't noticed the vampire standing near the door to his office.

Dios.

If he could miss the current Anasso (the ultimate king of all vampires) then his head was truly up his ass.

Styx was a six foot five Aztec warrior dressed in black leather with a sword big enough to carve through a full-blooded troll strapped to his back. And of course, there was his massive power that pulsed through the air like sonic waves.

It would be easier, and certainly less dangerous, to overlook an erupting volcano.

"Perfect," he muttered regarding his unexpected guest's bronzed face that had been carved on lean, arrogant lines that was emphasized by his dark hair that was pulled into a tight braid that fell nearly to the back of his knees. He didn't look like he was there to party. Which meant he wanted something from Santiago. Never a good thing. "Could this night get any better?" he muttered.

Styx arched a dark brow. "Do you want to talk about it?"

Share the fact he was no better than a eunuch with his Anasso? He'd rather be gutted.

And, speaking as someone who actually had been gutted, that was saying something.

"I most emphatically do not," he rasped, shoving open the door to his office and leading his companion inside.

"Thank the gods." Styx crossed the slate gray carpet, perching on the corner of Santiago's heavy walnut desk. "When I took the gig of Anasso I didn't know I had to become the Vampire Whisperer. I just wanted to poke things with my big sword."

Santiago veered past the wooden shelves that held the sort of high-tech surveillance equipment that only Homeland Security was supposed to know about, unlocking the door of the sidebar that was set beneath the French Impressionist paintings that were hung on the paneled walls.

"I hope you didn't come here to poke anything with your sword," he said, pulling out a bottle of Comisario tequila.

"Actually, I need your help."

"Again?" Santiago poured two healthy shots of the expensive liquor. The last time Styx had said those words the Dark Lord had been threatening to destroy the world and he'd been teamed up with Nefri in an attempt to find the missing prophet. "I thought we'd gone beyond the sky-is-falling to yippee ki yay, everyone back to their neutral corners so we could pretend that we didn't nearly become puppy chow for the hordes of hell?"

Styx hadn't become king just because he was baddest of all bad-asses. He was also frighteningly perceptive.

Narrowing his eyes he studied Santiago's bitter expression with a disturbing intensity.

"Does this have something to do with Nefri and her return to her clan?"

Nope. Not discussing it.

Santiago jerkily moved to shove one of the glasses into Styx's hand.

"Here."

Briefly distracted, the ancient vampire took a sip of the potent spirit, a faint smile curving his lips.

"From Viper's cellars?"

"Of course."

Styx's smile widened. Despite being predatory alphas, Styx and Viper (the clan chief of Chicago) had become trusted friends. It was almost as shocking as the fact that vampires and Weres had become allies. At least temporarily.

Which only proved the point that doomsday truly did make for strange bedfellows.

"Does he know you're enjoying his private stash?"

"What he doesn't know . . ." Santiago lifted his glass in a mocking toast before draining the tequila in one swallow. "*Salud.*"

"You know," Styx murmured, setting aside his glass. "Maybe I should try my hand at Dr. Phil."

Santiago poured himself another shot.

"You said you needed my help."

"That was the plan, but you're in a dangerous mood, *amigo.* The kind of mood that gets good vampires dead."

"I'm fine." Santiago drained the tequila, savoring the exquisite burn. "Tell me what you want from me."

There was a long pause before the king at last

reached to pull out a dagger that had been sheathed at his hip.

"Do you recognize this?"

"*Dios.*" Santiago dropped his glass as he stared in shock at the ornamental silver blade that was shaped like a leaf with a leather pummel inset with tiny rubies. "A pugio," he breathed.

"Do you recognize it?"

His short burst of humorless laughter filled the room. Hell yeah, he recognized it. He should. It belonged to his sire, Gaius, who had once been a Roman general.

Centuries ago he'd watched in awe as Gaius had displayed the proper method of killing his prey with the dagger. What a fool he'd been.

Of course, he wasn't entirely to blame.

Like all foundlings, Santiago had awoken as a vampire without memory of his past and only a primitive instinct to survive. But unlike others, he hadn't been left to fend for himself. Oh no. Gaius had been there. Treating him like a son and training him to become his most trusted warrior.

But all that came to an end the night their clan was attacked. Santiago had been away from the lair, but he knew that Gaius had been forced to watch his beloved mate, Dara, burned at the stake. And lost in his grief, Gaius had retreated behind the Veil where he sought the peace they supposedly offered.

Of course, it had all been a load of horseshit.

Gaius had allowed himself to be swayed by the promise of the Dark Lord to return Dara and he'd gone behind the Veil to betray them all.

And as for Santiago . . .

He'd been left behind to endure hell.

Realizing that Styx was studying him with an all too knowing gaze, Santiago slammed the door on his little walk down memory lane.

"Gaius," he said, his voice flat.

"That's what I suspected."

"Where was it found?" Santiago frowned as the Anasso hesitated. "Styx?"

Styx tossed the dagger on the desk. "A witch by the name of Sally brought it to me," he at last revealed. "She claimed that she worked for Gaius."

"We know he had a witch who helped him along with the curs." Santiago nodded his head toward the pugio. "And that would seem to confirm she's speaking the truth. Gaius would never leave it lying around." He returned his gaze to Styx. "What did she want?"

"She said she had been using Gaius's lair in Louisiana to stay hidden in case she was being hunted for her worship of the Dark Lord."

"More likely she knew that Gaius was dead and decided to help herself to his possessions."

Again there was that odd hesitation and Santiago felt a chill of premonition inch down his spine.

Something was going on.

Something he wasn't going to like.

"If that was the case then she was in for a disappointment," Styx said, his expression guarded.

"Disappointment?"

"She says that a week ago she returned to the lair to discover Gaius had returned."

"No." Santiago clenched his hands. This was supposed to be over, dammit. The Dark Lord was dead and so was the sire he'd once worshipped. "I don't believe it."

Something that might have been sympathy flashed through Styx's eyes.

"I didn't either, but Viper was convinced she was speaking the truth. At least, the truth as far as she knows it. It could be that she's being used as a pawn."

Santiago hissed. His clan chief possessed a talent for reading the souls of humans. If he said she was telling the truth then . . . *dios.*

"I witnessed him coming through the rift with the Dark Lord, but how the hell did he survive the battle?"

"Actually, he only survived in part."

Santiago struggled against the sensation he was standing on quicksand.

"What the hell does that mean?"

"This Sally said that Gaius was acting strange."

"He's been acting strange for centuries," Santiago muttered. "The treacherous bastard."

"She said that he looked filthy and confused," Styx continued, his watchful gaze never wavering from Santiago's bitter expression. "And she was certain he didn't recognize her."

Santiago frowned, more baffled by the claim that Gaius had been filthy than by his supposed confusion.

His sire had always been meticulous. And Santiago's brief glimpse of Gaius's lair beyond the Veil had only emphasized the elder vampire's OCD.

"Was he injured?"

"According to the witch, he looked like he was under a compulsion."

"Impossible. Gaius is far too powerful to have his mind controlled."

"It depends on who is doing the controlling," Styx pointed out. "Sally also said that he was obviously trying to protect something or someone he had hidden in the house."

With a low curse Santiago shifted his gaze to make sure the door was closed. No need to cause a panic.

"The Dark Lord?"

"No." Styx gave a firm shake of his head. "The Oracles are certain the Dark Lord is well and truly dead."

Santiago's stab of relief was offset by Styx's grim expression.

The Dark Lord might be dead, but Styx clearly was afraid something was controlling Gaius.

"You've spoken to the Oracles?"

Styx grimaced. "Unfortunately. Since my first thought was like yours, that he'd managed to salvage some small part of the Dark Lord, I naturally went to the Commission with my fears."

"And?"

The room suddenly filled with a power that made the lights flicker and the computer monitors shut down.

"And they politely told me to mind my own business."

He gave a sharp laugh. How many times had Styx been told to mind his own business? Santiago was going with the number zero.

"How many did you kill?"

"None." Styx's crushing power continued to throb through the room. "My temper is . . ."

"Cataclysmic?" Santiago helpfully offered.

"Healthy," Styx corrected. "But, I'm not suicidal."

That was true enough. The King of Vampires might approach diplomacy like a bull in a china cabinet, but he was too shrewd to confront the Commission head-on.

No. He wouldn't challenge the Oracles, but then again, Santiago didn't believe for a second he was going to sit back and meekly obey their command.

Obey and *Styx* was an oxymoron.

"If this is none of your business, why did you come to me?" he demanded.

"Because Gaius is one of mine, no matter what he's done," Styx said, his face as hard as granite. "And if he's being controlled by something or someone I want to know what the hell is going on."

"What about the Oracles?"

"What they don't know . . ." Styx tossed Santiago's words back in his face.

Santiago narrowed his eyes. It was one thing to sneak a bottle of tequila from Viper's cellars and another to piss off the Oracles.

"And you chose me, because?"

"You're the only one capable of tracking Gaius."

Santiago shook his head. "The bastard did something to mask his scent along with our previous bonding. I don't have any better chance of finding him than you do."

Styx's smile sent a chill down Santiago's spine. "I have full faith you'll find some way to hunt him down. And, of course, to do it without drawing unnecessary attention."

Great.

Not only was he being sent on a wild goose-chase, but he was in danger of attracting the lethal anger of the Oracles.

Just what he didn't need.

With his hands on his hips, Santiago glared at his companion.

"So you're not willing to risk the wrath of the Commission, but you're willing to throw me under the bus?"

"Don't be an ass." Styx allowed his power to slam into Santiago, making him grunt in pain. "If you don't want to do this, then don't. I thought you would be eager for the opportunity to be reunited with your sire."

Santiago held up a hand in apology. *Mierda.* He truly was on the edge to deliberately goad the King of Vampires.

"You're right, I'm sorry," he said. And it was true. Styx *was* right. He'd waited centuries for the opportunity to confront his sire. Now he'd been given a second chance. Why wasn't he leaping at the opportunity? "It's . . ." He broke off with a shake of his head.

"Yes?"

"Nothing." He pulled out his cell phone, concentrating on what needed to be accomplished before he could head out. "I need to contact Tonya to warn her she'll be in charge of the club."

"Of course."

"Where's the witch?"

"She's at my lair in Chicago. Roke is keeping an eye on her in case this turns out to be a clever trick."

Santiago sent his companion a startled glance. Roke was the clan chief from Nevada and was in an even fouler mood than Santiago since Styx had refused his return to his clan after the prophet had revealed he'd been seen in a vision.

"The poor witch," he muttered. "That's not a punishment I would wish on anyone."

Styx shrugged. "He was the only one available."

Santiago froze. "Is there something going on that I should know about?"

A strange expression tightened Styx's lean features. Was it . . . embarrassment?

"Darcy insists that I devote my Ravens to trying to locate that damned gargoyle."

Ah. Santiago struggled to hide his sudden smile. The Ravens were Styx's private guards. The biggest, meanest vampires around.

The fact he was being forced to use them to locate a three foot gargoyle who'd been a pain in Styx's ass for the past year must be driving him nuts.

"Levet is still missing?" he murmured. The tiny gargoyle had astonishingly played a major part in destroying the Dark Lord, but shortly after the battle he'd disappeared into thin air.

Quite literally.

"You find that amusing?" Styx growled.

"Actually I find it a refreshing reminder of why I'm happy to be a bachelor."

Styx's annoyance melted away as a disturbing smile touched his mouth.

"Who are you trying to convince?"

Santiago frowned. "Convince of what?"

"That you're happy?" the older vampire clarified. "From all reports you've been storming around here, making life miserable for everyone since Nefri returned to her clan behind the Veil. That doesn't sound like a man who is content with his bachelor existence."

Damn Tonya and her big imp mouth. Shoving his phone back into his pocket, Santiago held out an impatient hand.

"Do you have directions to Gaius's lair?"

"Here." Handing over a folded piece of paper, Styx suddenly grabbed Santiago's wrist, his eyes glittering with warning. "For now all I want is information. Is that clear?"

"Crystal."

"The Oracles won't be happy if they find out you're trespassing in their playground," Styx warned. "Stay below the radar, *amigo*, and be careful."

Santiago gave a slow nod. "Always."